The

Architect

A Traditional Regency Romance

Mary Kingswood

Sutors Publishing

Published by Sutors Publishing

ISBN: 978-1-912167-64-7 (paperback)

Version V1

Cover design by: Shayne Rutherford of Darkmoon Graphics

Author's note:

this book is written using historic British terminology, so *saloon* instead of *salon*, *chaperon* instead of *chaperone* and so on. I follow Jane Austen's example and refer to a group of sisters as the Miss Wintertons.

About this book

The duke, a struggling architect and a lady who loves to dance... but just who is sending seemingly random strangers to the duke?

At eight and twenty, Miss Sophia Merrington is the youngest of four sisters, not one of whom has yet found a husband. When her brother becomes heir to the Duke of Brinshire and moves to the vast country house of Staineybank, Sophia is the only one not happy to be there. What is the point of living in such a grand house when there is no dancing to be had? A chance invitation opens up all sorts of possibilities, but can she seize the opportunity and find herself a husband at long last? Or is she doomed to be an unmarriageable spinster?

The Honourable Simon Payne is estranged from most of his family, with his half-sister, Lady Juliet, his only support. Struggling to make his way as an architect, but finding no success, he's thrilled to receive an invitation to design an orangery for the Duke of Brinshire's house. But when he arrives at Staineybank, he's not expected and there is a rival architect already working on the design. Who has sent him there, and why?

This is a complete story with a happy ever after. A traditional Regency romance, drawing room rather than bedroom. Book 1 of a 6 book series.

About the series*:*

Book 0: The Duke's Heir *(a novella prequel)*

Book 1: The Duke's Architect

Book 2: The Duke's Portraitist

Book 3: The Duke's Gardener

Book 4: The Duke's Steward

Book 5: The Duke's Librarian

Book 6: The Duke's Enemy

Want to be the first to hear about new releases? Sign up for my mailing list at https://marykingswood.co.uk

The Duke's Household

The Duke's Household, Staineybank, Brinshire

Richard, 7th Duke of Brinshire

His family:

Lily nee Willaston, his duchess

Hester Merrington, his 'cousin'

His heir and family:

Richard Merrington, his heir

Mrs Richard Merrington nee Holt (Rowena), Richard's wife

Mrs Roland Merrington (Cora), Richard's widowed mother

Richard's sisters:

Miss Charlotte Merrington

Miss Augusta Merrington

Miss Maria Merrington

Miss Sophia Merrington

His guest:

Mrs Henry Hastings (Georgie), the widowed companion to Rowena

His employees:

Mr James Hammond, his secretary/memoirist

Mr Hammond Senior, his former secretary

Mr George Pyott, the comptroller

Mr William Godley, the chaplain

His servants:

Froggett, butler; Henry, Robert, footmen

Allen, Lily's lady's maid

Mrs Bright, the cook; Timmy, the kitchen boy

Ben Lovell, the gamekeeper

Contents

Prologue	1
1: An Unexpected Arrival	6
2: The Architect	18
3: Night And Morning	30
4: An Eligible Man	43
5: An Invitation	56
6: The Orangery	70
7: A Grand Ball	82
8: Disappointment	95
9: A Winter Walk	106
10: Waiting	117
11: Daughters And Sons	130
12: A Bridge Over The River	141

13: A Suitor 153

14: Courtship 164

15: Abandoned 174

16: A Question Of Marriage 186

17: Friends 197

18: A Visit From Mr Thwaite 209

19: Lord Edlesborough 220

20: Visitors From Newcastle 233

21: The Library 245

22: The Blue Parlour 255

23: Despair 268

Epilogue 279

Thanks for reading! 294

About the author 296

Acknowledgements 297

Sneak preview: Book 2 of Black Sheep: The Duke's Portraitist 298

Prologue

FINSBURY SQUARE, LONDON; JANUARY

The Honourable Simon Payne pulled his shawl more tightly round his shoulders and glared balefully at the fire burning fitfully in the grate. It was not the fire's fault that it had so little power to heat the attic room. It was doing its best, he supposed, but there were limits to what could be expected of any fire against the freezing cold air trying to creep through even the smallest crack in the windows.

He sighed, remembering sorrowfully the brilliant blazes of his youth. There was no chill in any room at Edlesborough, no matter how frigid the outside air. But all that had changed fifteen years ago, when he had asked to be articled to an architect, and his father had stared at him as if he had two heads.

"*Articled?* To an *architect?* Nonsense! It is the army for you, my lad. That is the tradition for younger sons in the Payne family, since you are hardly suited to the church. John and Matthew are promising in that way, and will take up the two livings I have in my disposal, so you must go into the army. It will do you good — make a man of you, and none of this drawing nonsense. I can get you into the Guards, so you will not have to fight."

"No, sir."

"Good. That is settled. Next year, when you are sixteen, you will—"

"No, sir. I will not join the army."

His father's eyes had bulged like a frog's. "You will do as you are told!"

"No. Juliet said she will take care of me."

That brought on such an outpouring of rage that the physician had to be called, and Mama had brusquely packed Simon off to London to join Juliet at once.

And here he still was, still trying to become an architect, still failing miserably. Yet Juliet's small annuity managed to keep him in paper and pencils, and so he still designed his great houses in the Greek style, although he toyed with Gothick designs sometimes, too. But no one wanted them. They were much admired, but the men of wealth who could afford them preferred the established names like Stewart, Holland or Wyatt. How was a man ever to become an established name if no one would engage him? Just one house would make his reputation, he knew it.

Mary Ann brought him his afternoon pot of tea. It was weak, of course, since the leaves had to be reused and by supper were barely colouring the water, but at least it was hot and would warm him inside. He sipped gratefully, moving closer to the fire. Another quarter of an hour and he could add some more coals to it. Then there would be his glass of wine at dinner to look forward to.

He had barely begun his first cup of tea when Juliet dashed in, unwinding a voluminous scarf, her nose red from the cold.

Simon frowned. "Thought you intended to be out all morning."

"Indeed I was, but I called at the post office and there were *three* letters, which have been there for an age, the fellow said. Since Christmas, almost! Just imagine, and two are for you from your mama, so I brought them at once. Quick, quick, quick! How much is it?"

She tossed two small letters at him which he tried to catch but missed. Swiftly, Juliet bent down to pick them up. "Hurry up, Simon! The suspense is killing me."

He ripped open the first letter. "A hundred!" he said, awed, holding up half of a bank note. Tearing open the other, he held the two halves side by side. "A hundred pounds, sister! We can have beef steak for Sunday dinner."

"Or a turkey, perhaps," she murmured. "Or what do you say to a bit of partridge? I am so fond of partridge. And a box of those wonderful bonbons that Haydocks have."

"Let us not be too ambitious," he said, laughing. "We cannot say how long this will have to last us. It is six months, two weeks and three days since the last note, and that was only twenty."

"She must have had all the aunts and uncles at Edlesborough for Christmas," Juliet said. "You know how she does it — feed them up, pour Papa's best claret down their throats and then gently fleece them at the card table."

"It was only fifty after last Christmas," Simon said.

"So it was. She has had a successful time of it. I wish my mama were still alive, to send me little presents like this. Yours is very kind, and Papa knows nothing of it. The letters were not even franked, but I do not mind paying the postage when the contents are so rewarding."

"Three letters, you said. What was the other? A bill? We can settle for the coal now... and the butcher."

"Oh, yes. In all the excitement, I had forgotten." She fished the third letter from her reticule. "I do not recognise the hand. It is not a bill, I think." Breaking the seal, she unfolded it and read it silently, before looking up with a frown.

"What is it? Not bad news?"

"No... good news, I think, but... strange. Listen. *'To the Lady Juliet Payne, Finsbury Square, London. With humble greetings, my lady. You do not know me, but I am bidden to request you to bring Mr Simon Payne to Staineybank in Brinshire at your earliest convenience, in order to discuss the design for an orangery. Please reply directly to me to confirm your preferred date of travel, and I shall arrange private transportation and accommodation en route suitable to your station. Respectfully yours, A Goodenough (attorney at law), Castle Street, Brinchester'*. What do you think of that?"

"An orangery? Nothing else?"

"It is progress, Simon. Nothing but stables and kennels so far, so an orangery is a step up. A gentleman client, at least."

"But Mr Thwaite may yet settle on a design."

"Two years you have been working on designs for Mr Thwaite, and for all his great fortune, we have seen not a penny piece from it, nor has he actually commissioned any of your designs. But this... transport provided... a private carriage, Simon, just think! And suitable accommodation on the way. Oh, to be eating at someone else's expense! And when we arrive, we might even be invited to stay at the house itself. Staineybank... I have never heard of it."

"Campbell," Simon said. "English Palladian style. Built 1722."

She chuckled. "Yes, but who lives there?"

"Duke of Brinshire."

Her eyes widened. "A *duke!* Oh, Simon, we must go! Even if nothing comes of it, we must go."

"Yes," he said. "Campbell's houses are always worth seeing, and I have never seen that one. Of course we must go."

She shook her head, smiling. "You are incorrigible, brother. Very well, I shall write to this... what is his name? Mr Goodenough, attorney at law, and make arrangements, and you will be able to see Staineybank. And I... I shall endeavour to take as long as humanly possible to discuss this orangery in the hope that the duke will feed and house us both in the meantime. A fortnight, at least, surely, or even a whole month. And if he likes your designs, and who could not..." She shivered in anticipation. "Just think, Simon — we might see out the whole winter in comfort."

"And warmth," he said with feeling. "I hope Staineybank is warm."

1: An Unexpected Arrival

STAINEYBANK, BRINSHIRE; JANUARY

Miss Sophia Merrington gazed at the image on the page before her and sighed. Such elegance! Such exquisite details! And, sadly, such extravagance. *'A light blue, or grey chemise robe, of gossamer net, imperial crape, or Spanish gauze, worn over white pealing satin, ornamented up the front with French bows and knots of silver'*, quoth the journal. White satin? Six shillings a yard at the very least, and possibly twice as much. The gauze would be a little less, and the bows and knots… she could make them quite small.

Then she read the next lines and despaired. *'A full melon sleeve, formed of the same material as the dress, and alternate stripes of white satin; finished with bows and knots of silver. A double roll of white satin round the neck of the robe, by way of tucker'*. Full sleeves in stripes of two materials? A white satin tucker? And then the journal went on to describe the diamond comb in the hair, and diamonds for necklace, armlets and ear-rings.

She sighed even more heavily.

The slumbering figure on the sofa stirred. "Georgie? Oh, it is you, Sophia. Have I slept for a long time?"

"An hour or so, no more. Georgie went to see about the jellies. The duke came in to look at you, but I chased him away."

"He fusses so, but I am perfectly well. Just... tired. And enormous."

"Not much longer to wait now, Rowena," Sophia said briskly. She was very fond of her sister-in-law, and was delighted that Richard had married such a pleasant, unassuming woman, but the whole household revolved around her. If she should happen to fancy a certain dish at dinner, an army of gamekeepers and poultry maids and gardeners and still room maids would be mobilised to provide the ingredients. If she sneezed, the servants were thrown into a frenzy of possets and tisanes and tinctures, followed by a stream of midwives and apothecaries and physicians, who all recommended different remedies and stood in the hall roundly disparaging each other.

And the duke was the greatest worrier of them all. Now that Richard was his official heir, the child Rowena carried would be the next in line, and oh, the hopes and expectations that rested on her to produce a son. Sophia could only hope for that, too, for then perhaps the trembling excitation that infected Staineybank would dissipate and they could all settle back into their usual activities. Not that there was much to look forward to in January, with the Christmas festivities past and not so much as an evening party on the horizon for months. It was dispiriting.

She sighed again.

Rowena heaved herself into a more upright position. "Now, what is making you sound so out of sorts? No ball to plan for, I imagine. What are you reading? Oh, this is pretty," she said, taking the journal from Sophia's hands. "White satin... French bows and knots of silver. That sounds quite delightful. Shall you have one like it made up?"

"I cannot afford it," Sophia said dejectedly.

"Not even with the additional allowance from the duke? He is very generous."

"Oh yes, the *duke* is generous, but Richard is not. I do not like to speak ill of my brother, for he is an admirable man in every other respect, but he is a nip-farthing, Rowena. Even you must admit it. He insists I must not overspend my allowance, not even by the cost of a single ribbon, and how can anyone be sure to keep to a specific sum? One must have clothes, after all."

"He is careful with money, it is true," Rowena said with a little smile. "Being a man, he does not quite appreciate the benefits of a new gown or slippers."

"Or diamond armlets," Sophia said with another sigh. "Just imagine how glorious that would be. With every movement, I should glimmer and sparkle."

She held her arms in the correct position and executed a complete figure with all the steps, and then sighed again. "When, oh when will there be a ball? I cannot tell you, Rowena, how I long for a proper ball, but not when I have nothing to wear."

"There will be no balls before Lady Day when your next allowance will arrive, but perhaps the seamstress might begin work a little early? She will know she will be paid, after all."

"Richard will not permit it," Sophia said dejectedly. "We are never to buy anything for which we could not settle the bill immediately, if required. Nor are we allowed to borrow money, and we are never, ever to gamble to defray debts. Oh, it is hard! There is nothing like a new ball gown to lift the spirits."

"Then you know the answer, Sophia," Rowena said with a quick laugh. "You will just have to marry a vastly rich man who dotes on you so much that he gives you all his wealth to spend on ball gowns and diamond armlets."

"*All* his wealth? But then we should be destitute and how should I survive without any new gowns at all?"

Rowena laughed out loud at her dejected tone. "There is no pleasing you! What you must do, Sophia, is what I was obliged to do for many years, and rework your old gowns. You have some very pretty ones that could be refreshed with very little effort."

It was a strange thing, but Richard had said precisely the same thing to her many, many times, and it had merely made her cross and long even harder for the new gown or gloves or fan. When Rowena said it, however, it sounded eminently reasonable and she could not think of a single argument against it.

Richard himself came in just then, with his sketchbook under his arm, and Sophia had no wish to hear any more about his precious orangery. For months now, he had been drawing up plans for it, so that Rowena might grow oranges and lemons and who knows what exotic fruits, and Sophia was tired of it.

Leaving them to their discussion, she slipped away to her room, and flung open the doors of the two presses that housed all her ball gowns. She had quite a collection now after eleven years of balls and she had bought at least two for each season. Laying them carefully on the bed, she counted thirty-one. Since each gown had danced its way through four or five balls apiece, that was... too difficult a sum to work in her head. She kept a notebook with every ball listed, and all her partners, and what they had danced, together with a few comments about the number of couples and the quality of the supper and any particularly memorable moments, so she could work it out from that.

After some concentrated effort with the notebook, she reached a final number — one hundred and forty-one. That was the sum of her life so far, one hundred and forty-one balls, any number of dances and partners and not a single offer of marriage. Even in the days of her highest bloom she had attracted no suitors, and now, at the advanced age of twenty-eight, it was unlikely that she ever would. She was a confirmed spinster, and even three older sisters in the same pitiable state was no comfort. What was *wrong* with them all, that no man wanted any of them?

She lifted up her favourite gown, her very first. Horribly outdated now, of course — such full skirts! So much material in it, and even Richard had agreed that she must wear silk to a ball. She pressed the fabric to her face, wondering if she would still catch the faint scent of the perfume she had worn on that unforgettable evening... No, it was gone.

With another sigh, she carried it to the window to examine more closely. Such a beautiful silk, that flowed over her hands like cool water. And so much of it... if it could be carefully unpicked, perhaps a new dress could be contrived? And there would even be enough left over for full sleeves, if she should want them.

Gathering up the gown, she rushed off to find Lily. The duchess was almost the same age as Sophia, and also came from a family at the lower edge of gentility, where finding the money for new gowns was a constant struggle. Even since her marriage to the duke, she still dressed frugally, and was adept at fashioning new from old.

"Have you never had to do this before?" Lily said, taking the gown to the window to examine it closely. "Richard must have been very generous with you."

"Not he!" Sophia said. "The trustees were generous, certainly, but as soon as Richard came of age, he leased Leahollow and marched us off to a poky little house in Norwich, and reduced our allowances."

"Oh!" Lily said, wide-eyed. "But perhaps there were debts to be settled?"

"No, he is just horridly cheeseparing. It is not so bad for my sisters, for Charlotte is as tight-fisted as Richard, Augusta is happy so long as she has a riding habit to wear, and Maria cares nothing for clothes when there are books to be read. Mama was the only one who understood, but even she could not sway Richard. His mind was entirely closed to the idea that one cannot exist on only two or three gowns a year. It is just not possible, not if one is to be respectably turned out."

Lily laughed. "Indeed, I cannot fault your logic, cousin, for my sisters and I suffered just as you do. Poor Papa! There were so many of us, and the boys had to be educated and mounted, so there was very little left over for unnecessary items like clothing. We were only allowed new gowns twice a year, spring and autumn, and then it was only one morning gown, one walking and one evening. We spent half our days unpicking and sewing anew."

"How dreadful!"

"Oh, it was a challenge we all relished. Happily for me, my godmother descended on us when I was about to come out, and insisted I needed a veritable mountain of gowns. Papa grumbled about it, and we only persuaded him in the end by telling him that good quality clothes could be handed down for year after year, and serve for several of my sisters."

"I imagine he did not grumble so much when you drew the duke's eye," Sophia said slyly.

"Oh, but he did! He was horrified, and I think he would have forbidden the match if Mama and my godmother had not pointed out all the advantages. And now Cordelia and Amabel have made very good matches, and John has his colours, in a far better regiment than he might have expected, and Henry is a midshipman. There is a living for Charles or Thomas, too, if they want to go into the church. The duke has been so kind to us... to all of us," she added wistfully.

Sophia said nothing, for she found Lily's story heartbreaking. To be forced to marry a man old enough to be one's grandfather! Lily had been eighteen to the duke's sixty-eight, and no matter how kind he had been and still was, for he was clearly fond of his young wife, it was indubitably a dreadfully unequal match. As for the advantages, those all accrued to others — Lily's brothers and sisters, and not to Lily herself, beyond the comfort of wealth and high standing in society.

But Lily never railed at her situation, except to say now and then that the grandeur and size of Staineybank felt oppressive to her. After her only child had died at the age of six, she had planned to leave it altogether and return to Cheshire, where her family lived, but here she still was.

Now she smiled, running slender fingers over the skirts of the ballgown. "This is a beautiful silk. It will make up afresh very well, you will see. We can look through the journals today, and talk to the seamstress tomorrow."

The two spent a delightful afternoon in the duchess's private sitting room, with journals lying open on every available surface, sipping tea and discussing fashions, for it was a subject of inexhaustible interest to both of them.

Dinner that evening was dominated as so often these days by discussion of the proposed orangery. It was intended as a wedding gift to Rowena, who had admired the Duke of Camberley's orangery at Marshfields, but at the present rate of progress the bride would be a matron with three or four children before it was finished. Not a stone had yet been laid, and the exact location had not even been determined.

As always with Richard, it came down to money. The duke was all for a grandiose scheme on a hill to impress visitors, lined with marble pillars. Richard was more inclined for a simple brick structure, on account of the cost of glass, and as for marble, it was not to be thought of. No matter how many times the duke pointed out that he would be paying for it and the estate could easily bear the cost and it would be a gratifying celebration of the birth of the next heir, it made no difference.

Sophia was glad to creep away to bed and dream of balls and the swirl of silken gowns, of rooms filled with waving feathers and sparkling jewels, and everywhere music and charming young men eager to dance. And surely there would be one, just one, who would look at her and truly *see* her.

***

The next morning, she awoke to steady snow, coating the gardens in white icing. By breakfast, the fall was reduced to a few stray flakes, but there was a flurry of activity amongst the men, anxiously discussing the roads, while most of the ladies had wisely decided to take breakfast in bed.

"Let us escape," Lily whispered to Sophia. "The seamstress will not be able to get up from the village today, but there is much we can do. I thought we might look at the rest of your gowns and see what else might be reworked."

Sophia could see no flaw in this enticing plan, so they left the men muttering about oxen and sweepers, and crept away to Sophia's room.

She was still unused to an entire room all to herself, having shared with Maria all her life. At first, she had confined her things to the accustomed half of the room, leaving ample space for Maria's piles of books, but she had soon realised the luxury of taking up every inch of space herself, if she wanted it. Not that she did. Oddly, the more space she had to fill, the less she wanted to clutter up every surface with abandoned bits and pieces. Only a few small ornaments, symmetrically positioned, graced the mantelpiece, her hairbrushes sat in a neat arrangement on her dressing table, a single journal lay on the bedside table in case she should be wakeful at night and everything else was hidden away in drawers and cupboards.

In under an hour, Lily had selected seven gowns that could readily be converted to a more fashionable style. Only two were ball gowns and one an evening gown, but Sophia could not deny that four new morning gowns would be very welcome, too. Their two lady's maids were summoned to give their advice, a pot of tea brought and all was going on in the most satisfactory manner when Froggett, the butler, came in.

"Beg pardon, your grace, Miss Merrington, but there's a Lady Juliet Payne and Mr Simon Payne just arrived."

Lily's face registered bewilderment. "I do not know them. Sophia, do you? No? Are they perhaps acquaintances of the duke, Froggett?"

"Not that I'm aware, your grace."

"Perhaps they are stranded by the snow... a carriage breakdown," Sophia suggested.

"I don't think so, madam," the butler said. "They seem to think they're expected... something to do with the plans for the orangery."

"Then Richard must have invited them," Lily said.

"Oh, yes, of course," Froggett said, brightening. "That will be it, and I dare say he forgot to mention it, what with the snow and all. It's a pity he's out with the oxen team just now. I'll let Miss Hester know. She can arrange rooms and deal with them."

"Oh, no, indeed, I must receive them myself," Lily said at once. "As a noblewoman, Lady Juliet will expect it."

The two visitors stood rather forlornly in the Marble Hall, their luggage in a puddly heap near the door, while an assortment of servants awaited instructions. Mr Payne was gazing around the Marble Hall with its array of pillars reaching imperiously to the high ceiling, his expression of awe one that Sophia entirely understood. She had never quite accustomed herself to the grandeur of Staineybank herself. Lady Juliet, oddly, was engaged in watching Mr Payne.

They were a strange couple. Lady Juliet was tiny, a doll-like figure of around forty, while Mr Payne, perhaps ten years younger, was a large man in every sense, both tall and broad of chest, and as handsome a man as Sophia had ever seen. No... that was not quite true, for there had been a man of ethereal beauty at her very first ball, but he had not even noticed her and she had never seen him again. Nevertheless, he remained an ideal of manhood, but she suspected that Mr Simon Payne, once unwrapped from the many layers of his winter travelling garments, might come very close.

"Lady Juliet, welcome to Staineybank," Lily said. "I am the Duchess of Brinshire."

It was, perhaps, an unnecessary introduction, for the flurry of bows and curtsies from the assembled servants must have suggested her rank, but Lady Juliet turned to her in some surprise.

"Oh! Duchess! I had not expected..." Only then, rather belatedly, did she drop into her own curtsy.

"You are here to see Mr Richard Merrington, I understand?" Lily said brightly.

"Well... I am not sure..."

"It is about the orangery, is it not? Then that is his project."

"Is it? I did not know that," she said vaguely. Then, in a sharper tone, "Simon, do not wander away when her grace is speaking."

"But it is a perfect cube," he said, his face alight with inner fire. "And the pillars... Corinthian, and the frieze is so elegant. Do you not think?"

"Well, I am sure, but do please pay attention when her grace is addressing you."

He turned puzzled eyes on her. "I am complimenting her house, Juliet. She cannot object to that, can she?"

Lady Juliet sighed, but Lily only laughed. "Actually, Mr Payne, I am very pleased that you admire Staineybank, but I find it oppressively grandiose myself."

"Oh no," he said solemnly. "It is beautiful. Campbell, you see. Wonderful architect."

"I am sure he was," Lily said diplomatically. "But if you are not here at Mr Richard Merrington's behest, who was it who invited you?"

"Goodenough," Mr Payne said. "Attorney. Brinchester."

"Mr Goodenough!" Sophia cried. "But there is no such person!"

"I assure you there is," Lady Juliet said robustly. "He wrote to us and then brought us here himself from London in the most commodious style. The carriage is still outside, awaiting our instructions."

"I am afraid it is quite true," Lily said. "Mrs Richard Merrington arrived here last year in precisely the same manner — a letter from a person calling himself Goodenough, who brought her here, whereupon he disappeared. There is no attorney in Brinchester by that name."

Lady Juliet turned and almost ran across the Marble Hall, wrenched open the door before the footman could reach it and raced outside. The others followed more slowly, knowing what she would find.

The drive was empty, only the twin tracks in the snow betraying that a carriage had arrived and had now left, making its way down the drive and not to the Staineybank stables.

"Then it is true," Lady Juliet said. "We have been duped. But *why?* Why would anyone play such a cruel trick on us?"

But no one had an answer to offer.

2: The Architect

"Do come inside," Lily said. "Let us at least offer you the hospitality of Staineybank. You will want hot baths and perhaps something to eat? Or drink? Do you have servants with you?"

"No. Just the two of us," Lady Juliet said, deflated by the discovery that they had been brought there under false pretences.

Lily waved a footman forward. "Henry will take your coats."

They unwound scarves and removed outer garments and gloves and various other impedimenta, and Sophia was pleased to see that Mr Payne was indeed a good-looking man, symmetrical of feature and with dark eyes of unusual brilliance.

Cousin Hester appeared just then, and Lily introduced the awkward guests. Whatever the difficulty, Cousin Hester could always deal with it unflappably. Sophia was not quite sure what sort of cousin she was to the duke — an irregular one, she suspected — but since she was still a spinster at the age of forty-one, she made herself useful running Staineybank.

"Lady Juliet? Mr Payne? Would you care to follow me?" Cousin Hester said in her soft voice.

She made for the stairs, with Lady Juliet and Lily dutifully in her wake, but Mr Payne was still craning his neck to view the magnificent ceiling plaster-work. The ladies stopped and turned on the stairs.

"Simon?" Lady Juliet said, sounding anxious. "Do come along. You may look around the house later, I am sure."

His face fell, and he almost pouted, like a schoolboy denied a long-anticipated treat. Sophia was tempted to laugh, for he was an oddity, that much was certain.

"Perhaps Mr Payne would like to view the principal rooms now?" she said. "I should be happy to show him around, and bring him to his room later."

"That is very kind, dear," Lily said. "Where are you putting Mr Payne, Hester?"

"I thought perhaps the smaller Chinese room? If you approve, your grace. Sir, if convenient, I shall order your bath for one hour from now. Would you care to step this way, my lady."

They vanished up the stairs, and the servants and luggage had disappeared, too, leaving Sophia gazing at the stranger, while he continued to revolve slowly, taking in every detail of the hall.

"I think we were not introduced properly, Mr Payne," Sophia said. "I am Miss Sophia Merrington. My brother Richard is heir to the duke — a second cousin."

"How do you do?" he said, bowing formally to her. "I am Simon." Then as an afterthought, he added, "Payne."

Automatically, she curtsied in response. "Shall we look at another room? The White Drawing Room is through here."

For a while, he prowled around the room, muttering excitedly under his breath at the statues in niches or the carved stone mantels that graced the twin fireplaces. Occasionally he would stretch out a finger to place the gentlest of touches upon an object of particular interest, straightening any ornament slightly askew, his manner almost reverent.

Then he looked up and gasped in awe. Sophia rather liked the painted ceiling, too, with its swirling colours and flying cherubs. When the ladies were yawning after dinner and watching the clock to see when they might expect the gentlemen to return and liven things up a little, Sophia would rest her head on the back of her chair and admire the ceiling. Richard's estate at Leahollow had some interesting plaster work, and a few good paintings hanging on the walls, but this scene, painted directly onto the ceiling, gave her a great sense of wonder. Imagine the skill of the artist, to create such a thing in place, lying on his back, just like Michelangelo! It made her very humble to be able to live beneath its extraordinary beauty.

"It is lovely, is it not?" she said.

"Yes!" He spun round to face her, alight with enthusiasm. "Magnificent! Incomparable! Better than Chatsworth."

"Oh! My goodness! I had no idea. I know nothing of art in general, but I like this very well. There is another, smaller painting on the ceiling of the dining room, if you would care to see it."

"Yes. I would. Very much."

They ambled from room to room, and perhaps because she had expressed an interest, he stopped muttering to himself and described to her all the interesting features. She did not understand much of it, for the vocabulary of art seemed to be largely Italian, not a language she had ever studied beyond a few simple songs, but she liked to listen to him. He had a pleasant voice, lighter than one would expect for such a large man, and his passion for the subject infused every word. And she could not help admitting that he was well worth looking at himself. With his face afire with enthusiasm, and his dark eyes shining, she liked him just as well as the painted ceilings.

Eventually, her curiosity got the better of her, and she said, "I have been trying to decide how you are related to Lady Juliet, but I cannot work it out. You are related, I assume? Or... married?" The ages were odd for a married couple, since Lady Juliet was some ten years older than Mr Payne, but it was as well to know at once.

"Ha! Not married. Brother and sister. Half... different mothers."

"And your father is...?"

"Earl of Edlesborough. Nasty, vindictive man."

"Oh!" Sophia said, shocked.

"Sorry but quite true. I hate him. Keeps us in poverty — his own children."

He pulled at the sleeve of his coat, and she could see now that although it was of good quality, it was shabby and frayed. His neckcloth, too, had a slightly grey tinge, as of linen that has been laundered too many times. Somehow, that was even more shocking, to Sophia's mind, that the children of an earl, a man who must be supposed to have a vast income, should not spend a little to keep his son and daughter clothed in a manner suitable for their station in life.

They had gone round most of the ground floor and had reached the library, where Mr Payne was distracted by the architectural drawings of Staineybank on one wall, when Froggett came in.

"There you are, Miss Merrington. Your bath is ready, Mr Payne, if you would care to step upstairs."

"Oh, goodness, I forgot to watch the time," Sophia said guiltily. "I am so sorry, Mr Payne, and half these rooms have no fires lit. You must be frozen. It is unconscionably rude of me to monopolise your attention in this way, but I was so enjoying your thoughts that everything else went out of my head."

He smiled at her, a warm smile that made her insides melt just a little. "My pleasure. Perhaps we might continue later?"

It was hard to catch her breath. "I am not sure... it will depend. Do go and warm up, and I will see you at dinner, if not before."

With another smile, he bowed and meekly followed the butler, while Sophia was left alone to calm her pattering heart and wonder at her own foolishness.

***

Juliet was waiting for Simon when he emerged, bathed and changed, from his dressing room.

"Oh, good, you got the message about knee breeches," she said, looking him up and down. "The duke is most particular, it seems, and we want to keep on his good side."

"The footman told me, and also not to be late. He sounds... difficult."

"Possibly, possibly. What do you make of it?" she said, pacing back and forth between the bed and the window. "Is it not extraordinary?"

"Beautiful," he said. "The brushwork on the drawing room ceiling—"

"Not the *house*, Simon. The letter! This letter from the supposed attorney — Mr Goodenough. I have been hearing all about it from the duchess. In June last year, Miss Rowena Hood... Hodd... no, Holt, that was it. Miss Holt received just such a letter inviting her to come to Staineybank, where she would discover something to her advantage. She was looking for a post as a governess at the time, so naturally she supposed that was what it was about. A man turned up — she was living in Oxfordshire at the time — gave her a purse of one hundred pounds, if you please, and carried her here in just such a style as we have been conveyed. Whereupon she discovered that no one from the family had ever summoned her, and the carriage, with the fraudulent Mr Goodenough, had vanished. Just as he did to us today. Is it not the most peculiar circumstance?"

Simon pondered that, frowning. "We did not get a hundred pounds."

"That is hardly the point, Simon dear."

"It would have been useful," he said sadly. "A hundred from Mama and another hundred from the attorney — we could have lived very well on that for months. Years, perhaps. All the bills paid."

"Yes, yes, but there was no money from the attorney, who is not an attorney at all. He is a rogue and a charlatan, and I do not understand the purpose of all this. There *is* a plan for an orangery, but this Mr Richard Merrington is to design it."

"She married him," Simon said, suddenly struck.

"What? Who married whom?"

"Miss Rowena Something, who got the hundred pounds. She married Mr Richard Merrington. Who is he? Oh, I remember, duke's heir. Second cousin."

"Is he? Did she? Simon, what does any of that matter? We have been brought here on false pretences, but we can still make something of it. We cannot leave until the snow has cleared, and that gives us an opportunity to talk to this Mr Richard Merrington about the orangery — offer him advice, draw up some plans of your own, that sort of thing. We must spin it out for as long as we can, for at least we will be housed and fed — and *warm*,

Simon! Look at that fire! And the scuttle full of the best coal, and it will be replenished every day. Oh, the bliss!"

"Plenty of hot water, too," he said, smiling. "I had a glass of brandy while I soaked in the bath, and now I feel very warm, inside and out."

"Oh, yes, brandy! There is none in my room, only sherry and some kind of wine, but yes, it does help. Let us see if we can spin this out for a week, at least. If the weather is obligingly bad, we may get ten days out of it, so enjoy the brandy, brother, and the dinner — two full courses every night, the maid assures me. The luxury! Better even than Edlesborough, I imagine."

"Are we invited to join the family for dinner?" Simon said, startled.

"Of course! The duchess sees us as children of the nobility — which we are, of course — and treats us as honoured guests. Is it not wonderful? She is so kind! So very young to be a duchess. How old is the duke, do you know?"

"I know nothing about him."

"But you knew this was his house."

"The house, yes, but nothing about the owner."

"Oh. Well, given the duchess's age, he cannot be much above thirty, I suppose. We shall find out at dinner."

***

Sophia looked forward to dinner that evening with more than usual interest. It was always the highlight of the day, to have everyone gathered together and all in their evening finery. Regular evening dress was not quite as gorgeous as ball wear, but she loved to see the gentlemen in old-fashioned knee breeches, as the duke insisted upon.

The White Drawing Room was already filled with noise when the Merrington ladies arrived in their usual cluster. They were often the last to arrive, for one could not rush the business of choosing the most appropriate attire for the occasion, and then there was the delicate business of sharing a lady's maid. Mama's maid, Souter, also attended to Charlotte, but Augusta, Maria and Sophia were obliged to share Kitty, which meant doing a lot of the work themselves. Not that they minded, for it was part of the pleasure of having sisters in lacing each other's stays, and arranging hair fetchingly, but it did mean that it took an excessive amount of time to be finished, and Mama and Charlotte would be pacing about on the landing for some time before they were all ready to go down. They always went down together, all five of them.

Sophia saw Mr Payne at once, for although he was the centre of a group, he was taller than most of the others. Only Mr Godley, the chaplain, could match him for height. It was clear that there was a lively discussion going on, for voices were raised, the duke's the loudest of all, and Mr Payne's expression was almost panicked.

In between the duke's protestations were the quieter but equally determined tones of Richard, mingled with the gently placating voice of Cousin Hester, always one to smooth over any difficulty. It was not quite an argument, perhaps, for Richard never argued, but it was clear from his face that he was displeased. It was what Sophia called his 'money' face, the disapproving look when he discovered that one or other of them had exceeded her allowance.

Augusta raised her eyes heavenwards. "Now what is the matter?" she murmured.

Lily had seen them arrive, however, and towed them directly into the middle of the group, breaking up the discussion neatly. "Here is Richard's family now. Do allow me to introduce them to you, Lady Juliet. This is Mrs Roland Merrington, and here are Miss Merrington, Miss Augusta, Miss Maria and — oh, you know Miss Sophia, of course. Ladies, this is the Lady Juliet Payne and her brother Mr Simon Payne. They have received a letter from the mythical Mr Goodenough. Is it not intriguing?"

In the courteous exchange of bows and curtsies and polite greetings, the argument was dropped, and in a very few minutes Froggett announced dinner and the company filed into the dining room in silence.

For a while, conversation was muted, the company's attention being absorbed by the dishes before them, and the business of handing round soup and carving the joints, but eventually minds turned to the events of the day. Mr James Hammond, the duke's secretary and memoirist, already knew the circumstances of the Paynes' arrival, but Mr Godley, the chaplain, Mr Pyott, the bailiff, and most of the ladies had to have it explained to them.

"But that is extraordinary!" Sophia's mama cried. "Another letter from Mr Goodenough, just like Rowena's! What does it mean? What can it possibly mean?"

"It means that someone is stirring up trouble," Richard said tersely.

"Yes, but *why?*" Mr Hammond said. "One such event might be allowed to pass unchallenged, and especially given the resemblance between Mrs Richard Merrington and his grace's first duchess. It is clear that someone must have observed Miss Rowena Holt, as she then was, spotted the resemblance and brought her here to please the duke."

"It is not only the duke who was pleased by the lady's arrival," murmured Georgie Hastings, Rowena's companion.

Everyone laughed, and Richard had the good grace to smile and admit that, indeed, he was excessively pleased that Rowena had come to Staineybank and been so obliging as to marry him.

"But that is nothing to the point," he said, as ever allowing no diversion away from his argument. "*Then* it was easy to see a reason for this false attorney to act, but this case is very different. How did he know that there was an orangery to be built here? We have only talked about it amongst ourselves."

"My dear Richard," Georgie said, shaking her head at him, "there cannot be a servant in the house who does not know of the plans, or that you have already been pondering the question for months without arriving at a definitive design. That means that most of Brinshire knows it, too, and a mischievous attorney might well feel that you need a gentle nudge from a *real* architect."

"But why this one in particular?" Richard said. "I mean no offence, Mr Payne, but I know the names of all the most distinguished architects and yours is not amongst them, nor are you known here. So why were you selected?"

"I cannot answer that particular question, boy," the duke said, "but certainly the Paynes are very well known to me. Not that I have ever met these particular scions of the family, but I know their father, the Earl of Edlesborough, well enough — as well as I wish to, at any event. You must be Cecilia's daughter, Lady Juliet — your father's first wife. You have a look of her."

Lady Juliet dropped her spoon with a clatter. "You knew my mother?" she said in awed tones.

"My dear lady, everyone knew your mother. She was the toast of society, you know. A great beauty, of course, and so lively. Always good company. She used to hold an afternoon party every other Thursday in the season, and it was *the* place to be, I can tell you. Such an eccentric crowd she gathered around her, not merely the cream of society but also

Negros and Russian peasants and the like, *interesting* people, you see. Artists, musicians, poets — she loved to have poetry recited in a grand, melodramatic fashion, and if it should be about love and dedicated to her, so much the better. Everyone adored her. Well, except her husband, of course." He frowned, suddenly. "Not sure why she married him, to be frank. A less well-matched pair would be hard to find. His second wife is much more suitable. I suppose she is *your* mother."

He turned his gaze on Mr Payne, who flushed and stammered something inarticulate.

"So why is it that Richard has never heard of you?" the duke said to Mr Payne, his brows lowering ominously. "He is something of an architect himself, in a small way." Here he threw a fulminating look at his heir. "Cottages, and such like nonsense, but you are supposedly a proper architect, are you not?"

It was Lady Juliet who jumped in to answer. "Simon is fully trained... articled and so forth... but he has yet to make his name. One day he will be famous and his work will be widely admired and copied, but he is still at the start of his career."

"What have you designed so far?" Richard said.

"He is working on a country house for a London client," Lady Juliet said. "It is magnificent, but work has not yet commenced."

"So... nothing, then?" Richard said.

"Nothing substantial built as yet," Lady Juliet said. "Some stables and such like, but you may examine his sketches if you doubt my brother's ability, Mr Merrington."

"I shall look forward to it, if you are here long enough," Richard said coolly. "Perhaps you should concentrate on your London client, Mr Payne, for your advice is not needed here. You have been brought to Staineybank under false pretences, unfortunately. There is no requirement here for an architect... *another* architect."

"But for comparative purposes... a second opinion, different ideas," Lady Juliet said eagerly. "There is no harm in that, is there? Perhaps my brother could sketch out a few suggestions, for his grace to adopt or not, as he sees fit. Not a competition, more of a... collaboration."

"But a competition would be amusing," the duke said, with a sudden smile. "Let him have a shot at it, Richard. After all, you have not managed to come up with a final design yet, so why not? It is no insult to you, for I might yet prefer your design to his, but I should like to see some other ideas. There is no rush to settle upon anything, but I should like this orangery to be a fitting monument to the birth of the next heir to the dukedom."

He beamed at Rowena and nothing more was said about it, but Richard sulked for the rest of the evening.

3: Night And Morning

Simon was happy to let the subject drop and enjoy the vast array of food the duke's table provided. Juliet looked triumphant, having gained her point of staying on, at least for a short time, and Simon could not object to that aspect of the arrangement. To be warm and well-fed and permitted to live amongst the glories of Staineybank, even for a week or two, was an unexpected grace for which he would give sincere thanks in his evening prayers.

He ate a great deal and drank a little, and tried his best to make conversation with the duchess, on his left, and another lady on his right. Evenings like this were a great trial to him. There were sixteen at table, and more ladies than gentlemen, which was always difficult. Gentlemen were much easier to remember. The duke was the easiest, for he was by far the oldest, with the imposing presence typical of men of rank. His heir was the young fellow who also claimed to be an architect. There was a chaplain — Mr Godley, an easy name to remember. A solemn young man, who was the duke's secretary, and... the other one. An older man. Simon could not remember anything about him, but he had the air of an employee, rather than a relation.

But the women! There was no getting them straight. The beautiful one in black was the duchess, still grieving the death of her son, and the one heavily *enceinte* was the heir's wife for whom the orangery was to be built, but beyond that he could not put names to any of them. Oh yes, the drab female who looked more like a housekeeper than family was the one who had shown them to their rooms. Hester, he thought. Hester Merrington. They were all Merringtons, the relations.

As for the rest, he had no idea. He had rather hoped to talk again to the pleasant Miss Sophia Merrington, who had shown him about the formal rooms, but she had arrived in the White Drawing Room in a gaggle of her sisters, all with identical brown hair and indistinguishable faces. The annoying habit of changing for dinner meant that he could not even recognise her by her gown. The duchess had introduced them all but so quickly that he could remember none of it. *'Miss This... Miss That... and you know Miss Sophia...'* That was all he had. For a moment, when she smiled at him, he thought he recognised her, but then the sisters shifted into a different arrangement and she was gone. It was maddening.

From time to time, when he was not struggling to make conversation, he looked surreptitiously down the table to see if he could recognise her voice or a mannerism, perhaps, but it was impossible. They all looked the same to him, and the sheer numbers pressed upon his spirits like a boulder. So many ladies! He was no longer used to ladies, apart from Juliet.

Eventually, to his relief, the duchess led them all away and the six men regrouped around the duke. Being the newcomer, Simon found he was the focus of all their attention. At first the questions were easy ones — had he ever been in Brinshire before, and what did he think of it? What were the roads like just now? Where had they travelled from and had they encountered much snow on the way?

But then they reached the sticky parts.

"How is Edlesborough these days?" the duke said. "I have not seen him in an age, but the newspapers report that he is still busy at the House."

"I cannot tell you, sir," Simon said. "I have not seen my father in an age, either."

The duke frowned. "But you must hear from him... or from your mother, at least. Writing to their grown children is women's work, is it not?"

"Not in my family, sir. Not to us, in any event. My father wills it so."

They all stared at him.

The duke grunted. "What did you do to upset him?"

"Juliet? Nothing, I imagine. She was but three years of age when she was sent away. I was fifteen when I refused to go into the army, as he had decided I should."

Another grunt. "That would do it. I do not scruple to tell you, Payne, that I have never liked your father. There is a deplorable meanness of spirit about him, a pettiness that one cannot approve."

"Most people would call him a very fine fellow," Simon said, rather cautiously.

"Oh, he keeps a good table, and serves the best wine, I know all of that. A most hospitable host, and society generally thinks well of him, but I—" He stopped abruptly, his brows lowering. "There is another side to him, and your case only confirms it. So you quarrelled and he threw you out, did he? Foolish man! He does not know when he is well off. I would give my right arm to have a son to quarrel with, but it was not to be. To some men is given an abundance and to others nothing at all. You have several brothers, I take it?"

"Five that I know about," Simon said, with a half-smile. "There may be more now. I do not keep up with the society announcements."

"I suppose he forbids you from going into society," the duke said. "You see? Petty, that is what he is, for all his fine shooting parties. He is a terrible shot, as it happens." He gave a bark of laughter. "Useless swordsman, too. His temper gets the better of him, and of course all that good living made him slow on his feet." Another laugh escaped him. "I believe you are well out of his clutches, young man. So tell me, what do you know of orangeries?"

After that, the talk was strictly business, and much more to Simon's taste. He had never seen an orangery, but he could talk with confidence about them, and the need for high windows and warmth and a suitable aspect. The gentlemen were interested and so the subject lasted until the butler brought a message from the duchess that she would be glad for the gentleman to join the ladies in the drawing room.

Simon was less glad, following the gentlemen with the usual nerves. At dinner, one might at least talk about the food, or deter conversation altogether by a studious attention to one's plate, but in the drawing room there was no escape. He felt as the hare must feel when the hounds are in full cry, with no shelter within reach. One could only sit quietly and hope to be overlooked.

He was not overlooked. One lady after another came to sit beside him, asking the same polite questions that the gentlemen had already asked. Well, he could answer those. No one asked about his father, which was a relief, and Juliet had clearly already explained their relationship, so he was not asked about his mother, or hers. There was music, too, which always lifted his spirits.

And then, at last, there was a call for the card tables and he was able to slide into a game of whist where there was virtually no need for conversation at all. It was somewhat nerve-wracking, for they were playing high, and he had visions of his mother's hundred pounds being swallowed up in a few days. Happily, she had taught her eldest son well, and he soon found his winnings mounting up. He ended the day fifty pounds better off and went to bed in an exceptionally cheerful mood.

He had barely dismissed the footman who was acting as valet when Juliet came in, still fully dressed.

"Well? Did you win?" she said anxiously.

"Cards? Yes. Fifty pounds."

"Oh, thank goodness! I lost twenty. I shall play with you tomorrow. There are some rapacious players here. That Mr Godley is far too mercenary for a man of the cloth."

"I dare say his stipend is not large, so he cannot afford to lose."

"Well, neither can I, but I shall be sure not to partner the duchess again. Very beautiful, but no head for cards at all. Goodness, look at that fire, Simon! What a glorious sight. Is this not the most comfortable place imaginable? If only we could stay here forever! Would you not like that?"

She sat in one of the two chairs arranged either side of the fire, curling her feet under her with a sigh of satisfaction.

"It would be wonderful," he said with sincerity. There was no painted scene on his bedroom ceiling, but the plaster work was intricate and elegant. "We must make the most of it while we are here."

"Yes, yes, but if we *could* stay... what do you think? Should you like that?"

"Of course, but it cannot be done."

He took the opposite chair, for she was clearly settling down for a long chat and when she was in this mood there was no dislodging her.

"That is precisely my point — it *can* be done! Look what happened to the previous recipient of a letter from Mr Fake Goodenough, the non-existent attorney at law."

"What did happen? Oh... she married the heir."

"Exactly so!"

"Is there another heir for you to marry?" he said, amused.

"Me? Nonsense! Heavens, Simon, I am above forty years of age with nothing to my name but that tiny house in Finsbury Square... *near* Finsbury Square, if we are strictly accurate, and a piffling little annuity. No one is going to marry me, but *you*... well, that is a very different matter."

Simon laughed. There was no other possible response.

"No, no, I am perfectly serious. Here we have a horde of unattached women running tame in the house, and the duke seems fond of them. He has not tried to throw them out, in any event. They must have some sort of dowry from their brother, and undoubtedly the duke can be persuaded to rustle up something extra for them. He seems to bleed freely — look at the way he wants this orangery to be a fitting monument to the birth of the heir. That means expensive, brother dear. If we can get our feet firmly under the table, we could be settled for life and think how blissful that would be. So if you could attach one of them, and she can wheedle a settlement out of the duke..."

"You mean one of the Miss Merringtons? The heir's sisters?"

"Of course, who else? Oh, make sure not to look at the girl with the reddish hair. She is companion to the heir's wife, an impoverished widow, and not to be thought of. The duchess has sisters, too, but none of them are here at present and we cannot depend on one arriving in time. My goodness, Simon, the duchess! She must be fifty years younger than her husband. The poor child! It is unspeakable!"

"My own mother was thirty years younger than her husband," Simon said mildly. "Married at sixteen to a man well past forty."

"Yes, well, that was not right, either," Juliet said robustly. "But she seemed... contented, would you say? She never complained, did she?"

"No, she never complained." But then she had never needed to express it in words. He had seen the strain in her eyes.

"Have you ever seen her? Since you left Edlesborough, I mean. You used to walk the streets at night quite a lot when you were younger, so I wondered if you went to meet her, or at least to loiter around the places where she might go."

"She told me never to try to make contact with her, so I never did. It was better so. Kendle would tell me if ever there were any need for contact... if she dies."

"Kendle? He is your father's tool, Simon," Juliet said. "As the heir, he must be. Has he ever made contact?"

"Only once. He wrote to tell me that he had given my address to Mama, but not to expect many letters, since she did not dare to defy Father openly. He put fifty pounds in the letter, too. Kendle is sound, Juliet. He does not defy Father openly, either, but he is a good man at heart."

"Fifty pounds? In one letter? Not cut up?"

"It was hand delivered. I suspect from the description that he brought it himself. Do you remember the stables I designed for the baron in Gloucestershire? He was a friend of Kendle's. The kennels in Yorkshire, too, although that never came to anything. He does what he can for us."

"That was years ago. Nothing since then... another fifty pounds would be useful," she said sourly. "Does it not grind you down, Simon, this dreadful poverty? You are an earl's son — a younger son, admittedly, amongst a veritable army of brothers and sisters, but still you should not be scraping to put food on the table."

"Nor would I be, if I had gone into the army, as he had wished," Simon said equably. "I should have been comfortably situated, probably married to a shrewish society wife, mired in the emptiness of the season and I should have been unutterably miserable. I had far rather live on cabbage stew and be able to do the one thing that makes me happy. I live in hope that one day, perhaps sooner than you might think, I shall be a famous architect and rich enough to keep you in comfort for the rest of your life."

***

Simon woke to the unusual sound of a footman creeping into the room. The bed curtains were swept aside and the spotty-faced youth called Robert was grinning down at him.

"Mornin' chocolate, sir. Cold outside an' snowin' again."

The cup of chocolate was dumped on the side table, slopping a little over the side. Simon hauled himself into a vaguely upright position, while the footman cheerfully rattled the fire irons and tipped coal onto the flames in a great clatter. It was just as well that Simon was not recovering from a surfeit of alcohol. As it was, he smiled. The bed was both comfortable and warm, the heat of the fire was already making itself felt and oh, the joy of a cup of chocolate in bed! What a glorious way to start the day.

"You wantin' me to lay out linens and such?" the footman said. "Press anything?"

"No, no. I can see to myself," Simon said. "Off you go now. You must have more important gentlemen to deal with."

"Only Mr Godley, and he's not prop'ly a gen'leman," the boy said. "Not like yourself, sir. An *Honourable*, you are. Son of an earl. Mr Godley's father was a grocer... or a butcher, I don't rightly remember."

"A respectable tradesman, then," Simon said, with a quick laugh. "What was your father's occupation, Robert?"

"Farm labourer, sir," he said grinning, "so I'm doin' better'n him, ain't I?"

"So you are, and if you work hard and learn to speak properly, as Froggett does, you might even end up as butler one day."

"Lor', sir, that'd be a fine thing!"

"So it would. Now off you go and see to Mr Godley, and try not to spill his chocolate into the saucer."

"Right you are, sir," he said cheerfully, not in the least chastened, but he took himself off and left Simon to enjoy his chocolate in peace.

Juliet, always an early riser, was already in the breakfast parlour, deep in a discussion with... what was his name? The duke's secretary. Another man was there, too, whom Simon had not seen before, an older man who rose politely at his entry. Then, when the other two seemed too engrossed in their discussion to make the introduction, he bowed to Simon.

"How do you do, sir? William Hammond at your service, father to this young man here. I had the good fortune to be secretary to his grace for many years until my retirement. Jamie has followed in my footsteps, but I help out with compiling his grace's diaries in preparation for publishing his memoirs. You must be Mr Payne, the architect."

"I am, yes."

"Delighted to make your acquaintance, sir. I hope your mission here is successful."

The butler came in just then and poured coffee for Simon, as Mr Hammond Senior tucked into his breakfast again.

"What precisely are his grace's memoirs?" Simon said. "Political?"

"The subjects of interest to his grace cover many areas," he said with a broad smile. "His grace commenced to keep a diary when he undertook his Grand Tour at the age of twenty, and has maintained the habit ever since. As you may imagine, in his grace's long and full life there is much to record, both of his public life, his observations of the world and also of personal matters. There is also correspondence of relevance to be reviewed, and newspaper reports of key events in which his grace played a part. There is much to be done to collate all of this information and distil it into a suitably succinct form ready for consumption by the world at large."

"A massive undertaking, I should imagine," Simon said.

"Indeed it is, and one must be something of a diplomat to ensure that no offence is caused. His grace expresses his opinions in his diary more robustly than he would if voiced aloud."

"I am not sure I would agree with you there, Father," said the son, his attention caught by the conversation. "The duke can be extremely robust when he wishes to be. He is not a man who smiles sweetly to a man's face and roundly abuses him in the privacy of his diary."

"So you think he would have called a certain Prime Minister *'a snake of the first order, who should be nailed by his treacherous neck to the stable door and left to writhe'* to his face, do you?"

"He certainly called him vermin, in the House of Lords, if you please, and said he would set his dogs on him if he ever set foot in Brinshire."

The father burst out laughing. "Did he so? He is a redoubtable old fellow, is he not? Who could not admire such spirit?"

"I could not, for one," Juliet said acidly. "I value a little civility, myself."

"Oh, to ladies, certainly," Mr Hammond Senior said, a twinkle in his eye. "A true gentleman will extend every courtesy to a lady, but gentlemen may exchange views more vigorously, and yet remain the best of friends."

"How very odd," Juliet said. "I should not call anyone a friend who was rude to my face. Do gentlemen never fall out with each other, Mr Hammond?"

"Certainly," he said, "but not on account of a few choice epithets after a glass or two with convivial friends. On points of honour... that is a different matter entirely. A gentleman will always defend his own reputation, or that of the ladies in his family."

"At the point of a sword, no doubt," Juliet said. "How very foolish men are."

"Undoubtedly," James Hammond said, with an edge of impatience. "Mr Payne, Lady Juliet and I have been puzzling over this letter that you received, asking you to come here."

"From the supposed attorney," Simon said absently, as he concentrated on buttering his toast liberally.

"Goodenough, who does not exist," Hammond said acidly. "Yes, that letter. Did you have not the least idea who it might be from?"

"If it is not from an attorney by the name of Goodenough, then no."

"But he accompanied you here. Can you describe him?"

Simon set down his toast with a sigh. Clearly he was obliged to earn his breakfast today. "A nondescript fellow, rather shabby."

"Age?"

"Hmm. Hard to say."

"Tall? Short?"

"Average, I should say."

"Thin or fat?"

"Neither thin nor fat. Middling brown hair, what I saw of it. Nothing distinctive about him."

Hammond huffed in frustration. "Which no doubt describes half the men in Brinshire."

"Is he from Brinshire?" Simon said. "He did not have the accent."

"Ah... interesting," Hammond said. "But of course that means he could be anybody. And the question remains — why? With Mrs Richard, the motive was clear, since she was the very image of the duke's first duchess, but with you, Mr Payne..."

The sentence tailed off into silence, but Simon understood him well enough. Why an unproven architect, rather than a more established man? And why an architect at all, when clearly there was already one in the family?

"It is a mystery," Juliet said impatiently. "Perhaps we may never know, so it hardly matters. No point wasting energy on fruitless wondering."

"I believe we must," Hammond said. "If this were the work of a random stranger, it would be no more than a curiosity, but it cannot be. The letter is quite specific in requiring someone to design an orangery. That means that someone known to the family wrote to your brother, Lady Juliet. Possibly someone within the family. So, again, and more strongly, I wonder why."

"Wrote to Juliet," Simon said.

"What?"

"Letter was to Juliet. Asked her to bring me here. Not written to me."

Hammond huffed in disbelief. "That makes no sense whatsoever."

It made no sense to Simon, either, so he disregarded it and turned his full attention on his toast.

4: An Eligible Man

Simon was enjoying his third or possibly fourth cup of coffee, and pondering the delights of a proper breakfast, in which mutton chops featured prominently, when Richard Merrington came in, nodded to everyone, scowled at Simon and then waited. Without being asked, the butler placed a plate of ham and the toast basket in front of him. A creature of habit, then. Detecting a chill in the atmosphere, Simon rose to retreat.

Without looking up from his plate, Merrington said, "I am required by his grace to show you my work so far on the orangery, Mr Payne, and discuss the requirements with you."

"I had sooner discuss the requirements with the duke," Simon said, prompting a hiss of alarm from Juliet.

Merrington frowned. "Nevertheless, those are my instructions, and therefore yours."

"I am at your disposal, Mr Merrington."

"Are you indeed?" he said, his tone flat.

Simon waited politely until Merrington had consumed his ham, two slices of toast with strawberry jam and a single cup of coffee. Then he followed him through several apartments he had not seen before, up a stair and into a large study, decorated in a lighter style than the other rooms he had seen.

"This is very elegant," he said, slowly spinning round to admire the delicate colours on the walls. "That table — Sheraton?"

"It is. I like the simplicity of his style."

"These paintings are good, too. Yours?"

"Not my work, no. I have no skill with oils. That set came from my estate at Leahollow, in Norfolk."

"Why do you live here if you have an estate in Norfolk?"

"Because I am the duke's heir and his grace requires me to be here," Merrington said tersely. Then, after a moment's silence, he exhaled slowly. "I beg your pardon. That was uncivil of me. You do not know the circumstances, after all."

"My fault," Simon said equably. "I am inclined to say whatever comes into my head."

Merrington gave a bark of laughter. "That is refreshingly honest. The truth is that I am not at all comfortable with my new position as official heir."

"New position? How is that? Is the duchess—?" He saw the expression on Merrington's face, and realised he was treading on dangerous ground. "None of my business, is it?"

"It is no secret. The duke has been married three times, has sired innumerable children, including four sons. All have died, the most recent only last June, a boy of six. At that point, his grace surrendered the battle and sent for me. Until then, I was quite happy as a lowly country gentleman with a modest estate."

"Leahollow. This one here?" He pointed to a framed pencil drawing hanging above the desk.

"Yes. It has been leased out for some years, since I preferred to live in Norwich."

"And here you are buried in the country again."

Merrington gave a rueful smile. "Indeed. I should not complain — indeed, I do not, for we are kept in the utmost luxury, and his grace has generously opened his doors to my entire family."

"And you met your wife here," Simon said, still prowling round looking at the pictures on the walls.

"Yes!"

There was so much animation in the single word that Simon looked at him in surprise, to see a smile of such warmth that he almost felt embarrassed. There was a man who adored his wife!

Almost at once the smile faded, to be replaced with a much more anxious expression. "If only this baby were born! The waiting is so hard."

"Hoping for a son?"

"I care nothing for that, so long as my wife survives the ordeal," he said savagely. "I *hate* this waiting, knowing that any day could be her last on this earth. The duke lost his first duchess that way, so naturally we are all... nervous." He heaved a sigh. "There is nothing to be done about it. God's will, and so forth." Another sigh. "Well, shall we make a start, Payne? I am to show you my sketches, and also the drawing I made of the orangery at Marshfields."

"Marshfields?"

"Home of the Duke of Camberley, to whom my wife is related. *Distantly* related... and on the wrong side of the blanket."

Simon chuckled. "There is one of those in every family, so they say. Not always acknowledged, though. Your family history is... complicated."

That brought a wintry smile. "So it is. My sketches are over here."

***

Sophia had breakfast with Mama and her sisters in their own little apartment, as usual. She was wild to go downstairs and find out more about the intriguing Mr Payne, and her sisters were so minded too, but Mama was adamant.

"This is the home of a duke, girls, and I will not have you scampering about chasing eligible men like hoydens. You will be dignified and restrained, and remain ladylike at all times."

"We can be dignified and ladylike just as well in the breakfast parlour as here," Charlotte said, not unreasonably.

"We are never hoydenish," Augusta said with dignity.

"Nor do we scamper," Maria said. "At least, I do not."

"None of us do," Charlotte said firmly. Being the eldest, she was the most certain of the rightness of her opinions.

"Nevertheless," Mama said, "it would be seen to be putting yourselves forward, and the duke would frown upon it. We must at all costs do nothing to give him cause to send us away. He is happy for us to befriend the duchess, and we make ourselves useful where we can. I am helping Cousin Hester and Charlotte is tidying up the household accounts, and I am sure the rest of you are finding ways to help out."

"I am exercising the horses," Augusta said quickly.

"Yes, the two mounts trained to accept a side saddle," Charlotte said, making the others laugh.

"Oh, the grooms can ride the men's horses, but only a lady can ride a lady's horse," Augusta said, her chin rising. "I am providing a necessary service, but I am not sure that Maria or Sophia are finding useful ways to occupy themselves. Maria lounges around in the library all day and I do not even know what Sophia does with herself."

"Wishes she were dancing," Maria said, with a sympathetic smile. "It is all very well for the rest of us, who are quite content to be buried in the country since we have our favourite occupations here, but Sophia must be missing Norwich and the assemblies."

Sophia sighed gustily. "Oh, the assemblies! And we cannot even get to the piffling little assemblies in Brinchester for this foul weather, and it will soon be Lent and there will be no pleasure to be had until Easter."

The ladies sighed in unison, for although Sophia loved a ball above all things, her sisters never missed an opportunity for dancing either, for how else were four spinsters ever to find husbands? And that thought brought Sophia back to the intriguing new gentleman at Staineybank.

"Is Mr Payne eligible, Mama, would you say?"

"Why certainly, dear! The son of an earl — how can you even ask the question?"

"I do not think he has very much money. He said his father keeps him in poverty, and his clothes are shockingly worn."

"Unmarried gentlemen are often careless of their appearance, Sophia. Once they start thinking of matrimony, they generally become very smart, and I am sure Mr Payne will do so, too. Bachelors spend their allowances on gaming and horses and... well, other things, but once they have a wife and children to support, they become perfectly respectable."

"What other things?" Maria said.

"Male things," her mother said, with pursed lips.

"Are you saying he is *not* respectable now?" she persisted.

"Really, Maria!" her mother said, rather flustered. "All these questions are most unbecoming. You need only know that Mr Payne is most eligible, and if one of you should have the good fortune to attract him, then your brother will enquire into his exact financial position, so you need not be concerned. His father will want him to be suitably settled, and what could be more suitable than an alliance with the Duke of Brinshire's family?"

"So we may try to entice him?" Charlotte said.

Her mother winced at such plain speaking. "You have my approval to get to know him better, and if he should like one of you... well, let us see what happens, shall we?"

"I wonder if he rides?" Augusta said.

"I am sure he will be very learned," Maria said. "One cannot be an architect without knowing a great deal."

"Only of art," Charlotte said loftily. "I doubt he reads poetry, Maria. If he is purse-pinched, he will be looking for a wife who knows how to keep house economically."

Sophia said nothing. She was more interested in whether Mr Payne could dance, but she was unlikely to find that out soon. The others soon fell into their usual man-hunting conversation, of strategy and the proper means of taking turns with him, which always resolved itself into Charlotte claiming the superiority of age and the others loudly denouncing any such idea. Sophia had heard it all before, and no matter what schemes they dreamt up, they always ended in disappointment. This time would be no different, she was sure.

And she would not mind a bit, if only she could dance now and then.

Glumly, she crumbled her breakfast roll and tried to count in her head the number of weeks until Easter, and the next certain assembly.

***

Simon spent the whole day with Richard Merrington. In the morning, he looked at his multitude of sketches and listened to his description of the discussions with the duke. He was most interested in the drawings of the orangery at Marshfields, home of the Duke of Camberley, which had inspired the original idea of building one at Staineybank. Merrington and his wife had visited the duke, who was recovering from illness and found the orangery a warm and congenial place to spend his days. Mrs Merrington had liked the place, and Simon could see why. Merrington's drawings showed a light and spacious room with high windows, filled with light, and a multitude of fruit trees dotted about. He had put the duke into his drawings, too, and his wife, which brought a sense of human scale to the magisterial dimensions of the building.

Yet when he saw Merrington's own designs for an orangery, he saw nothing magisterial. The simple brick structures had no grandeur or elegance, they were merely practical.

"Why so small?" he said, puzzled.

"The expense!" Merrington said brusquely. "The duke may not care how much this costs, but I do."

"Why?"

"Because... good heavens, do I have to explain it to you? The duke has a vast income now, but if he spends by the bucketful, he will very soon find himself in deep water. Or rather, *I* will find myself in deep water, when I inherit. There is nothing more miserable than an income inadequate for the wants of those dependent upon it."

Having lived for half his life on an inadequate income, Simon had no argument against this point of view. Instead, he said mildly, "Is he spending by the bucketful?"

"Of course he is! His kind have no idea of money. Apart from the orangery, he is setting up an establishment for the duchess in Cheshire, near her family, and according to his grace, nothing is good enough for her. She must have the biggest house in the county, the most servants, the largest stables to house the vast number of carriages she is to have. Then he has provided lavishly for my wife and me, not to mention accommodating my wife's friend as companion. And then there is my mother, and my four sisters, all eating their heads off here, while the duke encourages them in every extravagance, and has even talked of putting up additional dowries for my sisters. It is madness!"

"He must know what he can afford, surely?"

"On the contrary, he never thinks of money at all, in the wild assumption that it will always be there when he needs it, and Mr Pyott — the comptroller, you know — is the most supine fellow imaginable. *'Yes, your grace. No, your grace. Anything your grace wants.'* It is... oh! Listen to me, grumbling away as if I have any right to object to anything. I assure you, I am very grateful for my good fortune, Payne."

"When one has developed the habit of economy, it is hard to shake it off," Simon said neutrally.

"Exactly so! You understand the case, and you will appreciate why I do not rush to design some wildly extravagant monstrosity for this orangery. I should like it to be built, naturally, to please my wife, but it does not need to be grandiose."

"But it must be beautiful, surely," Simon said. "It must be in keeping with the splendour of Staineybank."

"It is a functional room, no different from the forcing houses in the kitchen garden," Merrington said dismissively. "A place to grow fruit, that is all, but the need for heat will make it expensive to maintain, so I am attempting to keep the scale at a level which will minimise the cost of fuel."

Simon made no further comment on Merrington's designs, determining that he would ask the duke for his thoughts on what sort of design he would like and let that be his guide. Having seen all of Merrington's sketches, he showed him his own designs and the rest of the day was spent in a comfortable discussion of the relative merits of renaissance styles and baroque, and the newly emerging picturesque designs.

***

Dinner that evening was another trial of Simon's patience, although of a very different nature. As soon as he crept into the drawing room, hoping to find a quiet corner from which to admire the painted ceiling, he found himself surrounded by a fragrant cloud of Merrington ladies. He did not even recognise any of their gowns from the previous evening, so there was not the slight hope of separating them in that way.

At least they were all unmarried, so he felt safe in addressing any of them as *'Miss Merrington'*, should he find himself talking to one in particular. But they hovered around him like a gaggle of geese, although somewhat more melodious. He had no need to scrabble about in his mind, presently overloaded with architectural matters, for suitable topics of conversation, for they maintained the flow of words by themselves, answering their own questions and twittering so happily together that he could not have found an opening for his own thoughts had he wanted one.

It was a relief to go into dinner, although he was not surprised to find two of the four sitting smugly to either side of him, and the others, showing discontented expressions, on the opposite side of the table. The meal drifted away with painful slowness, and he did his best, no one could say that he did not, but the sort of light-hearted conversation that Juliet said was favoured by young ladies did not come easily to him. He did his duty, ensuring that they were served from whichever dish took their fancy, and discussing the food doggedly, for that was easy enough to talk about, but beyond that his imagination struggled. Happily, however, the four continued to talk as much to each other as to him, even the two across the table, so his imagination was not greatly tested.

Eventually, the duchess rose to shepherd the ladies away and a blissful silence descended upon the dining room, as the butler and two footmen cleared the table and set out the port and nuts.

The port had gone round the table twice before the duke crooked a finger in Simon's direction.

"Come and sit beside me, Payne, and tell me what you think of Richard's efforts for this orangery, now that you have seen his designs. Are they any good, do you think? He tells me it is important to be practical, and take the costs into account, but I should not like anything paltry, not when it is a gift to the future duchess and mother of the next heir. What is your view?"

"Practicality is certainly important," Simon said cautiously. "However..."

"Yes?" the duke said eagerly.

"One would wish the edifice to be in keeping with the magnificence of Staineybank."

That brought a murmur of agreement from around the table. Not from Richard Merrington, Simon noted, but that was only to be expected.

"Now that the snow has stopped, Richard must show you about the grounds," the duke said. "He has his own ideas regarding a suitable location for the orangery, but I should like to hear your thoughts. You will want to see the best prospects, so be sure to view the south face of the house from the far side of the lake. So you find much to admire in Staineybank, do you, Payne? The entrance hall is well done, do you not agree?"

After that, the duke only wanted to hear praise of the house, and there was no more talk of the orangery.

***

The next morning, Charlotte appeared at the Merrington ladies' breakfast fizzing with excitement. Taking a stance as melodramatic as an actress on the stage, she flung her arms wide and declaimed, "What do you think? Richard is to show Mr Payne over the grounds this morning. I have it directly from Weston that they are to go all round the lake and then back past the forcing houses."

"It is to be hoped they wrap up well," Mama said. "The snow may have stopped, but it is dreadfully cold out there."

"Yes, yes, but do you not appreciate my meaning?" Charlotte cried. "I propose that we go for a walk ourselves. If we take the opposite direction, we shall be sure to meet them and then we may turn and walk back to the house with them."

"Oh, what an excellent idea," Mama said. "I have always thought that these seemingly spontaneous meetings outdoors offer by far the most fruitful opportunities for furthering an acquaintance. Gentlemen are so much more at ease out of doors, have I not always observed it so? Did Weston say what hour the gentlemen have arranged for their outing?"

"Directly after breakfast, he said."

"Then you had better make haste, girls. Quick, quick! Away with you now!"

Sophia was not keen on the idea of a walk in the snow, for in her experience such events led to one being cold and wet, with a red nose, but the pursuit of Mr Payne was too worthy an objective to be neglected. Accordingly, then, the four sisters donned their warmest clothing and stoutest boots, and set off to accidentally meet their quarry.

As she had suspected, the air was cold enough to freeze a girl's very bones, but the snow was not deep if one walked with care to avoid places where drifts had gathered. Augusta, of course, managed to walk through the deepest piles, so that the hem of her pelisse was soaked. Charlotte gently chided her, in her rôle as temporary mama. As the eldest, she was always in charge whenever the sisters ventured forth without Mama. If ever a woman had been born to be a wife and mother, it was Charlotte, with her stream of gentle admonishments and her housewifely instincts. It was a puzzle why no man had ever seen the possibilities in her.

Sofia herself could not quite see the attraction in motherhood. The improved status of being a married woman was a consideration, naturally, and she would quite like to be mistress of her own establishment, and not be merely the youngest, and frequently overlooked, daughter. But to spend one's life breeding, as Rowena seemed condemned to do, did not appeal. As for a husband, no matter how dutifully she chased after every likely young man, and a few less likely ones, too, it had to be confessed, she had never been greatly drawn to them as companions of her heart. There had not been a single one whom she could look at and say honestly that she would be content to meet him at breakfast every morning for the rest of her life.

Nevertheless, it was her bounden duty to do her utmost to marry, and so she set forth with her sisters in pursuit of Mr Payne. Their efforts were in vain, however. Once they caught a glimpse of him with Richard on the far side of the lake, and occasionally there was a faint drift of their voices far away, but the only person they saw was the gamekeeper, out with his gun. They returned to the house cold and wet, especially Augusta, and with bright red noses. The rest of the day was spent in bemoaning their ill-fortune, and planning the next stage of their campaign.

But on one matter they were all agreed, even Mama — from now on, they would eat breakfast with the gentlemen in the breakfast parlour, a far more comfortable method of pursuit than trailing about in the snow.

5: An Invitation

"A Greek temple?" Richard Merrington said in astonished tones. "Great heavens!"

"Roman," Simon said diffidently. "It is in the Roman style."

The gentlemen had gathered in the duke's study to examine Simon's first drawings of his proposed orangery.

"I suppose it will be filled with statuary and all manner of marble decorations," Merrington said.

"That is the general idea, and some suitable murals on the inner walls. A hypocaust for heating."

The duke laughed. "This is very different from your efforts, Richard," he said, leaning over the table where Simon's drawings were laid out. "I like it, and the setting is interesting, with the lake around it. It will look charming from the front of the house."

"That is the idea," Simon said.

"It will cost the earth," Merrington muttered.

"What does that matter, for Rowena?" the duke said, his brows lowering ominously. "It will be a suitable celebration of the birth of the heir. Have you any costings, Payne?"

"Not yet, Duke."

Merrington gave a *'Pft!'* of disgust, and walked out of the room.

"He is on edge at the moment because of Mrs Richard's imminent confinement," James Hammond said in conciliatory tones.

"That is no excuse," the duke said. "If you ask me, he is jealous of a man of real talent showing him how it should be done. These are proper architectural drawings, not those piffling sketches of his. And I never met a more penny-pinching man. When I am gone and he inherits all this, he will doubtless turn off half the servants and live on mutton dripping and stale bread. I cannot abide such parsimonious ways."

Simon said nothing, leaving it to Hammond to remonstrate gently with the duke.

When the drawings were shown to the ladies later, he was gratified to find that they were almost universally admired. The only naysayer, although in the mildest terms, was Mrs Richard Merrington herself, for whom the project was ultimately intended.

"It is quite splendid," she said, after the effusions of the others had died away somewhat. "It will be rather a long way to walk to enjoy it, however."

"There will be an admirable view from the front of the house," the duke said, his brows lowering again in the manner Simon had come to recognise as a sign of displeasure.

"Oh, yes, and it will be quite lovely to gaze out at it over the lake," she said. "But I shall want to sit in it, too. There is nothing so delightful as the sight of all those exotic trees flourishing and watching their wonderful fruits burgeoning day by day. To get there, I shall have to cross the stream by the bridge at the top of the lake and walk round the far side to the orangery."

"You will hardly want to be out there every day," the duke said dismissively. "It will be a pleasant stroll in the summer."

"Well, yes, but—" she began.

Simon put in hastily, "How about a bridge across the narrow part of the lake? That would be a shorter route to the orangery."

"Even more expense," Merrington muttered, but Simon was given leave by the duke to design a suitable bridge.

"After all, nothing is agreed yet," he said, glowering at Merrington. "I want to see all the possibilities before I make a decision."

Simon retreated promptly to his room, and settled at the table there, sketch book ready. How easy it would be to run up some elegant designs for bridges, and yet... He could not help recalling the endless hours he had spent talking to Mr Thwaite, discussing his requirements in minute detail and then modifying the plan of his great house accordingly. Not that he had yet agreed to build, but still, everything had been discussed.

Yet he had never talked to Mrs Merrington about the orangery. To Merrington, yes, and to the duke, but never to the lady in whose honour it was to be built.

He was still pondering this point when Juliet bustled in.

"This is very good, brother! The duke likes what you have done, and now there is to be a bridge, so—"

"She plans to *use* it, Juliet."

"What? Use what? Of whom are we speaking?"

"Mrs Merrington. I assumed it was merely a monument, an ornamental gift, but she wants to use it... to sit in it."

"And so she may, if she wishes. There is no law against it, I am sure. You can put some seats and such like inside it, I dare say, something comfortable, and she can go and sit there whenever she likes. What is the problem?"

"She wants to *'watch the fruit burgeoning day by day'*, Juliet. *Day by day*, do you see? She wants to sit in it every day. But it is away across the lake."

"So you will design a bridge for her. Simon, this is not a difficult task, but you must take as long as possible over it, for Richard Merrington will probably have his way in the end, and therefore we will not be here to see the thing built. Let us see if we can last a full month, at least."

"He wants to put the orangery with the forcing houses, which is much further away. That would not do at all. Mrs Merrington will not want to get herself rigged out for a long walk in the rain every day."

"Well, of course not! She will not go there in bad weather. But tell me, how are you getting on with the Merrington girls? You played whist with Miss Augusta last night."

"Did I? I cannot tell one from another."

She stared at him in disbelief, before bursting into laughter. "Really, Simon! What a tease you are! Now get to work on that bridge, but slowly, mind! You were far too quick with the temple design, so take your time with this. It is glorious to be warm and well-fed all the time."

She sighed with contentment, and he smiled, entirely in agreement with her.

***

Sophia's project to produce new gowns from old was proceeding apace. The duchess had thrown herself into the task with enthusiasm, and as

Sophia's supply of old gowns was gradually depleted, so the press filled up with delightful new ones. The seamstress from the village did most of the work, but Lily directed her and Sophia had little to do but agree to all the improvements. The outdated wide skirts and voluminous bodices disappeared, replaced with fashionably high-waisted bodices and narrow skirts. There was enough fabric left over for puffed sleeves, decorative trimming and elegant little trains.

It would be very satisfactory if only there were somewhere such charming garments might be worn.

The answer to that question arrived that very afternoon, in the prosaic form of the mail collected from Brinchester by one of the grooms. The snow having rendered the roads impassable for several days, the haul was rather larger than usual and the Merrington ladies and the duchess gathered in the cosy winter parlour to read them.

At first they seemed to be merely the usual missives from distant cousins and acquaintances from Norwich, with depressing news of how lively that city now was, with a great many parties to be held. The Merrington sisters were thrown into gloom by all the entertainments which were going forth without them.

"Now, girls, you know perfectly well it will only be musical evenings and card parties and the like," their mama said, in tones where her own disappointment vied with the need to be bracingly cheerful. "No assemblies, and no one would risk a ball at this time of year. We are much better situated where we are."

"But there are no parties at all here, Mama, and no dancing," Charlotte said plaintively.

"You would not wish to be dancing while the duke and duchess are still mourning the loss of their son and heir," Mama said sharply. "Perhaps after

Mrs Richard Merrington's confinement there might be some celebrations considered."

The sisters sighed, but the possibility of some future delight could not quite compensate them for missing the known entertainments of Norwich, and which they might even now be enjoying.

The duchess had bad news, too, although it was cunningly disguised as good news.

"Well! Elinor has a suitor! At least, so Amabel thinks. She says he is *'excessively attentive, and has called at the Grange every day, through the direst weather, bringing fruit from his own stores.'* They went out for a walk, you see, and were caught out in a nasty shower, not snow but very sleety. Sir Nicholas was most concerned that Elinor might take a chill and nothing assuaged his fears, seemingly, except baskets of pears. That is very promising! Oh, but it means that Elinor will not come to me later this month after all. Amabel says that matters are just at a delicate stage, and she does not think a separation just now would be a good idea. No, indeed! Elinor must stay, and see if anything comes of it."

"Your sisters?" Sophia said, trying to follow Lily's rapid words.

"Yes... did I not mention it? I am the eldest, but Amabel is next to me in age, and then Elinor. Amabel is married to Sir Maurice Hartwell — an excellent match, and now this neighbour of hers... Sir Nicholas... something-or-other... sounds as if he will do very well for Elinor. Goodness! How exciting! I shall miss her, of course, but how happy for me that I have you ladies to bear me company, for I should be very moped without you all."

But the best letter of all was one which was not revealed to the ladies until the evening, when they were all seated around the White Drawing Room.

"I have received an invitation from Camberley," the duke said in a loud voice, standing with his back to the blazing fire as he surveyed the room.

All conversation died away on the spot.

"The Duke of Camberley?" the duchess said. "Goodness! What does he want with you?"

"He wants me to help him celebrate his heir's fortieth birthday, that is what he wants, and you are invited too, my dear, and also Richard and Mrs Richard. There is to be a grand ball, and with the weather being so unreliable at this time of year, we are all invited to stay at Marshfields. It is a compliment to Rowena, to be sure, on account of her connection to the family. What do you think, Lily? Should you care to go?"

"A ball? Oh, no, I could not! It is too soon after—"

Tears filled her eyes, and the duke said gently, "Ah, of course! No need to distress yourself, my dear. Naturally we shall not go. I thought it might lift your spirits a little, but I quite see that it would not do."

"I cannot go, either, Duke," Rowena said, patting her swollen belly. "But Richard might like to—"

"Certainly not!" he cried. "Leave you at such a time? I should not have a moment's peace."

"Then the invitation must be refused," the duke said. "It is a kind thought, but Camberley will understand."

"Oh, but—" Sophia's mama began.

At the same time, Mr Payne said, "I should like to go."

All heads turned towards him.

"You?" the duke said. "What, pray, entitles you to go to Marshfields?"

"Not... not *entitled,"* Mr Payne stammered, flushing. "Should like to see the orangery, that is all. The one Mrs Merrington admired."

"What an excellent idea!" the duke said. "Then you will have a better idea of the thing. Ha! You can make sure that mine is better than Camberley's. You are Edlesborough's son, so there can be no objection. I shall let Camberley know to expect you."

"I had better go with him," Lady Juliet said quickly. "He is liable to forget to eat without someone to watch over him."

Mama had gone rather pink. "I am sure no one would quarrel with your dispositions, Duke, but perhaps it might be as well to send someone who can more properly represent the Merrington family. Mr Payne and Lady Juliet are wonderful additions to any society, naturally, but they are not connected with your grace. Besides, a ball can be of no interest to them. Whereas my daughters—"

"That is an excellent idea!" cried Lily. "The Miss Merringtons would love to dance at Marshfields, I am sure."

Sophia held her breath. Surely, surely, the duke would see the advantage of it? What was the point of sending a man like Mr Payne to a ball, or a spinster of forty or more? How much more sensible to send young ladies, particularly those who longed to dance.

"Two of them might go, I suppose," the duke said, frowning. "Only four are invited, and Camberley will have a houseful by the sound of it, so there will not be room for more than four. Payne, Lady Juliet and any two of the Miss Merringtons."

Sophia's spirits sank into her slippers instantly. That would be Charlotte and Augusta, by right of seniority.

"Oh, but my girls must have a chaperon," Mama tinkled, "and they are never apart, you know, Duke. So very close! We must all go."

"Not all!" Lily cried. "You cannot leave me here without a single Miss Merrington to bear me company. They cheer me up so."

"A mother cannot be separated from her daughters," Mama said firmly. "You will have Mrs Richard Merrington and Mrs Hastings for company, so you will not miss us at all, I am sure. Indeed we must all go."

"Or none," said the duke, his brows lower than Sophia had ever seen them.

Sophia made a tiny squeak of distress. To be so close to a ball, and yet to have the possibility snatched away at the last minute! It was more than a girl could bear.

The duchess turned to her with a smile. "Ah, you want to dance, Sophia, do you not, and put those new ball gowns to good use? I have a proposal, Duke. If Mrs Merrington were to take Sophia to Marshfields with Lady Juliet and Mr Payne, I should still have three sisters for company, and I believe I should be an acceptable chaperon for them. Do you not agree, Mrs Merrington?"

And Mama, little though she liked to concede the point, was obliged to smile and express her gratitude and pretend that nothing would please her more.

Sophia's sisters glared at her, but she did not care. She was going to a ball, and nothing could dent her happiness.

***

Simon found an unexpected advantage to the journey to Marshfields, in that there was only one Miss Merrington to contend with. With four sisters indistinguishable to his eyes, he could never be sure when he spoke to one which of them she was, and so he dared not initiate any conversation in case he had spoken the same words to the same lady previously. How stupid that would make him appear! And yet how stupid he must seem when he was so unwilling to speak. It was so much easier to converse with a lady in the morning knowing that she was the same person he had spoken to at dinner the previous night.

Juliet, naturally, was excited by the possibilities.

"Just think, brother! Two or three weeks in Miss Sophia's company! You have only to exert the least amount of charm and she will be in your hand, without doubt. At her age — she is twenty-eight, just imagine it! At her age, as I say, she will be desperate for a husband and here you are, just the right age for her and free as a bird."

"A lady who remains unmarried at twenty-eight must be very determined not to acquire a husband," Simon said, amused.

"Nonsense! All those girls are desperate to marry, that much is plain. What, did you think they like being spinsters so much that they have deterred all suitors? No such thing, I assure you. Their mama is very forthcoming on the subject. She has ten thousand to share amongst them, so they will each have two and a half thousand — a tidy sum! That would keep us in mutton for a long time, would it not?"

"Their brother would be foolhardy to agree to any of them marrying a penniless architect, Juliet."

"Oh, pooh! He will be happy to get rid of one of them, you may be sure. His mother says he is constantly bemoaning how expensive they are. Besides, there is no knowing but that the duke will settle something on them, too, and he is full of juice. This could be the making of you, Simon, if you would but exert yourself a little."

Simon was not minded to exert himself to Miss Sophia Merrington or anyone else. He was contented with his life as a bachelor, and if he would be happy to have the supply of mutton a shade more secure, there would be the constant irritation of another woman in the house, not to mention a string of mewling infants. He and Juliet rubbed along pretty well together, but that was largely because she made few demands on him. A wife would not be so forbearing, he was sure.

Nevertheless, Miss Merrington turned out to be a peaceful travelling companion. Her mother and Juliet found endless subjects for discussion, and maintained a constant stream of comments, but the daughter read her travel guide, speaking only to point out a distant spire as they drew near to a cathedral town, or a glimpse of some grand estate as they passed by its perimeter palings. If applied to, she would tell them how far they had come or how many miles to the next posting house, but otherwise she was blessedly silent.

On the second overnight stop of the journey, Simon entered the parlour secured for their use to find Miss Merrington the only occupant. She was seated at the table with her back to him, an untouched glass of wine near at hand, with her travelling writing box open, her pen flying over the paper. Her head was lowered as she bent to her task, and he found himself mesmerised by the sight of her pale neck. There was only a small gap between the frill round her gown and the lowest reach of the hair piled on her head, but a few wisps of hair had strayed from their fellows and lay tantalisingly across the divide. He could not say why those wandering curls attracted him so powerfully, but they did. In daylight, her hair was an indeterminate brown colour, but in the flickering light of the candles the errant strands looked pale and insubstantial, and he had the most inappropriate urge to touch them, to feel their silkiness and wind them around his fingers.

With a start, she looked up. "Oh! Mr Payne! I beg your pardon, I did not see you there. May I pour you a glass of wine?"

He shifted uncomfortably, aware that he had been staring at her. "No, no. I can pour my own. Pray finish your important letter."

"It is only to Augusta," she said, with a sudden laugh, laying down her pen. "Charlotte yesterday, Augusta today and Maria tomorrow, then back to Charlotte again."

With the wine in his hand, he sat down opposite her. "You write to one of them every day, then?"

"Oh yes! There is so much to tell them of all that we have seen. None of us has ever been on this road before, so they will want to know everything. It is very difficult to describe it all in words, I am finding. It is so much easier when we are all together for if one of us misses some important detail, one of the others will be sure to have observed it. But now I must be the eyes and ears for four people and it is not easy, let me tell you."

"You are not often apart, then?"

"Hardly ever," she said, with a sorrowful shake of her head. "I miss them abominably, but I could not refuse to go, could I? Not with a ball to be enjoyed. I shall have my work cut out to describe the occasion. The dances I can remember, and the ladies' gowns will be easy enough, but the setting! I shall be spending half my time counting the candles and the number of footmen instead of enjoying the dance."

"Then perhaps I can help you," he said, with a smile. "Shall I sketch the room for you? Then you would not need to count candles."

"How good you are! But I should not wish to keep you from the dancing, Mr Payne. You must have your share of the pleasure, too."

"Dancing is no pleasure to me, Miss Merrington. I have no intention of spoiling the pristine symmetry of the movements with my ineptness. Producing a drawing of the room will give me an excuse not to skulk in the card room, as I might otherwise do."

"You do not dance?" she said in astonished tones, just as if he had said that he ate babies for breakfast or admired Bonaparte. "Not at all? Not ever?"

"Not ever," he said solemnly. "I never had a dancing master to teach me, and so I never learnt."

"How sad!"

That made him laugh. "I have never felt the lack, I assure you."

"I suppose one does not miss something one has never known, but oh, if only you could understand the joy of dancing, Mr Payne! Do you walk... or ride?"

"I can ride, of course, but I have no horse, so it is not a means of transport in which I can indulge. I walk, naturally. Everyone walks."

"Yes, but do not mean a walk to get somewhere, nor a dawdling sort of walk, such as Mama likes, so she can talk at the same time. I am thinking of a brisk walk in cold weather, preferably of several miles' duration. Do you ever do that?"

"Sometimes."

"And do you not feel exhilarated, as if your whole body is thrumming with energy and you are at one with the world, your limbs energised and your lungs filled with clean air? Or a fast ride — that can produce the same effect, or so Augusta says. That is what dancing is like for me. Do you never feel like that, Mr Payne?"

"Miss Merrington, I do not. If I go for a long walk in London, brisk or otherwise, my lungs are filled with choking smoke and my limbs ache."

She smiled, shaking her head at him. "You have no soul, sir."

"Not as far as walks are concerned, no. But give me a hearty meal washed down with a good claret, and I engage to be as much at one with the world as even you might wish. And set me down in a house like Staineybank, with lofty ceilings and marble pillars and exquisite plasterwork, the walls hung with great works of art or adorned with statuary — that calls powerfully to my soul."

"Ah... I remember when you arrived how much you liked the house."

"Liked it? I was in awe — struck dumb with admiration."

"I do not remember you being struck dumb, precisely. I thought you were remarkably eloquent. However, I concede the point, and acquit you of having no soul. And now I must finish my letter, or poor Augusta will not know what has become of me."

She bent her head to her task again, and Simon was left with an odd little smile on his face and the strangest bubble of warmth inside him. What on earth did that mean?

6: The Orangery

Marshfields was vast, Sophia discovered. She had barely grown accustomed to the scale of Staineybank, but the Duke of Camberley's seat was enormous. The main body of the house was set around a square courtyard, while each corner sprouted a vast additional wing. Fortunately, a footman was stationed at the foot of every stair to direct a girl who might otherwise wander about for hours, at risk of missing something vital, like dinner.

The house was stuffed to the rafters with relations of the duke, come to celebrate the fortieth birthday of the heir. Sophia found herself sharing a room with two other young ladies, Lady Emma Something and Lady Maria Something Else. They tried to explain their connection to the duke, but Sophia lost track in a morass of cousinships. She had the same difficulty explaining her own connection to them.

"My brother is the heir to the Duke of Brinshire, and his wife is descended from a sister of the Duke of Camberley, Lady Rosalind Bucknell, who was thought to have died but did not, and her twin sister was

Caroline, the present Duke of Brinshire's first duchess. She *did* die! So I am sister-in-law to... um, a great-niece of the Duke of Camberley. I think."

At which point, the two girls' eyes glazed over.

The numbers filling the house meant that no one dining room was large enough to accommodate all the guests at once. The Staineybank party was assigned to a modestly sized room in one of the outer wings, known as the Blue Room, into which some forty people squeezed each evening. They were, so Lady Emma informed her, the third tier of guests, the most important eating in the State Banqueting Hall in the main building, the lesser beings in the marginally smaller Oak Dining Room.

After dinner, everyone separated into one of several rooms, depending on whether one wished to play cards, listen to music, play billiards or simply sit and chat in one of several drawing rooms. Sophia would have liked to venture to the music room, but she had no idea where it was. Mama was too overwhelmed to wander about and so stayed in their own wing, befriending two or three other matrons. Being accustomed to the modest proportions of Leahollow, and latterly the tiny Norwich house, Marshfields was terrifyingly large to her.

"Imagine if I should become lost and wander off into some unknown quarter," she said. "Why, I might never be found! It is better to stay here and not go too far afield."

Sophia would not have minded wandering around the house, for it was symmetrical enough that she did not fear to become entirely lost. Besides, there were plenty of people about. Still, she could not leave Mama, so she dutifully worked on her embroidery as her mama chatted. If only her sisters were with her! There were other young ladies about, and sometimes they came to sit beside her, which was pleasant, but not like having her sisters there. At other times, they stayed away and Sophia had no idea how to make friends with them. It was not something she had ever needed to do before. Still, even if she could not talk to them, she could covertly note what they were wearing. Not only was there the need to report fully to Charlotte, Augusta and Maria, but it was imperative that she fit in with the society in which she now found herself. One would not wish to be thought a dowd, but nor would one want to appear too grand. Fortunately, the latter was unlikely, for every lady, it seemed, was wearing her finest gowns and jewels.

One person who looked much as usual was Mr Payne. He still wore the same slightly shabby attire as at Staineybank, making Sophia wonder afresh if he were truly impoverished, or merely eccentric enough not to care about his appearance.

At one dinner, the third after their arrival, she found herself sitting beside Mr Payne at table. In all the strangeness of Marshfields and the loneliness of being without her sisters, he was a beacon of familiarity. Even though she hardly knew him, he smiled at her and felt like something close to a friend in this sea of strangers.

"How do you like Marshfields, Mr Payne? Does it meet your expectations?"

"I had no expectations, Miss Merrington. The description in the guidebooks did not inspire me with any great sense of anticipation."

"Oh! You do not like it?" she said, astonished. "But... it is huge, and... and very decorative, do you not agree?"

"Very decorative!" he said, eyes twinkling. "Excessive quantities of decoration, in fact. The northern wing is decorated in the Elizabethan style, the west wing in Rococo, the east wing in the modern style, apart from the library, and I cannot even describe the south wing." He shuddered. "But two of the corner wings are somewhat elegant."

"I see," she said, with a little laugh. "I rather like not knowing what may be round the next corner, but I suppose Staineybank does have a greater harmony."

"Staineybank is beautiful," he said. "Marshfields is... interesting, perhaps. No doubt in the days of the Plantagenets it was a simple courtyard house — a great hall with a kitchen wing to one side and public rooms on the other, but the owners have tinkered with it unmercifully. Externally, it has a degree of symmetry, but inside... although I take your point about a surprise around every corner. That does lead to some curious juxtapositions of ancient and modern, of the exquisite pinnacle of the craftsman's art next to... well, less felicitous pieces, shall we say. And then there is the orangery."

"Oh, have you found it? Lucky you! I should so like to see it, after hearing so much of its wonders. We were given a tour of the house yesterday, but there was no sign of it."

"The orangery is what I am here for, so I asked. It is where the duke likes to sit, which is probably why you were not taken there. He has not been well, so the orangery has become his retreat from the world, a warm cave to hide away from the frantic activity elsewhere."

"The poor man! There is nothing worse than being surrounded by people when one is unwell. I was determined to attend a ball once, even though I felt very sickly, and it was not a pleasant experience. The noise! And I was so hot, it was unbearable. I swooned and had to be taken home. Well, we all went home, and my sisters were very cross with me for spoiling their fun. The next day, I went down with influenza, and they got it afterwards, one after the other, even Mama, and so we went nowhere for six weeks. It was dreadful, and we were still at Leahollow then, so we were stuck out in the country, with nothing to do except wait for everyone to get better. The poor duke! I wonder he holds this ball if he is unwell. He could perhaps delay it until he has recovered."

"My understanding is that he feels he might not recover," Mr Payne said in a low voice. "He has been ill for some time, and although he is a little better, he is not a young man, and is feeling his age. Or so it is said below stairs. The footman who attends me is full of such gossip, and it could be moonshine for all I know."

This was too tragic for Sophia to contemplate, so she fell silent and since he seemed to have nothing further to say, they both turned their attention to their plates.

Later, Sophia settled with reluctance to her stitchery again while Mama talked to another lady of her anticipation of the impending grandchild. The other lady had around a dozen grandchildren, she said, although she seemed hazy as to the precise number, and had much to say on the subject of wet nurses and nursery maids and the necessity for the new mother to drink beef tea in vast quantities. Sophia could not summon the least interest in such matters, which all sounded most alarming to her ears.

When the gentlemen abandoned their port and masculine discussions, Mr Payne was among the first to enter the small drawing room where Sophia sat. He stood uncertainly on the threshold, surveying the room, and for a moment she thought he might decide there was no one of interest there and go in search of better company. However, his eye fell on her and with a little smile he headed straight for her.

That was a surprise! Before she had time to do more than school her features into an expression of polite welcome, he was upon her.

"Miss Merrington, since you have not yet seen the orangery, perhaps you would like to visit it now?"

An even bigger surprise, but of course there was only one possible answer. "I should love to see it, Mr Payne."

"Then allow me to escort you."

She jumped up at once, only to be held back by her mother's gentle voice. "Alone, Sophia? I think not."

She was immediately crestfallen. "Of course. Perhaps tomorrow we can arrange a party to go. I am so sorry, Mr Payne."

Mama gave out her tinkling little society laugh. "No, no, I do not mean to spoil your pleasure, Sophia, only to deter you from wandering off alone with a gentleman. You are so used to having your sisters with you, that you have seldom needed to consider such matters. If *I* accompany you, however—"

"That is perfect!" Sophia cried happily. "Although... I do not wish to take you away from your interesting conversation."

Mama laughed, tucking her embroidery needle neatly into the material, and folding her work into her sewing bag. "Lady Aurelia will forgive me, I am sure. We may continue our discussion later... or tomorrow, if the weather continues inclement. Lead on, Mr Payne. I confess to a great interest in seeing this orangery myself."

Mr Payne led them out of their satellite wing and into the main body of the house, and thence through a bewildering array of apartments, all decorated in a different style, muttering, *'Rococo... Jacobean... ah, Palladian!'* as they walked. Then there was a short, narrow passage before a footman guarding an arched door threw it open to allow them to pass.

It was like being in a strange sort of indoor forest. All around were the orange and lemon trees, set in giant pots on wheeled platforms. There were pineapple plants, too — she recognised them from an engraving she had once seen in a book — but many of the plants were unrecognisable to her.

The air was warm, and musty with the aroma of soil and a multitude of plants. The floor was tiled, and the high roof gave the room an echoey feel, like a cathedral. To one side was a solid wall, but the opposite side of the room was dark — glass, she saw, like a giant window looking out into the night.

"Oh!" she breathed, thrilled. "It is snowing."

"So it is," Mr Payne murmured beside her. "She will want to sit and watch the snow."

"Who will?" Sophia said, but he had walked straight over to the window, there to gaze out, mesmerised, at the steady snowfall.

Sophia and her mama followed, albeit rather nervously, for there was the sound of a harp playing somewhere in the orangery. They were not alone! The music stopped, and a lady rose from behind a bank of greenery, a vision of loveliness such as Sophia had seldom seen. She had grown used to Rowena's beauty, but here was another one to make her wish that she had been born with smooth skin, rosy lips and enviable symmetry of feature.

"Good evening!" said the vision. "Ah, you are with Mr Payne. Pray allow me to introduce myself. I am Lady Grace Skelton, daughter of the duke. You must be the Merrington ladies."

"Indeed, I am Mrs Roland Merrington, mother of Mr Richard Merrington, heir to the Duke of Brinshire," said Mama, instantly taking charge of the situation. "This is my youngest daughter, Sophia. I beg your pardon for intruding. We had no idea anyone would be here, and we so wanted to see the orangery that has been so much spoken of. The duke wishes to commission one of his own for his seat at Staineybank, in honour of my daughter-in-law."

"So we understand," Lady Grace said. "Do come in and meet my father. He does not cope well with crowds just now, but he will wish to welcome you to Marshfields personally."

In the far corner of the room, hidden by a range of bushes that rustled gentled as they passed by, they found the duke huddled over a card table, deep in a game of piquet with a well-favoured young man, who was introduced as Lady Grace's husband, Mr George Skelton. The duke himself was rail-thin, with the sort of grey tone to his skin often seen in those suffering a prolonged illness. He rose courteously to his feet, however, without any sign of unsteadiness.

"Mrs Merrington, and Miss Merrington, I am delighted to welcome you to my home, and to thank you for helping us to celebrate this milestone in my son's life. But your own son is to encounter a milestone of his own very soon, I understand — the birth of his first child, and the first of many, we must all hope."

"Indeed, and if it should be a son—"

"That would be a blessing indeed," the duke said gently, "but a daughter is a blessing of a different kind, is it not so? I have certainly been blessed in my own daughters, who are a great comfort to me in my old age."

"That is not what you said to us when we were younger, Papa," Lady Grace said, with a smile. "You called us troublesome creatures, if I recall."

"And so you were, when you were off in town spending my fortune on fripperies and doing nothing but enjoy yourselves at my expense. But then you all married and brought amiable young men into my life, and filled my house with delightful grandchildren, and so I forgive you. Will your son's firstborn be your first grandchild, Mrs Merrington?"

"It will, your grace."

"Then you have all the joys of that exalted state to come. Let me tell you, madam, there is only one felicity greater than the arrival of small children for a visit, except for their departure, when the house descends once more into blissful calm. Pray sit, and tell me of your son and his wife. Skelton, be so good as to pour some wine for Mrs Merrington and Miss Merrington."

Sophia declined the offered wine, and, leaving Mama to attend to the duke, she wandered towards the high windows to watch the snow falling outside. It fell straight down, like a white waterfall, the many candles burning inside illuminating those flakes nearest the window. Beyond, the garden lay in darkness.

"It is fascinating, is it not?" said Mr Payne, materialising at her elbow. "I could watch it all night, but should you care to look around? There are some interesting plants in here."

"I know nothing of plants," she said. "Tell me instead what you think of the room. It seems very elegant, to me."

"Yes, but a little plain," he said. "If it were me, I would add more statuary, and murals on the walls."

"What sort of murals?"

"Oh, plants... greenery, to make the place look bigger. One would feel as if one were in a tropical garden, stretching to the horizon. And there need to be more seats... a hammock, perhaps."

"A hammock! How lovely! One could sit here in the warmth with a book, and swing gently under the trees. Even if it were raining outside—"

"Or snowing!"

"Yes, or snowing, it would be cosy. But there should be birds singing, and perhaps a fountain plashing gently."

"A fountain! What an excellent idea. Yes, yes, that is just what she would like, I am sure. And canaries… a line of cages, perhaps along the back wall. Yes, I can see it now."

"Who would like it?"

"Mrs Merrington, of course."

"Mama? But—?"

He gave a bark of laughter. "I beg your pardon — no. Mrs Richard Merrington. The orangery at Staineybank is for her, is it not? And she wants to *use* it, which means she wants to sit in it, or play cards in it, like the duke, or… or…"

"Or entertain in it," Sophia said. "I like the way this one is connected to the house, so one may walk here at any time."

"Yes! Connected… so one might entertain in it. An additional drawing room, perhaps. A place to gather before dinner. You are a fount of good ideas, Miss Merrington."

They walked about the room together, as he described just what features might be needed, adding more and more decoration until she was moved to remonstrate with him.

"There will be no room for the plants at this rate, Mr Payne."

"By Jove, I believe you are right. I was a little carried away there, for a moment. Very well, no Gothick arch draped with vines, but I must have my statues of the Roman gods, and the bird cages and the fountain. Definitely a fountain."

"And a hammock," Sophia said, with a sigh of contentment. "There must be a hammock."

The duke overhearing these words, they were summoned back to his side again, and Mr Payne was called upon to describe once again all the delights he envisaged for the Staineybank orangery. The duke added his own embellishments to the scheme, so that it became both a peaceful retreat from the world and yet the hub of the entire house, a room for the display of great art and yet displaying elegant simplicity, a place of solitude and contemplation, but also capable of entertaining great crowds.

Sophia shook her head at the impossibility of it all, and was rather relieved when the duke's valet arrived to point out that his physician had ordered the duke to be in his bed an hour ago, which broke up the party instantly.

As they left the orangery, two footmen were already lurking outside to douse the candles. The duke's party disappeared down a wide corridor, leaving Sophia and her mama to follow Mr Payne back to the main part of the house. Much of the house was already darkened ready for the occupants to retire, just an occasional beam of light spilling from an open door, with voices and laughter emanating that suggested that not everyone was ready for bed.

Mama was not minded for a late night, however.

"You must get as much rest as you can tonight, Sophia, to recruit your strength for tomorrow's ball," she said firmly, leading Sophia past the interesting open doors.

Reluctantly, Sophia went to her room, although the prospect of the ball compensated to some degree for missing the excitements of the present evening. A ball! Dancing! Oh, the delight of it, and the anticipation was almost as good as the event itself.

Her two noble friends were already abed and fast asleep, so she undressed and climbed into bed as carefully as she could. Then she curled up and closed her eyes, ready for dreams to overtake her. But curiously, her last waking thoughts were not of cotillions or energetic country dances.

Instead, she imagined herself lazing in a hammock reading the fashion journals to the delicate sound of canaries warbling and a fountain playing.

7: A Grand Ball

Simon could not sleep, his head filled with designs for the orangery, his mind sketching away even as he lay in the darkness. When he eventually dropped off, he slept badly, waking again and again with the urge to begin drawing. As soon as the girl came in to light the fire, he was up, his pencil in his hand. He worked at it all morning, absentmindedly almost forgetting breakfast until Juliet came to fetch him, covering page after page with his ideas.

And yet, nothing satisfied him. Somehow, his designs were not right, but he could not quite put his finger on what was wrong with them.

In the middle of the afternoon, he tossed aside his sketch book and stood gazing disgruntledly at the snow-covered grounds outside. The skies were already darkening in preparation for nightfall, as a few stray flakes still fell. Occasionally a miniature avalanche was dislodged from a tree, falling with a soft whump.

He sighed. Perhaps if he found a quiet spot somewhere about the house he could sit and think, and clear his head. Then perhaps he would understand what his designs needed.

It was a futile endeavour. The house was vast, but unused rooms were in darkness, and those with enough light for sketching were filled with noisy groups of people, chattering excitedly, playing the pianoforte and even dancing. There was no possibility of finding the quietude he needed. He moved on from room to room, and then up the grand staircase, running his hands appreciatively over the polished mahogany handrail. Again he was out of luck, until he turned a corner and found himself in the Great Gallery.

When he had seen it before on his tour of the house, it had been a dreary place, panelled in dark oak, badly lit, with no objects of artistic merit, only a few badly-executed portraits of Bucknell ancestors in a variety of improbable costumes. Now, however, lamps illuminated the full length and innumerable girandoles stood ready to be lit. At the far end, several footmen had lowered a chandelier to fill the candle holders. Nearer to hand, two men on hands and knees were steadily creating a chalk pattern of vines and ducal coronets and lions rampant on the wooden floor. Along both walls, a selection of chairs and sofas had been arranged, and on one sofa, swinging her feet joyously, sat Miss Sophia Merrington.

Congenial company — perhaps that was what he needed?

Sitting down beside her, he said, "Preparation for the ball?"

"Yes! Is it not exciting? They are putting in the candles, and they are *eight hour* ones! Is it not wonderful? Eight whole hours of dancing!"

"Shall you not be exhausted by so many dances?"

"Oh yes, but it will be worth it. If I am exhausted, it will be because I have stood up for every dance. There is nothing more dispiriting, Mr Payne, than going to bed at the end of a ball still full of energy. I want to dance and dance and dance until dawn. Or until the candles burn out, I suppose, because at this time of year, even eight hour candles will not see the dawn."

"Then for your sake, I wish you a partner for every dance," he said, smiling at her, for such enthusiasm was infectious. "How fortunate I am to see the chalk pattern before you and your friends obliterate it with your lively steps. And I have my sketch book with me, so I shall attempt to copy it."

For a while they were silent, as his pencil flew over the paper. After the two chalk artists, he drew the footmen with the chandelier, and then he added in the chairs. Dissatisfied, he started another sheet, this time drawing little details — a nearby girandole, the curved arm of a chair, one of the chalk artists, hunched over his work, his face intent. Simon's slender fingers moved the pencil with quick, sure strokes.

"Have you always had such skill?" she said, breaking his concentration so abruptly that he started. "I beg your pardon. I disturb your work."

"The fault is mine," he said. "I am inclined to forget the world when I draw. But yes, I have always been able to draw, or at least, I never remember a time when I could not. I have never had a drawing master and the architect to whom I was articled taught me only the skill of architectural drawings."

"But people... people are hard," she said. "I can paint a vase of flowers, say, with sufficient accuracy that the gardener would recognise the precise blooms and not mistake a rose for a poppy, but I cannot capture the likeness of people at all well. My attempts are usually only recognisable by their clothes, or a favoured ornament. I painted Richard once, and Maria said, *'Well, it must be Richard, because that is his waistcoat and fob, but otherwise I should have supposed it to be the bishop.'* Which was very lowering, for the bishop is twice Richard's age, and very fat with red hair. But Maria's portraits are no better, and Charlotte does not even attempt them."

He had to smile at this tale of woe. "It is true that portraits are challenging, and I could not do it in watercolours and certainly not in oils. But a pencil... that is a very forgiving medium, to my mind. Charcoal is even better. It is just a line here, another line there, a little smudge of shading... not difficult at all. And because my main interest is drawing buildings, I have a good eye for perspective and proportion, which is half the battle when drawing people."

She nodded thoughtfully. "I can see that that must be so. Richard is very good at drawing people, too, and he draws buildings all the time. Mostly cottages and the like. That is how he became interested in architectural matters, when new cottages were needed for our estate at Leahollow, and he disliked all the designs he saw, so he designed his own. Being Richard, of course, he wanted to save money, too. He worked out the cost to the last brick, so that he could order just the right number."

"There is nothing wrong with being economical," Simon said, pulling out his knife and shavings box to sharpen his pencil. "Especially with labourers' cottages, where the need is for practicality, not ornamentation. Function is the most important object, whereas a man of wealth and rank wants to impress his fellows and display his position in society to the world. The cost of coal and candles is immaterial to him."

"But not to Richard," she said softly. "When he inherits, he will be the most parsimonious duke in the Kingdom."

Simon laughed and shook his head. "He will grow accustomed. It is easy to adjust from a modest income to great wealth. It is much harder to grow up in great wealth and have to adjust to poverty."

"Oh. I suppose it is." She gazed at him round-eyed, wanting to ask the obvious question but not quite daring to breach the protocols of never asking about money.

"You are wondering, I suppose, if I refer to myself," he said. "Indeed I do."

"But... your father is an *earl*," she whispered.

"True, but the title bestows upon a man wealth and power and the esteem of society. It does not give him wisdom or kindliness or generosity. It does not make him a good father. It clothes him in silk and ermine and puts a coronet on his head, but his character remains just as it always was, for good or evil."

She was silent for a long time. The footmen had long since finished wrestling with the chandelier, and the chalk artists had shuffled their way almost to the far end of the gallery. He started another drawing, this time of the stone fireplace with its ornately carved overmantel.

"Was he very horrid to you?" Her voice was so low as to be almost inaudible.

"He never beat me or anything of that nature. Mostly, he ignored me. I was the third son, so quite unnecessary in the scheme of things. My destiny was to go into the army, he decided. If he had chosen the church for me, perhaps I could have put up with that, and become a famous ecclesiastical architect eventually, but no, he had settled on the army. My younger brothers were bookish, so he deemed them a better fit for the church, thus I was to go into the army. It would make a man of me, he said. When I refused, he threw me out."

"Threw you out of... his study?"

"The house. I was banished from Edlesborough, with only a small bag of necessities and whatever money I happened to have saved. Fortunately,

I had enough to get a seat on the mail coach to London, where Juliet and a widowed aunt took me in. I had never met Juliet, since she left Edlesborough before I was born, but when I became interested in architecture, I wrote to her for advice. She lived in London, where so many architects live, and she encouraged my ambitions. She told me she would help if I chose to study the subject, so when I was banished, naturally I turned to her. And there I have stayed for the past fifteen years with Juliet my only true friend. Half my life was passed at Edlesborough, in great comfort even if there was not much affection to spare, and the other half in an unfashionable area of London, eking out an existence on a hundred and fifty pounds a year."

Another long silence, then she said, "I spend almost that much on clothes every year." Then, slowly, "You must have *some* friends, surely? Do you belong to clubs?"

"No, since my father and uncles never introduced me to any. It is true that I do have... well, acquaintances. Other architects, for instance. Neighbours we dine with or invite to card evenings. But not *friends.*"

"Mr Payne," she said, her voice strengthening suddenly, "I have not known you for very long, but even so, I consider myself your friend. I hope you would regard me in the same light?"

"Oh!" He was aware of a warmth within him that made him, quite involuntarily, smile broadly. "I should be honoured to so regard you, Miss Merrington."

A friend! A female friend, at that. How strange the ways of the world! He had left London in search of a commission, and instead he had found a most unexpected friendship.

***

Sophia was ready for the ball long before the appointed hour. While Lady Emma and Lady Maria were still driving their maids to distraction by dithering over which gown to wear and how to dress their hair, Sophia was already skipping down the stairs to the drawing room to await dinner. Naturally, she had pretended to dither over her gowns, too, for what self-respecting girl would not? But in fact she had settled on her present gown as soon as she had known of the ball, for its pale green silk skirt with spangled net tunic made it the most exquisite of all her ball gowns.

She had agonised a little over the correct ornaments, but seeing how formal everyone at Marshfields was even for a regular dinner, she had decided to throw caution to the winds and wear diamonds at her throat and ears, with a sparkling headband to match. Sadly, she had no diamond bracelets to wear, but she had some set with peridot which would look well with her gown.

The disadvantage to arriving early was the long wait for everyone else to arrive. Luckily, the first was a bouncy girl from Yorkshire with a mass of black curls who was just as excited as Sophia, even though she already had a husband, and therefore had nothing at all to hope for from the ball beyond the pleasure of dancing. She chattered away, relieving Sophia of any need to speak, apart from an occasional *'Oh, yes, indeed,'* and *'I quite agree.'*

Eventually, everyone else appeared and dinner commenced, only one course tonight, which caused some grumbling from the men. Lady Juliet's lighter tones could be heard berating her hapless dinner companion.

"There will be a hot supper later, so you will not starve."

"It is all very well for you," the young gentleman complained. "At supper, you ladies are kept supplied by the good offices of the gentlemen, and we are so busy attending to your needs that we are lucky to get any left-over scraps when you have all sated yourselves."

She only laughed. "I shall keep a jelly or two for you, Lord Daniel."

"Invalid's pap," he muttered.

"Well, a lobster patty, then. You cannot turn up your nose at that, now can you?"

"Rather have a good slice of mutton, frankly. I shall be glad when this wretched ball is over and we can eat properly, and no nonsensical jigging about and pretending we are enjoying ourselves, either."

She shook her head, not at all discomfited. "There is no pleasing you, sir."

Sophia laid down her knife and fork as she puzzled over this conversation. A wretched ball? Nonsensical jigging about? It was incomprehensible to her, although she saw a number of the gentlemen nodding their heads in agreement. How strange men were! Lord Daniel, whoever he was, looked a pleasant sort of man, a little younger than she was, and surely capable of jigging about for a few hours without great distress. Was it truly such a trial to a man?

But perhaps he was married already, and therefore saw little point in it. She wondered idly if she herself would lose interest in dancing if she were married, but such a state seemed so impossibly out of reach that she could not imagine it.

Dinner was soon over, and the true purpose of the evening could begin. Sophia was filled with the usual flutter of excitement. A ball was such a delightful well of possibilities. Tonight her life might change utterly. All it would take is one man — just one — to *notice* her, not merely as a dancing partner but as a person... as a woman... as a potential wife. Surely there was one man in the world whose eyes would light up when they saw her? But she must not get her hopes up too high. There had been several over the years who had appeared to favour her, but nothing had ever come of it. It was not smiles in the ballroom that mattered, it was whether he would appear the next day, still smiling, and the day after that... So far, in almost eleven years, not one had ever lasted the course.

Still, tonight might be different, who could say? There was always hope.

Sophia and her mama found seats near the mid-point of the Great Gallery, where they could watch the arrivals and were well placed for prospective partners to notice Sophia. She discovered that, while she had spent the past days identifying possible gentlemen of interest, her mother had spent her time with the matrons more fruitfully.

"Never mind the men," she said to Sophia in a low voice. "Time enough to find out about them if they show an interest. It is the girls — your rivals — we need to watch. Now, that one in pink—"

"So pretty!" Sophia sighed.

"Betrothed," Mama said crisply. "The two blonde girls with the woman in puce have no dowries, so we need not regard them. The one in blue with the sapphire pendant — goodness, do you suppose that is real? Heavens! Well, she is a widow with three children, so she is not likely to be a problem. But that one... do you see who I mean?" She angled her fan to point discreetly. "The girl in white with that long curl over one shoulder... what a flattering style that is! It might do for Charlotte, since her hair is a little longer than yours. Anyway, the girl in white is an earl's daughter with twenty thousand, so she will be popular. And the girl with the peculiar headband — such an odd arrangement! I am glad none of *my* girls succumb to such monstrosities. You all have excellent taste."

"We had your example to follow, Mama," Sophia said. "You are quite the best dressed chaperon here."

"Oh... well... my goodness! You flatter me, my dear, for I am sure... one does one's best, but on such a modest jointure, one is somewhat constrained. We are mingling with ducal families here. There is no comparison."

"They may spend more money on their clothes, but not to such good effect," Sophia said sturdily, for she was sure that her mother was as well-dressed as anyone there. "If you had the jewels that some of them wear, you would look finer than anyone. Tell me about the girl with the headband."

"Oh yes! Only five thousand at present, but her brother is heir to a man of great wealth from Cornwall or Devon or some such outlandish place, and as soon as he inherits, she will have more. But I do not think she is very pretty, do you? She looks sulky."

In this way, they passed the time as the Great Gallery filled up and the musicians took their places and began to warm up their instruments. Some of Mama's friends joined her and brought an end to the discussion, but Sophia did not mind. If she could not talk, she could watch the swirl of silken skirts and the sparkle of diamonds and admire the shapely legs of some of the gentlemen, on display in their evening breeches and stockings.

And then — oh joy! — the musicians fell silent, the leading couples began to take their places in the first set and there was a gentleman bowing before her, an older woman, his mother, presumably, making the introduction and Sophia was swept into the lower reaches of the set. Mr Cadell... she must remember everything, so she could report to Maria... no, it was Charlotte's turn for the next letter. Mr Cadell... perhaps thirty years of age, neatly dressed, she could say no more than that, and with sadly spindly legs. Hair a nondescript brown colour, arranged in what he probably thought was a fashionably Brummell-like style but in fact looked as if he were leaning into a stiff breeze. Features… hmm, attractive eyes, nose a little too large and mouth too thin-lipped.

But he proved to be adept in the dance when the movement finally reached them, and an easy conversationalist. She discovered that he was a Surrey neighbour of the Duke of Camberley, had three brothers and two sisters, and he was the second son, with two good livings to his name. He was at pains to tell her that his pasturage was the best in the county and his income was no less than a thousand a year. Yet even as he danced, his eyes were assessing the other young ladies, settling often on the earl's daughter in white, the one with a dowry of twenty thousand. Ah well, Sophia could not compete with *that.*

Her second partner was the same Lord Daniel who had so disparaged the very idea of a ball. Yet in the event, he proved to be a most agreeable partner, setting himself to entertain her and not boring her with inane flattery or dull tales of his prowess in the hunting field. He was a son of the Marquess of Pentavon, he told her, when she asked, and said nothing more about himself, turning all her questions aside with a little smile and, *'Oh, I am not a very interesting person, Miss Merrington. But do tell me more about your home in Norwich. I have never been there, but the cathedral is magnificent, so I hear.'* She passed a pleasant a half hour, and returned to her place by her mama well pleased with him.

There was another source of pleasure, too, for she had spotted Mr Payne wandering around with his sketch book, amiably recording every detail of the evening for her. He seemed to be following her about, so that when she and her partner moved down the set, so did Mr Payne, and when they danced their way back up again, he followed, all the while drawing furiously. She could hardly wait to see the results.

After Lord Daniel, she was solicited by a taciturn and rather stout Mr Withers, and then a very tall and aristocratic Lord James, although she never caught his surname. After that, she was obliged to sit out, but to her delight, Mr Payne came to sit beside her, to show her his numerous sketches. Some of them were of details — a lady's fan, a turban, a vase of flowers — but most were of the dancers.

"Why am I in so many of the drawings?" she said, puzzled. "There are more than twenty couples in most sets, but I seem to be well to the fore on almost every page."

"I have been trying to capture the movements of your gown as you dance, and your feet also, and the way you hold your arms. It is illuminating to repeat the same sketch, to see if I am improving. Do you see? This was my first effort, which does not, to my mind, encapsulate the exuberance of your dancing, but this one here is much better, do you not agree? And this last one... I think I have caught you perfectly."

"I certainly look as if I am enjoying myself," she murmured, amused.

"Oh yes! I have generally hidden away in the card room on the rare occasions when Juliet has dragged me to a ball, so it has been a revelation to me how much enjoyment you derive from the simple act of dancing. Miss Merrington, I believe that gentleman is waiting to speak to you."

She looked up to see Lord Daniel hovering awkwardly nearby, twisting his hands about.

"I wondered..." he began, his voice rather high, before he coughed and began again in a more normal tone. "I wondered if perhaps... if you are not otherwise engaged... if I might secure your hand for the Cotillion after supper."

A second dance! Oh, such joy! She stammered her acceptance, he smiled with obvious pleasure, bowed and walked away, leaving her in a glow of happiness.

8: Disappointment

Simon was enchanted with Miss Sophia Merrington. The night of the ball was, perhaps, the first occasion in his existence when he had tried to put himself in another person's shoes, to see as she saw, to feel as she felt, and it was a revelation.

From the moment when she had declared herself to be his friend, he had felt a heightening of interest in her. That, after all, was how one treated a friend, was it not? One took an interest in their affairs, and so it was with Miss Merrington. She looked forward to the ball, and so he began to look forward to it, too. She wanted to dance all night, and thus he wanted that for her. And when he first saw her face that evening, a little flushed with excitement, eyes sparkling with anticipation, her hair arranged in a charmingly elaborate style for the occasion and her gown... there was something magical about a ball gown, its sole purpose to add a swirl of soft movement to every step its wearer takes. He could not wait to begin drawing her.

As the evening wore away, he followed her about with his sketch book, attempting to fix the lively motions of the dance in simple pencil strokes. How hard it was! The poses of her arms, the precision of her steps, the constant changes — all so difficult to capture in one frozen moment. He was never satisfied. If he managed her hands accurately, her feet were out of alignment, and if the feet were right, the gown was all wrong, and her face—! Those glorious expressions that flitted across her features and were instantly gone. How on earth was he to distil such splendour into mere drawings? Impossible! Yet he was compelled to try.

But as he sat in bed the next morning, the multitude of sketches laid out on the covers around him, he recalled one expression in particular, when the young man — she had called him Lord Daniel — had claimed a second dance. He had no chance of capturing it with his pencil, but there was something in her face at that moment that he had never seen in her before, something endearing but frightening, too. He could only describe it as *'hope'*. She had been given hope, and in that instant he saw her whole life laid bare, a life of waiting, endlessly waiting for that one man to come along and ask for a second dance, with all its implications. Perhaps nothing would come of it, but he could see the thought in her head as clearly as if she had spoken the words — *'if he likes me enough to dance with me a second time, perhaps he will like me enough to fall in love... to marry me'*.

As her friend, he should be hoping for such an outcome for her too, but his heart was not in it, somehow. He could not quite explain it, even to himself, but he was not at all satisfied with the idea of her marrying Lord Daniel. He was younger than she was, for one thing, and... well, obviously he was not right for her. Just why this was so, he could not say. He simply knew it, in some unfathomable way.

So when Juliet came bustling in, in her inimitable way, fully dressed already and chiding him as a lazy slug, he was not minded to be charitable.

"Leave me alone, Juliet. I am not feeling energetic this morning."

"But you should be, after such a successful evening. Even without dancing, you managed to be attentive to Sophia Merrington the whole night, sitting out the supper dance with her and then taking her in to supper. Well? How is it going? She must be well on the way to falling in love with you by now."

He could only laugh at such optimism. "Oh, it is as simple as that, is it? I pay attention to her, talk to her for half an hour and feed her lobster patties, and she will just fall into my hands."

Juliet rolled her eyes. "Simon, how many times must I explain it to you? She is twenty-eight years old, with no fewer than three older sisters still unwed. She will fall at the feet of any man who shows an interest."

"She would have to be desperate indeed to fall at *my* feet," he said, but smiling as he spoke. "Be realistic, sister."

"You are not so ineligible, brother. You are the son of an earl, after all."

"For what *that* is worth," he said harshly. "Juliet, I am penniless, entirely dependent on you to survive, and although I have a profession, of a sort, it has not brought me very much money. Precisely two hundred pounds, in fact, for those stables in Gloucestershire, and that was a higher than usual fee as a favour to Kendle. We have eaten my entire income long since. Or burnt it, perhaps. Coal is so expensive."

"Pft! What is that to the purpose? She will have two and a half thousand from her brother, and the duke is bound to give her something extra. We shall manage very well on that until you are established in your career."

"That just makes me the worst kind of fortune hunter. Even if I liked her, it would be dishonourable in me to offer for her when I have not a feather to fly with."

"But you *do* like her," Juliet said slyly. "Do not deny it, for I can see it with my own eyes."

"Dishonourable," he said firmly. "Beyond the pale. Unprincipled. Contemptible. Shameful. Despicable."

She gave a bark of laughter. "Yes, yes, yes, I know. Men do it all the time, despite these protestations, and do their wives regret it? No, they do not. Just a little more effort, brother dear, and you may secure Miss Merrington... or one of her sisters, if you prefer. I am quite easy on the matter. There is nothing to choose between them. Just secure one of them, that is all I ask."

"There are some serious heiresses here," he said. "I wonder you do not set your sights on a girl with twenty thousand."

"Let us not get over-ambitious. The rich ones all have fathers who would not take kindly to a son-in-law with pockets to let, but Richard Merrington will be glad to dispose of one of his sisters, I assure you. His mother says that he grumbles constantly about the expense. He will get his wife to wheedle money out of the duke, for she is wondrous great with him, and then you will be able to live in comfort until you make your name."

"You have it all worked out," Simon said disconsolately, seeing that she would not be deterred.

"So I have, and my arrangements always work out for the best. Have I not always looked after you, Simon? All that is needed is for you to do precisely as I say, and all will be well. Now, get out of bed, for the sun is up and so are the Merrington ladies, and you are just wasting the day."

"I do not know why you are so set on me marrying," he said, with a burst of anger. "We are quite happy as we are, just the two of us. When I have made my name — that will be the time for me to look about me for a wife, and one with more than two and a half thousand, too. What is the great rush?"

"Simon, I am heartily tired of being poor!" she said with asperity. "With a wife who brings a little money to the table, we could be a trifle less poor."

"Only until the children come along and then we should be considerably poorer, and a house full of bawling infants is hardly conducive to my work. It is madness, Juliet. We may not have much money to spare, but with Mama's little gifts and your annuity—"

"What annuity?" she spat.

"But—?"

"I know I talked about an annuity, which would have been lovely, but Aunt Tabitha left me a sum of money and most of it is gone, frittered away to no good effect, it appears, on your articles. If we do not find another source of income soon, we shall be obliged to take in lodgers, and I suppose you will complain that *that* is not conducive to your work, either. Well, if you want the peace and quiet, you had better find a paying client for your designs, Simon, and if you want to eat, I suggest you put that handsome face of yours to work and find yourself a well-dowered wife."

So saying, she swept imperiously from the room, leaving him shocked and bemused in equal measure. No wonder she was so keen for him to marry! This needed some thinking about... no, there was nothing to think about. He still could not in good conscience offer for Sophia Merrington, when he had not a penny to his name. It was utterly wrong, but he could not help wondering... what would happen if he were to do so? Would she even accept him, and if he were to marry her...? It was a strange thought.

He had always assumed that all women were managing females, as Juliet was, but she at least understood his need for a quiet life so that he could concentrate on his work. A wife would be far more intrusive, although he had to admit that Miss Sophia Merrington was not a disruptive sort of female. She did not chatter all the time, and when she did talk, it was to ask sensible questions or make rational points, such as when she had seen the orangery as a place to entertain guests. That had sparked all manner of ideas in his mind! She was more like a muse to him, whereas most women were irritants, like persistent bluebottles who would not leave a man alone.

His final thought was that if he had to marry at all, he could do far worse than Sophia Merrington. She was his friend, after all, and he could at least talk to her, could he not? He could test the waters and see if he could divine whether she might be receptive to an offer from him. After all, if she had formed an attachment to him, he would be obliged to marry her, would he not? Then it would become the honourable thing to do.

Throwing aside the bed covers, he dressed quickly and took the stairs two at a time. She was not in the breakfast parlour, nor in any of the public rooms in that wing of the house. Nor was Mrs Merrington there, or anyone who might know where to find her.

He wandered about the house for some time until he chanced on the Great Gallery, and there she was, on the same seat where he had found her yesterday. The scene was very different now. Only a few lamps were lit, far down the gallery where a couple of housemaids on their knees were scrubbing away the last of the chalk dust from the floor. Two footmen were removing chairs in a desultory fashion. Sophia's exuberantly swinging legs were gone, too, now decorously still on the floor, and her hands sat motionless in her lap. As for her face, he had never seen such a woebegone expression.

"Why so sad, Miss Merrington?"

"Oh... oh, Mr Payne. Good morning... or is it afternoon already?"

"I believe it is past the noon hour," he said, sitting down beside her.

"Everything is so flat the day after a ball," she said disconsolately, her head drooping. "After all the anticipation, and then the event itself... it is all over. Finished. Gone for ever."

"But still in your memory," he said. "You may reflect upon your triumphs of last night with some satisfaction. You stood up for almost every dance, after all."

She turned her face fully towards him, and he was struck by how pale she was. "Is that your definition of a triumph, sir?" A little smile washed across her face, almost instantly vanishing. "I wish it were so. Oh, do not mistake me, for I enjoyed myself prodigiously and was fortunate in having agreeable partners. Well... most of them, anyway."

"Not the short, fat one who never said a word."

She giggled. "Oh yes, Mr Withers! He was not very easy to talk to, it is true. And there was Mr Caplin, who prosed on forever about his new horse. And the clergyman who kept apologising for his missteps, although he was funny, in his way. One does meet some odd people, sometimes."

"There was one who solicited you for a second dance."

"There was! Lord Daniel... oh, what was his name? Torbuck, that was it. I wrote them all down as soon as I got back to my room, so that I could remember."

"For the next letter to... who is the fortunate recipient who will be told of the ball?"

"Charlotte, but there is too much to put in one letter, even though it will be franked. Apparently there are a *dozen* peers of the realm in the house at present, and a couple of Members of Parliament, too, so there is not the least difficulty in getting a letter franked. Or several letters... I expect it will take three or four to my sisters to convey every detail of the evening properly."

"What is *properly*, Miss Merrington?"

"One must name all one's partners, naturally, and describe each one, and who they danced with after. Then there are the other young ladies, and who *they* danced with. And then there are the ladies' gowns and jewels to be listed in full, especially any detail which is especially fashionable that might be copied. Naturally, there are all manner of other incidents to be related which might interest or amuse them, like the footman who spilt red wine down someone's very fancy waistcoat, did you see that? There was an older lady who fell and showed a great deal more than she would have liked to, I am sure. Oh, and the girl who did not know the steps and her partner was valiantly whispering *'Left!'* or *'Right!'*, and she invariably went the wrong way and bumped into that supercilious fellow... Lord James Something. And then she apologised for quite half an hour and he said, *'It is of no consequence, madam'*, at least a dozen times, although he was very cross and went quite red in the face in the effort to be polite. It was so funny." She paused, and then looked up at him with a shy smile. "Remembering all this has quite cheered me up, Mr Payne. Thank you."

"I am very glad of it. You were so looking forward to the ball that it was very upsetting to see you so downcast. Perhaps before long there will be a ball at Staineybank to look forward to?"

"I do not think so, for the duchess is still in mourning for her little boy, and besides, there is no ballroom there. There is not even a gallery! It would have to be a very small ball. But you are quite right — I should not be downhearted, since I had a splendid evening, all your wonderful drawings will remind me of the occasion and there will certainly be balls in the future — the Brinchester assemblies start again after Easter. Yes, I shall think about that and not sad things. After all, I should be inured to disappointment by now."

"Was it such a disappointment?" he said tentatively, wondering if he was walking into a quagmire by asking, but too curious to refrain. She was his friend, after all, and he wanted to know everything about her.

"A little. One always hopes, you see, that there will be consequences. One dances and one might even have a partner who embodies all that is agreeable in a man, and so one hopes... and sometimes, after the assemblies at Norwich, there would be a caller the next morning. There he would be, sidling into the drawing room with a posy of flowers or perhaps a book of poems by the particular poet he had mentioned the night before, and there would be wine handed round and cakes, and he would stay perhaps even longer than the customary fifteen minutes. And that would be the end of it. One might pass him in the street a month or two later, and exchange bows and move on as near strangers. Even if a man seems keen enough by candlelight, in the full light of day he becomes insubstantial and fades away to nothing. Or perhaps it is I who fades away, who knows?"

"Poor Sophia!" he said softly, unthinkingly taking her hand in his. "Are you so keen to marry?"

"Of course! What other respectable occupation is there for a woman? We cannot take up a profession, as a man might. If we are forced to work, we must become dreary governesses or companions, and even if we are lucky enough not to be brought so low, we remain dependent on a father or brother forever. Richard is very good and, despite his grumbles about the expense of four unmarried sisters, he would never turn us out. But now that he is married, we are of less and less importance to him, becoming eventually merely the spinster aunts to his children, who will save him the cost of a governess. I want my own home, Mr Payne. I want to be a wife and mother and mistress of my own establishment, someone of importance in my own world, however small that world might be, and not merely a peripheral part of someone else's life."

"Even peripheral parts may lead useful, productive lives," he said. "And happy lives, too, I wager. You are not unhappy, are you?" She shook her head. "Do your sisters feel this way too?"

"They do. We are of one mind on the matter, and yet not one of us has ever received even a single offer. What is wrong with us? What is it about us that renders us repulsive to the male sex?"

That was one misapprehension which could not be allowed to stand. He was not sure if it was wise, but he must... he *must* speak to reassure her. "Nothing! There is nothing at all repulsive about any one of you, and a man must be blind not to see all your good qualities. You have been unfortunate, perhaps, Sophia, in never meeting the one man who looks beneath the surface, and sees not merely one pretty girl amongst any number of other girls almost as pretty, but the beauty within... who appreciates your goodness and quick mind and strong character. And even if a man understands what a treasure you are, he may not be in a position to do anything about it. Honour and the disparities of rank or wealth may keep him from speaking. But never doubt that you are admired... you are very much admired..."

As he spoke, his grip on her hand tightened but she made no move to break free. Instead, eyes wide, she gazed up at him trustingly as each impassioned word brought him closer to her... closer and closer until their faces were but a handspan apart. He felt himself drawn inexorably towards her… so close that he felt her warm breath on his cheek, heard her rapid breathing… so very close…

A crash from the other end of the Great Gallery made them spring guiltily apart. One of the footmen had dropped a chair, and the other was loudly berating him.

Sophia jumped to her feet, and Simon sprang up too.

"Miss Merrington…"

"I must go," she said at the same time, rather breathlessly. "Mama will be looking for me."

And with a whisk of her skirts she was gone, leaving Simon trembling and distraught, angry with himself for his lack of restraint, but also yearning for the kiss that so nearly was.

9: A Winter Walk

Sophia fled. She cared not where she went, so long as it was far, far away from Mr Payne — the oh-so-dangerous Mr Payne, who had nearly kissed her! And she had nearly let him! What on earth was the matter with her? Surely she knew better than to allow herself to be drawn into such scandalous behaviour? She was eight and twenty, for heaven's sake, not some green girl fresh from the schoolroom.

Instinctively, she avoided the busy parts of the house for she was not sure she could sit and serenely make idle conversation when her heart was still racing and she could scarcely catch her breath. Eventually, she found herself at the far end of one of Marshfields' satellite wings, where a window with a cushioned seat and a concealing curtain offered a respite. She curled up there, looking out at the wintry sky, the snowy grounds and, just below her, the roof of the orangery. Lights showing through the roof windows and the glow of a brazier suggested that the duke was enjoying his own sanctuary from the crowds. At least he was warm! She pulled her shawl more tightly around her, glad of its thick, woollen comfort.

For some time she tried to make sense of her feelings. She was not outraged by Mr Payne's presumption, as she might have been with another man — as she had been when that slimy fellow with the yellow teeth had tried to press himself upon her at a card party in Norwich once. She had made the mistake of going alone to the ladies' retiring room, and had found him lurking in the corridor outside when she emerged, and not so much as a servant in sight to call upon to render her aid. She had managed to push him away, and fled back to the drawing room, but then she had been angry and complained to Mama about it.

She was not angry now! If she were to be honest with herself, her strongest feeling was disappointment. She should have liked to be kissed by a man whom she wanted to kiss. It was difficult to say precisely why she wanted to kiss him, but she was quite sure that she did, and that it would be a pleasant experience.

Was she in love with Mr Payne? In all honesty, it was not a question she could answer satisfactorily. He was very good looking, of course, and an imposing figure of a man — tall and broad of chest. He looked too large to be an artist, which was an odd thought, for why should artistic talent be confined to the small and delicate of frame? Perhaps it was his eyes which drew her most? They were dark, but clear and bright, and filled with an amused twinkle when he talked to her. Or was it his hands, with their slender fingers, wielding a pencil so masterfully?

She sighed. It was hard to say. All she knew was that she liked him, and she had wanted him to kiss her. Still wanted that, to be truthful. Their abrupt sundering left everything dangling, like unfinished business.

Yes, she would definitely like to kiss him.

After a while, when the cold had begun to seep into her bones, she reluctantly made her way to her own wing of the house to see if she could find Mama. She discovered her in her usual chair near the fire, embroidery frame in hand, but her companion today was not one of the other matrons.

Lord Daniel! That was a good sign... surely?

"Oh!" she said, startled.

"Miss Merrington. Good day to you," he cried, jumping to his feet with a wide smile. "I trust you have not suffered any indisposition after your exertions on the dance floor last night."

"No... thank you... how kind in you to enquire. I am quite well. And you, sir?"

He chuckled. "Never better, I assure you. I enjoyed our dances very much, so I came to enquire..." Another nervous laugh. "As I have already said. Um... your mama has been telling me all about your new home at Staineybank."

"Do sit down, Sophia," Mama said brightly. "Lord Daniel will bring forward another chair, I am sure."

"Oh... of course, ma'am... certainly."

He rushed about doing her bidding, and sat with them for another half hour, at least, although Sophia was so well entertained that she forgot to watch the clock. Mr Payne was driven entirely from her thoughts, as well as any lingering disappointment after the ball. Lord Daniel had danced with her twice, and now here he was, enquiring after her, doing the pretty... *courting* her! For what else could it be, this deliberate seeking out of her company?

Inside her was a little thrill of anticipation. Perhaps, just perhaps, something might come of this? For the first time in years, she felt a quiver of hope.

***

Simon sat motionless in the Great Gallery, his breathing ragged. What on earth was he doing? However much Juliet might urge him towards Miss Merrington, however much they needed her dowry to stave off utter penury, it was impossible when he had no estate, no fortune, no income at all. Her brother would, quite rightly, send him to the rightabout. And yet... he liked her. He liked her very well indeed.

The maids had long since finished scrubbing the floor, and the last of the footmen disappeared, too. Perhaps it was the servants' dinner hour and the guests were too indolent to stir from their firesides, for there was not a soul about. Simon rose and paced across the room, his footsteps echoing hollowly in the high-ceilinged room.

He executed a few steps of the cotillion as he went, smiling as he remembered. She was so light on her feet! How delightful to watch her dance her way through the evening, to see her shining eyes and heightened complexion, her wide smiles. She loved to dance, and he had loved to watch her, to imagine her feelings as she whirled and pirouetted.

Never before had he wondered what it might be like to be someone else. He had always been wrapped up in his own concerns, never giving a moment's thought to anyone else, not even Juliet. But then she had always bent herself to accommodate his wishes. Sophia was different, an independent being who gave no thought to him, and why should she, when he had nothing to offer her? Yet she fascinated him, and he wanted to know everything about her. What did she feel? Of what did she dream?

He had some answers to those questions now. She dreamt of a husband, her own house, children at her feet. She dreamt of the position in society that only marriage could give her. Oh, if only he could oblige her! How delightful that would be! He would not even mind the inevitable children, if they had Sophia's softly curling brown hair and creamy skin. How adorable they would be, miniature versions of their lovely mama.

That was foolish. He must not be carried away with impossible dreams of his own. But there was one thing he could do for her, and that was to provide the ballroom at Staineybank that would give her the opportunities she craved. A ballroom... not the orangery, for that would be full of plants, and would be too warm and sultry an atmosphere for exuberant dancing. But a gallery... that he could provide, and if he could combine it with the orangery...

Fired with enthusiasm, he rushed off to find his sketch book.

***

For the two days that remained to them at Marshfields, Lord Daniel fluttered around Sophia. It was, perhaps, putting it too strongly to describe it as courting, but there was *something* between them, that much was certain, and even Mama was filled with optimism.

"This is very promising," she said, as they knelt on the floor finishing their packing the night before their departure. "He is so attentive! And no doubt his father will provide him with a little estate of his own when he marries, which will be very useful for the children, although I imagine you will spend much of your time with his father at Pentavon Castle, and in London, of course. How delightful for you! I have made sure that he knows precisely how to find Staineybank, so I am confident that we shall see him there before too long. It is a pity he is a younger son, and his older brother is already married with a son of his own, so there is nothing to hope for there. Still, his father will want him to make a good match, and sister to the future Duke of Brinshire is as good a connection as a younger son may expect. Once Richard inherits, you may claim the title of Lady Sophia, you know, and then you would be Lady Sophia Torbuck."

"Would I not be Lady Daniel Torbuck, regardless of my own title?"

"No, not unless you insisted upon it." Mama sat back on her heels. "You would have higher rank than your husband, in such a case."

"Do you truly think he will come?" Sophia said in a small voice. "I do not want to get my hopes up if—"

"I know, I know, we have been disappointed before, have we not? I cannot think what it is about you girls that makes you so unlucky with men. But he does seem quite keen. He will want to talk to his father first, but then, perhaps, we shall see him at Staineybank."

Sophia could not be so sanguine, but nevertheless, the memory of Lord Daniel and the possibility of a spring wedding beguiled the long drive back to Brinshire. It helped to distract her from Mr Payne, sitting in the carriage a mere arm's length away from her. Whenever she looked at him, and especially at his enticing lips, she remembered the moment when he had leaned towards her... had so nearly kissed her. It was fortunate that he gave no sign of remembering it, seeming lost in thought for the whole journey.

At Staineybank, she found that nothing had changed except that Rowena had grown even larger.

"I cannot wait for this to be over," she said to Sophia, as the ladies retreated to the drawing room after dinner. "Only another month, if I am lucky. I waddle about like a duck — so undignified. I should feel better if I could get out into the garden, but we have had snow almost every day this past week. Not much, but enough to keep me indoors."

"We had snow in Surrey, too," Sophia said. "Apart from the ball, I had no exercise at all. I should love to walk about the gardens a little. Shall we make a firm plan to do so tomorrow? I do not think we shall have any more snow, and there is not much lying on the ground to deter us."

"Eleven, straight after breakfast," Rowena said. "I always take my walk at eleven."

Before Sophia could reply, her sisters began to lay out Mr Payne's drawings of the ball on a table, and she was applied to for all the little details which had already been related by letter but must be gone over again and again. She was not loath to oblige them, for although there had been so many successful balls in the past, this was the first at the home of a duke, and the names of the various lords must be repeated. There was something very satisfying about telling one's sisters that one had danced with the son of a marquess or a duke, rather casually as if one did so as a regular affair and therefore it was a perfectly commonplace event. But there was no escaping the mention of Lord Daniel Torbuck, and her tentative hopes in that direction, for Mama was not at all reticent about it.

Yet somehow those days at Marshfields already seemed hazy, like a distant memory of a summer's day, something long gone and become a shadowy, ephemeral thing. Had Lord Daniel really paid her so much attention? And even if he had, did it mean anything or was it mere politeness, or simply filling the hours until it was time to begin the journey home? Back in the solid walls of Staineybank, Lord Daniel had no substance, a half remembered dream that had vanished in the light of day.

The next day, Sophia breakfasted early and then returned to her room to finish unpacking, or rather, since the maids had unpacked already, to rearrange everything to her own systematic order. It was odd how unsettling it was should a hairbrush be misaligned, or a nightgown be folded incorrectly. Having removed every gown from her press and replaced each in its proper position, she was just beginning on her chest of drawers when Rowena's head appeared round the door.

"Ah, there you are! It is past eleven, dear. I have gathered the others for our walk, but I should not wish to exclude you, if you still wish to come."

"Oh, yes! Give me a moment to put on my stoutest boots. Are we going far?"

"Richard will not permit me to go far, or to wander from the approved path," she said, pulling a face. "Out by the front door, through the parterre to the bridge, then along the lake as far as the summer house and back on the path to the garden door. Always the same way. I cannot wait until the summer, when I shall be able to walk anywhere I wish."

Provided with suitable footwear and her warmest cloak, Sophia followed Rowena down the stairs to the hall where Charlotte, Augusta and Maria, and Rowena's friend Georgie already waited. Froggett signalled to a footman to open the heavy front door and then they were out in the crisp, wintry air. The steps had been swept clean, but on the drive an inch or so of snow still lay, rutted with the marks of wheels and hooves. Georgie gave Rowena her arm as she descended the steps, still damp and slippery, but once on the drive Rowena shook off her helper, and strode away.

"Is she always so independent?" Sophia asked, as Georgie shook her head at her friend's retreating back.

"More so at the moment because she feels so helpless," Georgie said. "She is so used to being active that all this waiting is driving her a little insane. Richard does not help, of course. He is so nervous and protective of her just now that he would have her stay in bed until her confinement if he could. But the physician is very keen on fresh air and healthy exercise, so she has her walk every day."

"But only on the prescribed route."

Georgie rolled her eyes. "That is Richard's doing, naturally, and of course the duke backs him up. The heir and all that. Still, only another month or so of this nonsense, thank goodness."

From the drive, they followed the path round the side of the house and entered the parterre, which Sophia thought was the least interesting part of the garden. It was part of the original formal pleasure grounds, but she preferred the more romantic landscape of the upper river, with its pretty Palladian bridge and miniature waterfalls, and then the sinuous curves of the lake.

At the bridge, Rowena stopped to allow the others, slower walkers, to catch up with her.

"I have never yet managed to reach the far side of the bridge," she said gaily. "Once, just once, Richard permitted me to venture onto it, but it came on to rain, so we turned back. But one day I shall cross this river."

Laughing, she turned and set off again, reaching the top of a short flight of steps before the others had even begun to move. She started down the steps, and then, with a terrifying shriek, she fell, tumbling away out of their sight.

Sophia gasped in horror. Georgie had already begun to run, so she ran too, finding Rowena sprawled at the bottom of the steps, looking confused.

"Goodness! How foolish of me to miss my step like that! Georgie, give me your hand, will you?"

"Are you hurt?" Georgie said breathlessly.

"No... I think not. Just... surprised. Help me up, will you?"

"Are you sure? Wait a moment, catch your breath," Georgie said.

"I am fine," Rowena said, trying, and failing, to haul herself into an upright position. "I just missed my footing, that is all. If I could just get up..."

"I think you should stay exactly where you are until we can fetch help," Georgie said firmly. "Sophia, will you run back to the house to find someone?"

"Augusta is the fastest of us," Sophia said, and her sister nodded and ran off.

Meanwhile, Charlotte began to shout, "Help! Help!" in a clear voice.

"What are you doing?" Sophia said sharply.

"There may be a gardener about," Charlotte said. "Maria, why do you not go towards the kitchen garden and see if you can find help? I will run down towards the lake, in case anyone is about there."

They left in opposite directions, the cries for help gradually fading.

"This is a great deal of fuss about nothing," Rowena said, having got herself into a sitting position. "Sophia, you will give me a hand to rise, I am sure. Oh, this stupid baby! If only I were not so large!"

"Are you sure there is nothing broken?" Sophia said.

"Quite sure. I shall be a trifle bruised, I imagine, but nothing worse than that. If I could—"

A man's voice sounded from across the river. "Are you in trouble, ladies?"

"Who is that?" Georgie called out.

"Ben Lovell, miss, the gamekeeper."

"We should be glad of your help, Ben," Georgie cried.

He stepped forward out of the shade of overhanging shrubs, so that he could be clearly seen. "I'll come over the bridge and be with you in a moment."

With a wave, he disappeared into the foliage again, but his footsteps could be heard scuffling through fallen leaves on the far side of the river, then heavy boots on the bridge, followed by lighter steps on the snow-covered path. He was a big man of about fifty, sallow of complexion, hung about with game bags, and a gun slung over one shoulder. Laying these objects aside, he knelt down beside Rowena.

"Are you injured, ma'am? Shall I carry you?"

"No, no! If you could help me to rise..."

Between Georgie and the gamekeeper, they got Rowena to her feet and began very cautiously to help her up the steps and back to the house by the shortest way. Sophia had nothing to do but walk anxiously in their wake, staying a little behind so as not to crowd them and puzzling over what had caused Rowena to trip and fall, for the steps were smooth and even, and although there was snow on them, it was not so much as to cause a sure-footed person to slip.

However, when she reached the step where Rowena had fallen, the snow had been all scuffed about as she had tumbled down, and there, no doubt buried in the snow before but clearly visible now, was the long handle of a rake. There was no need, then, to search further for the cause of Rowena's accident.

10: Waiting

By the time Rowena had walked slowly back to the front door, the nearest entrance to the house, leaning heavily on Georgie and the gamekeeper, Augusta had raised the alarm, and footmen were streaming down the steps. Not far behind them was Richard, his face ashen, who at once replaced the gamekeeper in supporting his wife carefully up the steps.

"What happened? You are not hurt? Any pain?"

His voice was high with anxiety, and beneath the tumbling words was the deeper question — *is the baby hurt?*

"My foot slipped, that is all, and I fell down the steps."

"What steps? Where? How far did you fall?"

"One of those short flights beside one of the little waterfalls on the upper river. I must have slipped down... oh, perhaps three or four steps."

"Three or four... but is there any pain?"

Is the baby hurt?

"I am a little achy where I fell... my arm and left leg, mostly. I shall have some splendid bruises in a day or two."

As they reached the top step, the duke appeared, with the same terrified expression and the same litany of questions, and the unspoken one — *is the baby hurt?*

"Froggett? Where is Froggett?" the duke cried. "Ah, there you are. Send for the physician at once. *At once!*"

"Already done, your grace," Froggett said, wringing his hands.

"And the midwife," Richard said. "Just in case."

And there it was, the unspoken fear brought into plain sight.

"Yes, yes, an excellent idea," said the duke, walking helplessly alongside the little group escorting Rowena, his arms spread wide as if to shield her from trouble. "Just to check that all is well."

"Ow!" Rowena said, stopping abruptly.

"What is it?" Richard whispered. "A pain?"

She laughed suddenly, the sound echoing in the cavernous entrance hall. "The baby kicked me."

They all laughed then, in relief. A kicking baby must be a good sign. He was unharmed, then!

"Ah, the little fellow does not like being tumbled down steps, I dare say," the duke said, indulgently. "He is registering his displeasure."

Sophia watched them to the bottom of the stairs, but by then half the household had appeared wanting to know what had happened, so, after sending a footman to find Maria and Charlotte, she took everyone into a parlour to tell the tale and listen to the ladies' prognostications. Cousin Hester was sure the baby would be born deformed, but Mama laughed that off.

"He is very well protected inside his mother, I assure you," she said.

The midwife arrived first, half running up the drive. A few minutes later, the apothecary arrived in his gig. And two hours later, the stylish carriage of the physician from Brinchester pulled up outside the house. All three were agreed that Mrs Richard would be somewhat bruised, but there was no serious damage caused and the baby inside her was perfectly well.

"He has a fine, strong kick," Dr Percival said with a smile, as he sipped Madeira in the duke's study. The whole household had crowded in to hear the verdict, and now there were sighs of relief all round. Even the duke was smiling.

Dinner that evening was a strange affair. Rowena kept to her room and Richard, too agitated to be in company, stayed with her. The rest of the party was surprisingly merry, aware that disaster had narrowly been averted.

Sophia was less merry. The image of the rake lying beneath the snow haunted her. How long had it lain there, waiting to catch an unwary walker? And what should she do about it? If she told anyone, there would be an almighty fuss, some hapless gardener would be dismissed without a reference and she did not want to be responsible for anyone losing his employment for a simple mistake. Yet she could not leave the rake lying there. Another snowfall would bury it again, and someone else could fall, with more serious consequences.

She had still not resolved the problem when she went to bed that night. She picked up her book and prepared to read for a while to put herself to sleep, but after a few minutes she closed it again. She knew clearly what she must do. Tomorrow, she would retrieve the rake and take it back to the head gardener. There was no need to mention that it had caused Rowena's fall. Instead, she would just say that she saw it lying and thought it best to put it back where it belonged.

With that thought, she settled down to read, but the house was not quiet.

First, there were rapid footsteps along the passageway outside her room, followed by knocking on someone's door — Mama's she thought. Then low voices, and more footsteps. All was quiet for a while, then there was a gentle knock on the door.

"Sophia?" The door opened and Mama's head appeared, lit by a flickering candle. "I saw the light under your door, so I thought you might still be awake."

"I am. What is it?"

"Rowena's pains have started and Richard is in a state."

"It is too soon, surely!"

"Only a month or so, which is not disastrous. The midwife is sent for, but I have sent Richard down to the library to pace up and down, or get drunk, or whatever men do in such situations." She sighed in exasperation. "Anything but sitting outside Rowena's room agonising loudly and distracting her. Will you sit with him for a while? By and by, I will wake Charlotte to come and take over from you, but for now, let the others sleep. Will you go?"

"Of course. What did Papa do when you were labouring?"

She laughed. "He went shooting! He was not a great one for such sport as a rule, except as a courtesy to guests, but whenever my time came, off he went with his gun. Then he would come home to hear that he had another daughter. Not that he ever blamed me, but he was especially pleased when Richard was born. He bought me the diamond parure, if you remember. I only ever got a necklace or a bracelet for you girls. Go on, off you go. Weston is with him, but he is almost as jumpy as Richard is. There is nothing like a lady's presence for soothing a man, is there?"

Richard seemed to be following Mama's suggestions to the letter, for Sophia found him prowling about the library in an elaborately embroidered banyan and slippers, a brandy glass in his hand, his nightcap askew on his head.

Weston's face brightened perceptibly when he saw Sophia. "Shall I fetch you something to eat, madam?" he said.

"Good idea," she said. "It is likely to be a long night."

Richard groaned. "It is too early! More than a month, everyone said, but now this fall has set things off and who knows how it will end?"

"We shall just have to await the outcome with patience," Sophia said briskly. "Getting yourself into a state is not going to help Rowena one little bit. She would be happier to know that you were dealing with the situation with fortitude."

Richard stopped prowling and glared at Sophia. "Have you ever been in love, sister? Have you ever felt such a connection with another person that your life is immeasurably better when she is in the world, and would be insupportable without her? No, of course you have not. You sail through life without a care for anyone. So do not presume to lecture me about fortitude. There can be no fortitude where Rowena is concerned."

A tart reply was on Sophia's lips, but she swallowed it. There was no point in quarrelling with Richard. He was quite irrational about Rowena, and there was nothing to be done about it. Instead, she persuaded him to sit down, and began to read snippets from the London newspapers, which she hoped might distract him. He said nothing, but perhaps the sound of her voice soothed him, for at least he seemed calmer.

Unfortunately, the door was flung open and the duke swept in, full of the tale of how his first duchess had died in childbed.

"It was just the same with Caroline — she started early, and all seemed well, but then—"

"Thank you, your grace, but that is not helpful," Sophia said firmly. "Rowena is a different person, the circumstances are different and we look forward to a different outcome. Just think, in a few hours' time, you may be holding the next heir to the dukedom in your arms."

"I have held four such in my arms," the duke said tersely, "and now they all rest in God's arms."

"Then let us see what God decides to do this time."

The duke glared at her, unwilling to concede even the slightest possibility of a happy outcome, but a moan from Richard brought him to his senses.

"There, there, boy! You must not take everything I say so literally. Maybe your sister is right, eh? Rowena is a fine, healthy young woman. No need to anticipate the worst."

"I cannot bear it!" Richard said with a groan. "How much longer will it be?"

That was another question to which there was no answer, so Sophia wisely did not attempt one.

The night passed in painfully slow increments. Never had the hands of the clock moved with so little energy! Richard paced, the duke worked his way steadily through the brandy decanter, Weston hovered anxiously and Sophia read from the newspapers, if only to fill the heavy silence. Even when Charlotte appeared, still yawning, Sophia read on, for it seemed to help. Whenever she paused, either Richard would start up his agitated maunderings or the duke would talk about his first wife, so she plodded on.

Sometime after three by the clock, Mama came in, causing Richard to jump to his feet in an agony of hope and terror.

"She is doing very well, but it is a slow business. You had much better go to bed, Richard."

"I could not possibly sleep!"

"No, but— Well, never mind. Sophia, what are you doing here? No need for you when Charlotte is here. Off to bed with you, child."

"Very well, Mama, but you will wake me if there is any news?"

"Of course, but it is not likely to be before morning."

Richard groaned again.

Sophia handed the newspaper to Charlotte, with the adjuration to keep reading, and went to bed.

***

As soon as he returned to Staineybank, Simon was consumed by his new ideas for the orangery. Or Sophia's ideas, if he were being honest. She was his inspiration, now. On the journey back from Surrey, he had never had the solitude to gather his thoughts, but now he retreated to his room and began to draw.

He took all his meals there, aided by the ever-cheerful footman, Robert, who brought trays periodically, conveyed Simon's apologies at the dinner hour, and brought the interesting gossip from below stairs. Mrs Richard had had a fall, he reported first, followed by the good news that she and the baby appeared unharmed. The next morning, almost quivering with excitement, he brought word of the latest developments.

"Started early, ain't she? Bound to be trouble. Lor', but the duke's in a right pother, and who'd blame the poor man? Not me. Mr Froggett says it's history repeating itself all over again, cos she looks so like his first wife. The duke's, that is, not Mr Froggett's. He's not married. I mean, who'd have the old fussbudget, eh? Poor lady! Shouldn't be much longer, though. Midwife says it'll be today. One way or the other."

Simon was not much interested in Mrs Richard Merrington's baby, except that if it should die, there would probably be no orangery for a while. And if the lady herself were to die, no orangery at all, he supposed. But still, the muse was upon him, so he drew on, first the rough sketches and then he began work on the full drawings.

Hiding in his room did not protect him from Juliet, however, who interrupted him numerous times to bring him the latest news.

"You do not need to tell me this," he said, trying not to sound too exasperated. "Robert keeps me fully informed."

"Did he tell you about the gardeners? There is some trouble, apparently, but I cannot find out what it is about."

Without looking up from the table where he was working, he said, "He mentioned something about it, but I was not attending."

"Not attending! Really, Simon, you are hopeless. Ask him about it, next time he comes. I took a stroll through the kitchen gardens, but all seemed perfectly normal to me. The snow is melting fast, did your Robert tell you that? There might be rain later. That will keep the roads well mired in mud, so we shall not be able to go home just yet. I am not quite ready to go back to cheap coal and tallow candles. How are you getting on with Sophia?"

"I have not seen her since we returned."

"Hmm, well, everything is a little topsy-turvy just now, but do not leave it too long. Be sure to come down for dinner this evening. Now that the oily Lord Daniel is no longer encroaching, you should have a clear field."

Simon lifted his head to stare at her, bemused. "I am not sure that the son of a marquess can be said to be encroaching, sister."

"Well... encroaching on your territory, then. Sophia is yours, and once this wretched baby business is out of the way, you can get on with securing her."

"The wretched baby business, as you call it, is a matter of life and death to this family, Juliet. Have a little compassion."

She had the grace to look a little shame-faced. "I know, I know. I am not unsympathetic, I assure you, but our own situation is, if not quite a matter of life and death, almost as dire. We are facing destitution, brother. I might even have to sell the house."

"Is it truly as bad as that?"

She nodded slowly. "The hundred pounds from your mama was very timely, and will stave off the creditors for a while longer, but we must have a source of income soon or matters will become desperate."

"You kept all this to yourself," he said quietly. "If I had known—"

"Now, what could you have done?"

"I could have found salaried employment — as a secretary, or some such. I could still have worked on my designs in my spare time. You should have told me."

"I always supposed that you would have established yourself by now. I cannot understand why no one engages you. Still, perhaps Mr Thwaite will settle on one or other of your designs for him... or this orangery, perhaps. Then your name will be made."

"And we will be rich."

"Precisely." She gave a gurgle of merriment. "In the meantime, you will marry Sophia Merrington, and her dowry will buy us a little more time."

After she had gone, Simon sat for a long time, twisting the pencil in his hands and pondering the situation. Even with his abbreviated education, the formal part cut short at the age of fifteen and continued somewhat erratically by Juliet and her Aunt Tabitha, he understood the gentleman's code of honour. His father, he supposed, had inculcated that much into him, with the aid of his tutors and the masters at Eton. Even the exigencies of his present life were not sufficient to cause him to set aside those principles.

And yet... if he did nothing, and the duke rejected his orangery design, and Mr Thwaite decided against his great house, what then? Lodgers in the house, or perhaps no house at all.

He shivered. He would have to do it, he supposed, and felt a little burst of excitement at the thought. If he had to marry, and it seemed that he did, then who could possibly suit him better than Sophia, who drew him so powerfully? Ever since the almost-kiss, she had haunted his mind, rather. In odd moments, when he surfaced from a prolonged bout of thinking about his orangery, her face rose unbidden in his mind. Such an agreeable person, who always looked well, talked intelligently, and yet was capable of remaining silent. Yes, she would suit him perfectly.

So that was settled. Sophia Merrington would become his wife and her two and a half thousand pounds would pay for coal and mutton and claret — he hoped there would be claret — for a few years. But what then? If he was still not earning, there would be Juliet and Sophia and a string of growing children to be fed and shod and educated, and eventually the money would run out.

No, he could not do it. He could not draw a lovely girl like Sophia into poverty. That was not the action of a gentleman. But if he could just secure one, at least, of his current projects, that would be a different matter. He would know soon enough whether the duke would accept his design, but he must bring Thwaite to the point, once and for all. He determined that he would write to him and ask him, very politely, to make a decision.

Then he would know what to do.

***

Sophia woke to find that nothing had changed. Rowena laboured on, and Richard, dressed now, although somewhat haphazardly, still paced about the library. The duke, having emptied the brandy decanter, snored gently on a chaise longue.

As the day wore on, the household gathered in the library awaiting news. Cousin Hester and Charlotte, busy below stairs for most of the day, came and went, and Mama and Georgie stayed with Rowena, but everyone else was there. Sophia, Augusta and Maria sat in a little group, talking in low voices. Mr Hammond, the duke's secretary, and his father worked on papers in the study next door, but with the door wide open to hear any news at once. Mr Pyott, the comptroller, sat placidly reading the newspaper, a glass of wine at his elbow, enjoying a respite from his usual labours. Mr Godley, the chaplain, read the Bible. Only Mr Payne was absent.

Lady Juliet Payne crept in last of all and, after ascertaining that the baby had still not put in an appearance, sat quietly in a corner by herself. Even after many days in her company at Marshfields, Sophia did not feel she knew her well, for Lady Juliet's age put her firmly into the orbit of the older matrons. Now, as she had no one to else to talk to, Sophia crossed the room to sit beside her.

"I hope Mr Payne is not entirely knocked up by the journey," she began. "He was not at dinner last night, and he did not come down to breakfast this morning."

She smiled. "Indeed, he is perfectly well, merely caught up in his designs for the duke's orangery. He was inspired by the one at Marshfields, and is working on a superior design to his first attempt."

"I shall look forward to seeing it," Sophia said. "He is so clever at drawing. I love to watch him work! But I dare say he is secretive about it, as Richard is. He shuts himself away in his room when he is working."

"Simon does that too," Lady Juliet said. "Especially when he is finalising the architectural drawings, he likes to be undisturbed so that he can concentrate." Charlotte came in just then, whispered something to Augusta and Maria, throwing them into gales of laughter, before bustling out again. Lady Juliet smiled. "How lucky you are to have sisters!"

"But you have sisters, too!" Sophia burst out before she could stop herself. "I am sure Mr Payne mentioned it once — three younger sisters, he said."

"Oh yes, but I have never seen them. I left Edlesborough when I was three, you see."

"But why? Oh, I beg your pardon. Pray ignore my vulgar curiosity."

Lady Juliet laughed. "It is a natural question, but I cannot answer it, not properly. My mother died, and it was deemed best for me to live with... well, I called her Aunt Tabitha, but she was Mama's cousin. She was a widow, living quietly in London with no children of her own, and... and I was sent to live with her."

"Yet you have never seen your three sisters?"

"I have never seen any of my family since that day. I have two older brothers, Andrew, the heir — Viscount Kendle — and Luke, and then after

Simon, there was John, Matthew, Rachel, Elizabeth and Martha. There may be more by now, but we could never afford the society newspapers, so we never heard."

"You could look it up in Debrett's Peerage," Sophia said.

"I have never had a copy."

"There is bound to be one here somewhere," she said, waving a hand at the multitude of shelves laden with books. "Froggett is over there — he will know."

Within a very few minutes, the butler had located a copy, with an apology that it might not be the latest edition.

"It is only five years out of date," Sophia said. "We have the latest at home. Mama is insistent that we keep up with all the families to which we are connected. Here are the earls, Lady Juliet. When was your father's title created?"

"The earldom? 1698."

"Hmm..." She thumbed through the pages. "Here we are. *'James Edward Payne, Earl of Edlesborough, Viscount Kendle, Baron Landrick.'* There! It will all be in there."

She handed the book to Lady Juliet, who read it avidly for a few moments, then gave a little gasp.

"What is it?" Sophia said.

But just then, Mama entered beaming from ear to ear.

"My felicitations, Richard! You have a fine healthy daughter."

"And Rowena?"

"Tired, but very well otherwise. You may see her in a little while. Are you awake, your grace? It is a girl."

And in all the excitement of the news, Sophia quite forgot to see what had surprised Lady Juliet in the Peerage.

11: Daughters And Sons

Simon was satisfied with his new designs for the orangery. An uninterrupted afternoon had seen the last of his detailed architectural drawings finished, and he could not but be proud of what he had accomplished. Whether the duke liked his ideas or not, he felt he had produced something quite out of the ordinary, which met both the duke's requirements and his own aesthetic standards. It was good, and he was pleased with it.

Mindful of Juliet's instructions to pay some attention to Miss Sophia Merrington, which he was by no means averse to complying with, he allowed Robert to lay out his evening attire, and, thus arrayed, went down to dinner. He discovered at once that Mrs Richard Merrington had produced a daughter, and although there was the expected disappointment in the presentation of a female infant, still, there was satisfaction in the safe arrival and the promisingly healthy state of the mother. The physician from

Brinchester had pronounced that all was well, and so there was an air of relief, if not quite celebration, in the assembled company.

One of the inexplicable, if pleasing, results of the visit to Marshfields was that Simon no longer struggled to distinguish Sophia from her sisters. He could not quite account for it, but now, whenever he saw them in a group, he could pick out Sophia with unerring accuracy. He drew her aside now, pleased that she seemed less twittery than her sisters.

"I congratulate you, Miss Merrington," he said. "You must be delighted at the arrival of your niece."

"Oh yes, if it will stop Richard from melting into an incoherent puddle," she said, with a wry smile. "We are all so tired of him being wound so tight he might explode at any moment. In a few days, or perhaps a month or two, we have the greatest hopes that he might become rational again."

"Poor fellow!" Simon said. "It must have been a great trial to him."

"A greater trial to Rowena, I should imagine. She, after all, is the one who has gone through the inconvenience of being *enceinte*, and then suffering the trial of labour, and must now be called upon to sustain the infant, until such time as a wet nurse can be engaged. I confess, none of it inspires me to hasten into matrimony."

"I thought your greatest ambition was to marry," he said in surprise. "Has your sister-in-law's experience soured you?"

"Not exactly, for I must marry," she said sombrely. "What else is there for a gently bred woman to do with her life, after all?"

"Juliet has never married, nor seems to feel the need for it," he said, after a moment's thought. "She is quite content to be a spinster."

"Only because she has you," Sophia said at once. "She devotes herself to a man just as she would as a wife."

He had no ready answer, indeed he was so flummoxed by the thought, that he neglected to secure Sophia's company for dinner which was announced shortly thereafter, and was obliged to sit between two of her sisters. Fortunately, the excitement of the new baby meant that conversation was general around the table and he was not required to talk beyond the gentlemanly obligation to enquire if he was required to reach any dishes for them.

After the withdrawal of the ladies, the gentlemen's talk was more sober. The duke's disappointment in the baby's sex was repeated again and again, no matter how many times Mr Hammond and Mr Pyott pointed out that Mrs Richard had conceived so soon that she would certainly have another baby on the way before too long. But Mr Godley's well-meaning pronouncement that it was God's will did not mollify the duke in the slightest, and an explosion of rage sent the chaplain scurrying from the room.

"Foolish man!" the duke muttered, when his ire had subsided to mere smouldering embers. "I cannot imagine why I put up with him. I shall write to the bishop and tell him to send him somewhere... the navy, possibly. He can be a ship's chaplain, and see if that knocks some sense into his head. Or the army! Ha! He can go and preach to Napoleon, if he likes. I cannot abide a prosy parson, always prattling on about God's will. God's will, indeed! As if I am not perfectly aware of God's will. Have I not suffered under His will for these many years? Damnable business! I should have liked another son before I die, but I suppose the wretched man would tell me to be grateful for what I have. Not a single living child of my own, that is what I have. Four sons and three daughters of my blood, and all gone to the churchyard. Well, maybe Richard and Rowena will fill the nursery again, and give me the heir I need. *Damnable* business. Where has the port got to? Send it up this way, will you?"

It seemed likely that the duke would settle down to get well foxed, so Simon slipped away as soon as he decently could. Sooner or later, the duke would remember the orangery and ask to see the new designs, but this was not an auspicious moment, when the man was so upset.

As soon as he entered the White Drawing Room, one of the Merrington sisters approached him to ask him about Marshfields. For a moment, he panicked — was it Sophia? But then he realised it was not. Maria or Augusta, he thought, for Charlotte was a little different... her nose, he suspected, although he could not be sure. But there was one way to find out. His sketchbook, with the drawings of the ball at Marshfields, was still sitting on a table, and there were a few sheets still unused. After asking a footman to find him a pencil, he began to draw.

"Why do you keep looking at me?" she said suspiciously. "You are not taking *my* likeness, are you?"

"Indeed I am, Miss Merrington. I should like to take the likeness of all four of you on one sheet, and then you may each of you add your name to it. It will make a fine picture, I think."

She clapped her hands together excitedly. "Charlotte! Maria! Sophia! Come here, for Mr Payne is going to draw all of us."

Ah, so this was Augusta. The others had been chatting in low voices to each other, their heads of identical light brown hair close together, but now they rose and twittered across the room.

"Draw us?"

"All of us?"

"At once? How exciting!"

Their voices were slightly different, but he would need to know them much better before he could distinguish one from another by their speech alone. Sophia... yes, he could be sure of Sophia, but the other three still troubled him.

"How would you like us to sit?" one of them said. Was it Charlotte?

"Perhaps if you all sit on this sofa, I can bring over a chair from which to observe and draw you," he said.

Giggling, they arranged themselves, then realised they were in the wrong order and shuffled themselves about. Now Sophia was at one end of the sofa, not in the middle. Were they in age order? He rather thought they were.

"But what pose do you wish us to assume?" one of them said... Maria, perhaps.

"No pose."

"But you want us to be still, presumably? So we must adopt a pose." Charlotte, he thought.

"No need. Just do as you normally do. Talk to each other."

Even though they talked incessantly as a rule whenever they were together, the instruction to talk silenced them. They sat, pulling puzzled faces at each other, while he pretended to draw, for he had no wish to capture them with such unnatural expressions. But gradually their natural ebullience rose to the surface, and they began to talk again. His pencil flew over the paper as he attempted to capture their differences. No, he had not quite caught them. He turned the page and began again.

"Is it done?" Sophia said, as they all fell silent and turned hopeful faces to him.

"Not yet. It will take me a few attempts to perfect it."

By the fifth attempt, he was reasonably satisfied, and yes, there were definite differences. Charlotte's nose was a shade more pronounced, Augusta's mouth was a little wider, Maria's chin a touch more pointed and his Sophia's eyes—

His Sophia? Well! If only it could be so, but although he was happy enough to oblige Juliet in most things, that was a step too far. But so tempting... *his Sophia.* How glorious that would be! When she was with her sisters, she was just one of a chattering mass of womanhood, but by herself, she was a peaceful and most agreeable companion. Unlike most of her sex, she was easy for him to talk to. That day when she had shown him around Staineybank, for instance, and listened with seeming interest to all his ramblings. Or the visit to the orangery at Marshfields, when she had filled him with ideas. Yes, she would make an excellent wife for him, and—

"Is it nearly finished, sir?" Sophia said, rousing him from these pleasant thoughts.

"Um... I believe so. What do you think? Have I captured your likenesses well enough?"

They praised his efforts with satisfactory enthusiasm, and it was Sophia who said, "You are so clever, Mr Payne. You have captured us to the life."

He persuaded them to sign their names, each to her own likeness, and he was pleased to see that his guesses were correct. They whisked his sketchbook away to show it around the room, and he was left to himself for a while. He had been so engrossed that he had not noticed the other gentlemen returning, but now the room was noisily full, the card tables set out and all the places filled. The duke was smiling now, and the duchess was in good spirits, her companions keeping her well entertained.

After a while, one of the card tables broke up as Miss Hester Merrington and Mrs Hastings went off to check on the mother and infant, and ensure that Richard was not plaguing them too badly, and the Miss Merringtons got up a round game with Mr Godley and Mr Hammond. Mrs Merrington brought Simon's sketch book back to him.

"What a talent you have, Mr Payne," she said. "This is a charming composition. Would you consent to a framing, so that it might be hung on the wall for everyone to admire?"

"If you think it worthy of such treatment, ma'am, then I should be honoured."

"You have not signed it yourself. Does not the artist always sign his work?"

"That squiggle in the corner is my sign — an 'S' and a 'P' combined."

"Ah, I see it now. How ingenious! I thought that was just a part of Sophia's necklace. Excellent! I shall ask Cousin Hester to recommend a framer, or perhaps Mr Hammond will know." Almost without a pause, she went on, "Is Lady Juliet unwell?"

"Not that I know of," he said, startled.

"Good. I wondered, you see, when she did not appear for dinner, but I am relieved to hear that all is well."

She bustled away to join her daughters, leaving him puzzled. Juliet not at dinner? Now that he thought about it, there had been two empty chairs at the table. The new father was one of the absentees, dining with his wife, but had Juliet been the other? He could not recall seeing her at all that evening. After their altercation earlier that day, when she had talked about taking in lodgers, there had been no sign of her and that was most unlike her. In particular, she never missed a meal! What on earth had become of her?

He slipped out of the room and up the stairs to her room. When he knocked, a thread of a voice bade him enter. He found Juliet curled up on her bed, still in her day dress, her face white and wan.

"My dear, whatever is the matter? Are you ill?"

"No," she whispered. "Not ill... I have received a blow, that is all. I shall make a recover before long."

"What has happened? What can I do?"

"Nothing. There is nothing anyone can do." She sat up abruptly. "The most dreadful thing, Simon. There, read that."

She pushed an open book towards him.

"'*The English Peerage*'? What are you—? Oh, it is Papa's entry. *'James William Payne, Earl of Edlesborough, Viscount Kendle, Baron Landrick. Born... succeeded his father...'*. Is there a point to this?"

"Read on."

"Very well. *'Married Cecilia, eldest daughter of Sir Henry Rushbury of Shrewsbury, by whom he had issue Andrew, Viscount Kendle, Luke and Juliet.* All your dates of birth are there. Well?"

"Read on."

"Oh. *'...which marriage was dissolved by act of Parliament.'* Good God! But... but she *died*... so we thought. Dissolved! Great heavens! And you never suspected?"

"That my mother was divorced? No, I never suspected *that!*" she said, with such bitterness in her voice that he was shocked. "Aunt Tabitha always said that she died in childbed, and naturally I never enquired further. Why would I? It would not have occurred to me that she might *lie* to me. And then, we never moved in the sort of circles where anyone would have known otherwise. I wonder if that was why I was sent away, so that I would not know the shame of my mother's wickedness."

"If so, it would have been the first time Papa ever did anything for the benefit of anyone but himself," Simon said tartly. "More likely he simply wanted to remove any reminder of her. He could not get rid of the boys — his heirs, after all — but he could send his daughter away."

"And then several years later, when the scandal had abated, he married again and had you and all the others. Oh, I forgot — that was why I was looking in the Peerage, to find out if we have any previously unsuspected brothers and sisters."

"We do!" he said, looking down at the book again, surprised. "Mark and Ruth, aged twelve and six respectively, and two others who died as infants, not even named."

"There might even be more," she said. "The book is several years out of date."

"So there might. Poor Mama! Ten children, and possibly more! She must be quite worn out."

"At least she is alive," Juliet said.

"But your mama is alive, too... or at least, she did not die in childbed all those years ago."

"Then where is she?" she said in despairing tones. "Why did she abandon me? If she still lives, why did she never make the least push to find me? *Your* mama is constrained by Papa's prohibitions, and your brothers too, I suppose, but *she* was not, not after..." Her voice died away to nothing.

"After the divorce? No, she would have been free of his authority, but I imagine the shame would keep her away from society and therefore away from London. And how would she find you?"

"Through the family lawyers, I imagine. I am her daughter, after all. She must be dead, Simon. I cannot believe that she would not try to find me. We could have been together all this time. I could have had a mother who loved me, and not—"

"Not Aunt Tabitha?" he said, smiling suddenly. "She was not the most maternal woman, was she? Kind in her way, but she could be harsh... unforgiving."

"I think she did not understand children," Juliet said. "She had never had any of her own, or any contact with them, so when I was foisted on her, I am not sure she knew what to do with me. I suppose she meant to be kind, by telling me Mama was dead. Such a scandal! My own mother, being so wicked that her husband divorced her! It does not bear thinking about. What do you suppose she did?"

"The usual thing is breaking the marriage vows."

"What does that — oh! You mean that she—? With another man? Heavens!"

"You know, I think you are right," he said. "There must have been the most fearful scandal, the whole thing dragged through Parliament. Everyone would have known."

"Of course, but—?"

"Well, the duke knew her, so he might remember what happened. He might even know what became of her afterwards."

She jumped to her feet, and paced rapidly across the room and back. "The duke! But I cannot ask him about it. It would be too shaming."

"No, but I can. She is not my mother, after all, but it is to do with my family, so I have the right to know."

"He might not tell you."

"In which case we are no worse off, but he must remember something of it. He remembered your mother very clearly, so he will know something. If you give me permission, I shall speak to him privately and see what I may learn. He might even know where she is now, and then *you* could contact *her*. Think how splendid that would be, if we could find her, Juliet. To meet your mother after all these years... would it not be a fine thing?"

"If she even wants to meet me," Juliet said gloomily.

12: A Bridge Over The River

The following morning, Sophia and her sisters were permitted a brief visit to congratulate Rowena and admire their new niece. Richard held the sleeping baby in his arms, gazing down at his daughter with a beatific expression on his face.

"Is she not perfect?" he murmured, as the sisters cooed over her. "Look at her tiny fingers... and such long eyelashes! She is the most beautiful creature."

Sophia stared at the wrinkled little face and blotchy skin, saying all that was proper but rather shocked that she was not, in fact, perfect, despite the delightful little hands now curled into fists and the eyelashes that would be the envy of her friends, if they survived to adulthood. Wisps of dark hair peeped out from beneath an overlarge cap, and occasionally her lips made little movements as she slept. Perhaps she dreamed... did babies dream?

And of what could their dreams be filled? Milk, she supposed and the strangeness of the world, so new and so filled with noise and light and colour and movement.

Rowena was sitting up in bed, her breakfast tray still before her. She looked tired and very pale, as if she were recovering from the influenza.

"What do you think of her?" she asked, smiling as the sisters left the baby to Richard and surrounded the new mother instead.

"So small!"

"So delicate!"

"Beautiful!"

Sophia scratched around for something true to say. "She seems to like sleeping in Richard's arms."

Rowena rolled her eyes. "She has a perfectly good crib, but he dotes on her... quite the besotted father."

"And you... how are you?" Charlotte said. "Was it awful?"

"No... well, it was unpleasant, of course, that cannot be denied, but well worth it. She is the sweetest baby, and I am sure the next one will be a boy."

The others jumped in to agree with her, but Sophia stayed silent. Producing babies was the whole purpose of marriage, and presumably one grew accustomed to all the inconveniences of it, but it did not greatly appeal to her at that moment. As for the pressure to produce a son — she was thankful she was never likely to marry into the peerage, and thus be expected to provide the all-important son and heir.

"Such a relief that all is well after that dreadful fall," Maria, ever the most tender-hearted of the sisters, said. "Such an anxious time for everyone."

"But so fortunate that the gamekeeper was near at hand to help us," Augusta said.

"The duke gave him five guineas to thank him for his services," Charlotte said.

And that reminded Sophia of the rake, which had been driven quite out of her head by other events. She should go back to the spot where Rowena had fallen, and examine the rake more closely. She did not want anyone else to know about it, however, for the duke was bound to make an almighty fuss when he heard. So when the sisters went downstairs again, and settled down to their usual occupations, she made an excuse to slip away, quickly donned her outdoor clothes and made her way out of the house by a garden door.

The rake was gone. Sophia stood on the exact spot, her cloak pulled tight around her to keep out the chill February air, and stared at the step, but there was no doubt about it. Where the rake had lain, half on the step and half on the grassy bank to the side, now there was nothing but a stray leaf or two. The snow had all melted, so there was no possibility of the rake being buried. Someone had tidied it away.

The crunching sound of booted feet in the woods across the river recalled to her mind the gamekeeper who had been so fortuitously nearby. Perhaps the path through the trees was a regular route for the outdoor servants, and one of them had spotted the rake.

"Who is there?" she called out.

The footsteps stopped, then began to come nearer, and there again was the gamekeeper.

"Oh, it is you! Lovell, is it not?"

"Aye, Ben Lovell. Are you in trouble, miss?"

"No, but... I should like to ask you a question, if I may."

As before, he came over the bridge to Sophia's side of the river. Again, he had a gun over one shoulder, and a game bag hung from his waist. This time, he had a couple of pointers at his heels.

"I thought it was mere chance that you were passing by the other day when Mrs Richard Merrington fell, but now I see that you often pass this way," she said.

He replied easily, "Aye, I go that way several times a day, going back and forth to the game store. No reason I shouldn't, is there?"

"Of course not!" she said hastily. "I meant only — Well, never mind. It was fortunate you were here to help, anyway."

"I hope she's going on well," he said politely. "And the babe, too."

"They seem to be very well, both of them."

"Lucky, after a fall like that," he said. "Could've broke her neck. You said you had a question for me."

"Yes, I do. After Mrs Richard's fall, I noticed a rake lying on the steps, which must have been what tripped her. I wondered if you had noticed it... or know what happened to it?"

"Aye, I saw it. When I came back to collect my bags after helping the fallen lady, I saw it there, where it should never have been. What was anyone doing with a rake just there? Makes no sense, and dangerous, too. Took it back to the gardeners, didn't I? Started a right to-do, that." He chuckled, his sallow face looking suddenly less dour. "They all swore it weren't them as left it there. Thought they were going to set about each other with shovels."

She laughed. "Oh dear! I was afraid of something of the sort. I planned to take it quietly back to the head gardener and simply say I saw it lying, without saying where. I hope no one was turned off because of it?"

He shook his head. "Couldn't agree who it was, so no one lost their place. They need to be more careful with their things, don't they? Be a fine thing if I were to leave my gun lying about, wouldn't it? If that's all, miss...?"

She hesitated, but the question worried away inside her. "Do you think...? I mean, is it worth mentioning to anyone? The duke or my brother, for instance? It was just carelessness, surely, that the rake was left there, and I would not wish anyone to get into trouble for such a simple mistake. It *was* just a mistake, was it not?"

He looked surprised. "You don't think it was deliberate, do you?"

"I cannot see why anyone would do that, but Rowena took the same walk at the same time every day, so if anyone did want to cause her harm—"

"No one wants to harm her," he said sharply. "A lovely lady like that, and all the family's hopes resting on her and the new babe — no, it's impossible. Put that idea right out of your head, miss."

She agreed to it, thanked him again, and followed him back to the house.

***

Simon's designs for the orangery were completed, but, mindful of Juliet's instructions to spin out their stay at Staineybank for as long as possible, he made no effort to present them to the duke. Instead, he occupied himself with sketching ideas for the interior. But inevitably the day came when the duke looked down the dining table at Simon and remembered why he was there.

"Anything new to show me, Payne? You must have some fresh ideas for this orangery after all this time."

"I have, your grace. After seeing how the Marshfields orangery was arranged, I have come up with a completely different plan that I believe would suit Mrs Richard Merrington very well, and would be an enhancement to Staineybank itself."

Richard, who had resumed dining with the family, snorted at this, but the duke merely nodded easily.

"Tomorrow at noon, in my study, Payne."

When Simon arrived, sketchbooks in hand, he found that he faced an audience of five. Apart from Richard and the duke himself, the duke's secretary, James Hammond, and Mr Hammond Senior were both there, and also Mr Pyott, the comptroller.

"The key feature of the Marshfields orangery," Simon began, "is that it is attached to the house. That means it can be used all year round as an additional room. The Duke of Camberley uses it as his private retreat as he recovers from illness, and even in the depths of winter it is warm and comfortable. Mindful that Mrs Richard wishes to be able to use her orangery every day, I have ventured to modify my original design to connect it to the house. The new design retains an imposing location on the far side of the lake, but now it is connected to the house by way of a bridge... thus."

"A bridge!" Richard said. "What on earth is all this likely to cost, Payne?"

"I will address that point in a moment. You will see that the bridge and orangery will be visible from every room at the front of the house, and—"

"We already have a bridge over the river," Richard muttered. "An elegant little bridge, too, not a monstrosity like this. And this huge window in the centre — it is preposterous! Why must you make it so large?"

"Because the bridge contains a gallery," Simon said diffidently. "There is no gallery at Staineybank, and every great house should have one, in my opinion. And it will make an excellent ballroom, too."

"A ballroom! Great heavens, why not just throw out a new wing, while you are at it? Or perhaps you would prefer to knock down the whole house and start anew?"

"Knock down a Campbell house?" Simon said, shocked. "No, indeed! But I hope my suggestions are in keeping with his work."

The duke began to laugh. "You like this house, I think, Payne?"

"It is a glorious house, your grace. I would not change anything about the original, but Mrs Richard wants to be able to use her orangery every day, and this is a way in which it could be done, while providing an additional feature."

"A ballroom..." the duke said thoughtfully. "Why a ballroom?"

"It is a great pleasure to young ladies to dance, and there is no place for a proper ball in the current design."

"It is certainly ingenious," Mr James Hammond said. "More spectacular than any of us had envisaged but very much in keeping with the grandeur of Staineybank."

"And her grace would like to hold balls here, perhaps," the duke said. "She loves to dance — or she did before the tragedy."

"So do the Miss Merringtons," Simon said, with a sudden smile as he recalled Sophia's enthusiasm at Marshfields.

Richard had been pacing about the room, his anger visible on his face. "It is ridiculous! Staineybank is big enough already without adding on vast extravagances like this. And knowing Payne and his love of marble, it would cost five or six thousand, I should think."

"Oh no," Simon said. "With the correct facings to match the main house and a suitable interior, it could not be done for under ten thousand, I imagine."

"You imagine? Then you have not even costed it properly?" Richard said, aghast.

"Not yet, no. For a labourer's cottage, perhaps, the sum would need to be calculated with some precision, but to enhance a ducal seat — what value would you put on that, Mr Merrington? Does the exact cost matter so very much? Would you choose to put in a smaller window in the gallery to shave a few guineas from the overall price, knowing that every time the duke walked past that window he would think, *'For a few pounds more, I could have had a view all the way down the lake, instead of the tops of the trees?'*"

"Would it overlook the whole lake?" Mr Hammond said. "That would be quite something — a place for the ladies to take their exercise on a dreary day, yet still be able to enjoy the lake."

"You like it, then, Hammond?" the duke said.

"I do, your grace. It would make a worthy addition to Staineybank, assuming it could be afforded."

The others murmured their agreement.

"Well, Richard?" the duke said. "You have seen the accounts. Can I afford to spend ten thousand without undue hardship?"

"It will not stop there, sir. There will be delays, complications, additional expenses..."

"Suppose it costs fifty thousand? Can I afford it?"

"I cannot at all recommend such extravagance, sir."

"Richard, what is my annual income?"

He hesitated, hands on hips, as his desire for parsimony warred with the need for honesty. Then he sighed. "Twenty thousand or so."

"And my expenditure?"

"Currently twelve thousand or so with the London house closed up, but with the duchess's new establishment—"

"That will come from her settlement, so does not affect my own estates. So, the surplus every year is in the region of eight thousand or so, correct? Which means that in under two years, this scheme of Payne's could be paid for with no diminution to my income, correct? So I can easily afford it, would you not agree? Richard?"

Pyott, the comptroller, coughed deprecatingly. "If I may remind your grace, the surplus income has been accumulating for some years now, so you already have the required sum available immediately. Even if it should amount to fifty thousand."

The duke laughed. "So let us have no more talk of whether it can be afforded, eh, Richard? I am sure your habit of watching the pennies was useful to you in your previous life, but you must get used to a different way of managing now. This orangery is a compliment to your lovely wife, who is a future duchess, and nothing is too good for her, and no expense will be spared to provide her with a home worthy of her. I said this orangery would be a competition between you and Payne, but so far you have not shown me anything worthy of a duke. Now that we have established that the cost is not a consideration, why do you not make another attempt? If you dislike Payne's orangery and gallery, then design something you like better, and I will choose the one I prefer. Now off you go. Take some of these sketches to show your wife. Hammond, we have some letters to attend to, I think."

Richard disappeared, with only one fulminating glance at Simon as he went, and Pyott left, too. Simon gathered up the remaining sketches, but he had not forgotten Juliet's difficulty.

"Your grace, may I ask you a question on a different matter?"

"Of course, boy. Anything you like. Of course, I might choose not to answer you," he said genially, making the Hammond father and son chuckle.

"You might not know the answer," Simon said. "It is about Juliet's mother."

"Cecilia," the duke said, his face softening. "Such a delightful lady. What about her?"

"Juliet was told that she was dead, but—"

"Ah. Was she now? Understandable, I suppose."

"Perhaps. But since she is *not* dead, I wondered if perhaps you knew what became of her... after the divorce."

"Lord, I forget. Hammond, you are working on my diaries. Have you come across it? The Countess of Edlesborough — the divorce was such a scandal it must have been mentioned."

"What year was it?" James Hammond said.

"Good question. Must have been... oh, sixty-five, sixty-six, round about then."

"I have not seen any of your grace's papers from that era. Father, have you done any work on his grace's notes for that period?"

"Aye, some. I recall the incident at the time, and I believe she went abroad, but I'm not sure any specific place was mentioned. It was a huge scandal, though. There were some cuttings from the newspapers about the business in Parliament. There was a baron cited as the gentleman concerned, although your own notes, your grace, seemed to doubt it, but he didn't contest the case."

"He was in love with her, poor fellow, so he wanted her to be free of Edlesborough. Farrance, that was his name, and he swore he never touched her, which might have been true." The duke chuckled. "He was always bird-witted. Married, of course, and was too hen-hearted to leave his wife for her, but he allowed Edlesborough to think he was the one who cuckolded him. Edlesborough was a fool, too. He thought I was Cecilia's lover at one point. I disabused him of *that* notion. Called him out... he lasted ten seconds, as I recall. The easiest duel I ever fought."

"Rapiers?" James Hammond said, sounding amused.

"Naturally. The gentleman's weapon, and needed a bit of skill, not like pistols. Just point and shoot — where is the skill in that? But a well-matched sword fight — ah, that was something else altogether. That was for real men. Difficult to stop, though. I saw men set out ready to fight until first blood, but once they were well into it, they tended to forget. Twice I had to get a man out of the country in a hurry when he got carried away and killed his opponent. Foolishness. Control is everything in a duel."

"How many have you fought in?" James Hammond said.

"Only three, but I was second for any number of friends. Well, the same friends over and over, if the truth were known. We were a hot-headed set, to be sure. But to your question, Payne, I never heard what became of Cecilia after the divorce. Never met her again, sadly. Ah, she was a lovely lady, and with a different husband... but there, in those days there was none of this romantic nonsense about falling in love. Girls married where their parents told them and that was the end of it, but Cecilia... well, she was never happy, poor girl. Too lively for Edlesborough, that much is certain. It was inevitable that she would get herself into trouble sooner or later. There were men enough willing to console her."

"Yet you were the one who fought a duel over her," James Hammond said, amused, "even though you were not one of those who consoled her."

"Did I say that?" the duke said, eyes gleaming with merriment.

"You did!" Hammond said. "What was it you said? That you *'disabused him of the notion'* when he accused you."

The duke rumbled with amusement. "Oh, when we fought over her, that was true enough, but later… well, having been accused and challenged over it, I saw no reason not to make it true. But it was a fleeting affair, and I had nothing to do with the divorce. She had long since moved on to someone else by then. Poor Cecilia! I hope, wherever she went, that she found happiness in the end. As for Edlesborough, he found a wife more suited to his temperament. Quiet little thing, your mother, Payne. She gives him no trouble, I imagine."

"As you say, sir."

Nothing more was said, and Simon was left to reflect on the difficult lives of aristocratic wives, and wonder whether it was better to be lively, like Cecilia, and end up cast out of all good society, or to be meek and timid like his mother, living always in fear of a mistake that would bring down retribution on her head.

13: A Suitor

In the garden, the first signs of spring began to emerge from winter's iron grip. Snowdrops edged the paths, and here and there in sheltered spots primroses brought their own sunshine to the shrubbery. Sophia and her sisters took advantage of a milder spell to explore further afield than the formal gardens, venturing across the river to explore the woods beyond.

They returned one day to see a mud-bespattered travelling chaise being driven away to the stables, as footmen laboured with several items of luggage.

"Visitors?" Charlotte said.

"Ooh, exciting!" said Augusta.

"Who can it be? No one is expected, I think," Maria said.

"Cousin Hester did not mention any arrivals," Charlotte said. "Perhaps it is one of the duchess's sisters."

"There was a coat of arms on the chaise," Sophia said.

"Ooh, nobility!"

"Quick, quick, let us find out who it is."

Augusta's longer legs took her up the front steps before any of the others, where she almost crashed into Froggett. He smiled paternally at her, and beamed at the three following close behind her.

"Who is it, Froggett?" Charlotte said. "Anyone we might know?"

"It is the Lord Daniel Torbuck, madam."

The sisters gasped in excitement. Sophia gasped too, with a queer shivery feeling, as if she were about to succumb to the influenza. *Lord Daniel!* He could only be here to see her, surely? But no — she must not assume that every acquaintance who happened to appear at Staineybank had arrived on her account. That would be foolishly presumptuous of her. Perhaps he was just passing, or brought a message from his father to the duke, for these peers all knew each other.

The others, whispering together in awed voices, were in no doubt. "Oh, Sophia! How wonderful for you," Maria breathed.

"Where... where is his lordship, Froggett?" Sophia said, her voice unnaturally high, but she could not quite master it, not yet. The shock was too overwhelming.

"Upstairs putting off the dirt of his journey, madam," Froggett said, his smile widened. "Her grace wishes you to know that she and Mrs Roland Merrington will expect you in the White Drawing Room whenever you have divested yourselves of your outer garments."

The White Drawing Room! The most formal room in the house, used only in the evenings, or for very important guests. So Mama and the duchess were according this visit its proper solemnity.

The sisters tore up the stairs to hurl away cloaks and pelisses, bonnets and gloves. Kitty was waiting for Sophia, a fresh gown already laid out, one of her newest ones.

"Madam said you're to wear this one, Miss Sophia," she said, eyes shining with excitement. "I'm to make sure your hair's neat, too."

Sophia understood. The arrival of a potential suitor was too important a matter for an ordinary day dress. She submitted meekly to Kitty's ministrations, although it was hard to be still when she was quivering with anticipation. What would he say? Would he be eager to see her again or restrained? And how should she respond to him? She was pleased to see him, naturally, but... somewhere deep inside her was a fluttering of alarm. She might be on the brink of receiving her first offer... she could even be married by midsummer. Heavens! After so many years of dashed hopes, she was not at all sure how she felt about that.

When Kitty was satisfied that her appearance would bring the appropriate credit to the family, Sophia left her room, to find her sisters waiting on the landing for her, eyes wide with delicious anticipation. Arm in arm, they descended the main staircase in a sedate manner, for heaven forfend that they arrive out of breath or dishevelled in any way. Froggett was loitering at the foot of the stairs, awaiting their arrival. He led them at a stately pace into the Marble Hall, where Henry and Robert stood ready to throw open the high doors to the White Drawing Room.

Froggett led them through, and bowed as they entered.

"Ah, here they are, Lord Daniel," Mama trilled, from her seat at the far side of the room. "My girls."

And there he was, looking just as he had at Marshfields, jumping to his feet and smiling, smiling... he saw the four of them, his eyes scanned them, the smile slipped and the strangest expression flashed across his face. It was almost as if he were horrified... but how could that be?

"Lord Daniel," Sophia said, stepping forward into the room. "What an unexpected pleasure to see you again so soon."

She did not ask why he was there. Presumably he would have some reason prepared, but she left that to him to articulate.

His face cleared, and the odd expression was replaced with a wide smile. “Miss Merrington... how delightful! I was just telling your mama... and her grace... how you had told me so much about Staineybank and its glories, that I had to see for myself.”

Well, that excuse would do as well as any other. “Campbell,” she said.

“I beg your pardon?”

“Campbell, I believe. The architect. It is magnificent, is it not?” He blinked at her, and seeing that he had nothing further to say on the subject of architecture, she went on, “You had a tolerable journey, I trust. Have you come far?”

“From... from Gloucestershire... near Cheltenham... my father’s seat at Pentavon Castle.” He fell silent, looking behind Sophia at the doorway where her sisters, she presumed, still stood, waiting to be introduced, and there was that odd expression on his face again. Surely she had mentioned her sisters? She was certain she had. He could not be surprised by them. But she had not introduced them...

“Oh — allow me to make my sisters known to you, Lord Daniel. My eldest sister, Charlotte... and Augusta... and that is Maria.”

The three made their curtsies, then they sat in a row on a sofa, near enough to hear the conversation but not so close as to be required to participate. Sophia sat beside her mother, with the duchess nearby, while Lord Daniel pulled up a chair to sit beside her, and after that all was easy. Sophia and Lord Daniel chatted as comfortably as they had at Marshfields, the conversation helped along by the occasional word from Mama or the duchess. And in no time, the afternoon had flown by and it was time to dress for dinner.

***

The irrepressible Robert brought the news to Simon with his evening washing water.

"Lord Daniel Torbuck, he is. Son of the Markiss of... of Something. Very happy to see Miss Sophia, he is."

"The Marquess of Pentavon," Simon said automatically, although with a frown. Lord Daniel here... that could only mean a serious courtship. He was not sure he liked the sound of that.

"Oh, you know him, then?" Robert said, pouring water into the washbowl, and only slopping a little over the side. "I s'pose all you great families know each other."

"I met him at Marshfields."

He had danced twice with Sophia at the ball, and then hung around her, and if he had now come to see her again, that was surely a good thing. Perhaps he would propose and then she would have the husband and children and a house of her own that she craved so badly. Although Torbuck was only a younger son, so unless he had a profession, he would be dependent on his father. At least *his* father would support his son, he thought morosely, unlike Simon's.

When he descended to the White Drawing Room, Torbuck was already there, with his expensively fashionable clothes and immaculately white neckcloth. Simon had no desire to cut a dash, but he envied Torbuck his supplies of new linen, or the skilled laundrymaid who kept them looking so.

Torbuck was making polite conversation with Godley, the chaplain, and Hammond, the secretary, but he willingly turned to Simon when he drew near.

"We met at Marshfields, as you might recall," he said. "Payne, Simon Payne."

"Ah yes. How are you?"

"Well. Have you come from Pentavon?"

"I have, yes."

"Motte and bailey. Original. Very interesting place."

Torbuck burst out laughing. "It is a damnably uncomfortable place to live, I assure you, all howling draughts and dampness. Never warm, even in midsummer. Give me a cosy modern house any day."

The Merrington ladies arrived just then, Mrs Merrington a little in front and two pairs of sisters behind her, arm in arm, as usual looking almost identical. Simon was amused to see a slightly panicked look on Torbuck's face, and realised he could not pick Sophia out of the group. What an awkward dilemma for him! How was he supposed to court her when he could not recognise her?

Taking pity on him, Simon murmured, "What a pretty gown Miss Sophia is wearing! That shade of blue sets off her complexion perfectly, does it not? And the amber cross is charming."

Relief flooded Torbuck's features. "Yes... indeed. Charming... quite charming."

He stepped forward to speak to Sophia, who blushed and lowered her head shyly. She was certainly charming, or at least she was managing to charm Lord Daniel. Simon was surprised at the intensity of the pain that shot through him as he watched them. Even though his head told him very clearly that he could never aspire to her hand, his heart, it seemed, was paying no attention. He had come, by insensible degrees, to regard Sophia a s *his*, in some indefinable way. Not as a wife, but as a friend... one for whom he felt a great affection. Now he saw that for the presumption that it was. She would never have been his, never, and the thought left him with an emptiness inside.

Juliet appeared at his shoulder, and drew him aside, whispering, "He is as fine as fivepence, would you not say? Look how he smirks at her! He will cut you out, if you are not careful, brother."

"I can hardly compete with the son of a marquess, sister," Simon said glumly.

"You are the son of an earl," she hissed. "Besides, I doubt he has much of an allowance. He is the third son, you know. His father probably has a living or two for him, but his prospects are no better than yours, and you are a great deal handsomer than he is."

Simon only shook his head.

"What about one of the others?" she went on. "Charlotte is a good manager — always in the kitchen, that one. Augusta would be too expensive, for she would not be happy without a horse and we cannot afford so much as a pony and gig, never mind a string of hunters. Maria... she is bookish, so she might—"

"For heaven's sake, Juliet!" he burst out. "I wish you would leave off this idea of me marrying."

"Oh." Her lip quivered. "Then what is to become of us, brother? Are we to starve?"

"We will find a way," he said. "I have written to Mr Thwaite, so he might yet commission me properly, even if the duke dislikes my orangery."

"Mr Thwaite!" she said savagely. "After two years? He is sporting with us, brother. No doubt it amuses him to keep us on a string, but it is not very amusing to *me.* Not at all amusing. Simon... truly we must do something. If you will not marry, then we must find another way."

Dinner was announced just then, and Simon followed the throng into the dining room. Dinner was generally the high point of the day for him, for the duke's table was always groaning with the finest delicacies that the expensive man-cook could produce, washed down with an excellent claret.

As an additional boon, the excessive number of ladies meant that he was rarely called upon to involve himself in anything resembling conversation. One or two of the Merrington girls liked to sit beside him, but since they were perfectly capable of carrying any conversation single-handed, he had no objection. Tonight, he was relieved of even that slight disadvantage, since Lord Daniel was the focus of all their female enthusiasm, and Simon found himself seated between Godley and Pyott, and thereby not required to speak at all.

It would have been quite blissful if it were not for the fact that he was positioned opposite Sophia and her beau, and therefore was obliged to watch the courtship progressing on its inexorable way. He could not deny that they appeared very well suited, for all was ease and openness between them. Whatever they talked about, they discussed the subjects with equal interest, neither of them being overly talkative or unduly reticent. They laughed together, too, at some shared joke, and that was almost more than he could bear. He was not much of a jokesmith himself, but the facility with which Torbuck was able to make Sophia laugh burned him inside. Oh, to be witty or droll or merely to know a few amusing anecdotes with which to beguile a beautiful woman! But he had no aptitude for it, and the thought left him quite dejected.

When the ladies had withdrawn, and the remaining company had rearranged itself around the port decanter, the duke turned at once to Lord Daniel.

"Well, Torbuck, so you have an interest in one of Richard's sisters, eh?"

"Well..."

"Excellent, excellent! I shall be glad to see them settled. Very pretty behaved girls, all of them. Which one do you have in your eye?"

Torbuck cleared his throat and adjusted his neckcloth by a minute amount. "Miss... Miss Sophia Merrington, Duke."

"Ah! She the pretty one, eh? I cannot tell one from another — these girls all look the same to me."

"The Miss Merringtons are all very pretty," Godley said, his Adam's apple bobbing.

"Well, of course they are, foolish man! All the Merringtons are good looking, it runs in the family. How much will she have, Richard?"

"Two and a half thousand, sir."

"Two and a half? What sort of paltry dowry is that for a girl who will be sister to a duke in the fullness of time?"

"The girls get an equal share of their mother's ten thousand," Richard said tersely, clearly uncomfortable discussing his financial affairs in company around the dinner table, and Simon could hardly blame him. The duke was outrageous, sometimes.

"Good heavens, boy, have you not put in a penny piece of your own? I cannot abide such cheeseparing ways. You can do better than that, now that you have a decent allowance. If you make it five thousand, I will put in another five, and the same for the other girls when their time comes. What do you say to that, eh?"

"No one could ever accuse your grace of cheeseparing," Richard murmured, to a ripple of laughter. "I am not sure that I approve of you frittering away my inheritance, even on so worthy a cause."

"Indeed it is a worthy cause," the duke said. "I am very fond of those sisters of yours who have brought a smile back to my dear duchess's lovely face, so I am prepared to indulge them a little, and surely by now you know that I am not going to leave you purse-pinched, boy? The Duke of Brinshire short of the readies? I hardly think so! Torbuck, how is your father going on these days. I have not seen him for an age."

"He is well, apart from the gout," Torbuck said.

"And your mama? And your Aunt Lavinia? My goodness, but she was a lively one, in her youth. A dreadful flirt." He chuckled, a deep rumble in his throat. "Ah, but she was such fun. I never understood why she married Crosby — such a dry old stick. He was no fun at all, keeping her secluded in the country as he did. And what about that wild uncle of yours — Herbert or Hubert or some such. Now, *he* was trouble, if I remember rightly."

After that, there was no shifting the duke from his reminiscent mood until Froggett came in to say that the duchess wished to know if the gentlemen would be joining them soon, for the ladies were ready for their tea, and then there was a general exodus. Simon drifted through in the wake of the crowd, and was immediately scooped into a game of whist with the duke, Hammond and Godley. It was an awkward combination, for Hammond and Godley were crafty players and the duke, although less crafty, nevertheless expected to win, and Simon could not afford to lose. It did not help that he had the other table, where Sophia and Torbuck were clearly well pleased with each other, in his view the whole time, an unsettling distraction. He went to bed happy to be only a few pounds down, and made a mental note to manoeuvre himself to a more fruitful table next time.

He was in bed not long after midnight, to lie restlessly in the dark, haunted by a pretty face surrounded by brown curls, eyes alight with excitement and entrancing red lips that smiled for another man.

14: Courtship

Sophia slept surprisingly well. Her sisters had been inclined to linger in her room to discuss the interesting development, but she had chased them out and climbed into bed, expecting to lie awake for hours thinking about Lord Daniel. But the next thing she knew was the girl quietly re-making the fire the next morning.

She knew instinctively that she must wear another of her newest gowns today, and had one already laid out when Kitty arrived with her washing water, earlier than expected.

"You're to be done first today, miss, and then Miss Souter's to do your hair."

Miss Souter was Mama's own maid, only deployed for the younger sisters on important occasions. This additional attention, and the more elaborate style Souter deemed appropriate, meant that Sophia was the last to be ready. Mama and her sisters were waiting for her on the landing, for it was absolutely necessary that they go down to the breakfast parlour together, for moral support. Sophia had never thought much about this habit, but now she wondered how it would feel if she were obliged to go everywhere by herself. As she would if she were married, she supposed. What a strange thought!

Lord Daniel was already in the breakfast parlour. He rose as they entered, and there was that odd expression again as he saw them. What could it mean?

For a moment, no one spoke. She thought he would speak first, but it seemed he had the same thought for he merely smiled, a slightly hesitant smile ranging over the five of them, and not settling on Sophia herself. Fortunately, Mr Payne was also there and had also risen at their entrance.

"Mrs Merrington, good morning!" he said cheerfully, pulling out a chair for her. "Pray sit here. And Miss Sophia... there is a chair beside Lord Daniel. Miss Merrington... Miss Augusta... Miss Maria..."

He pulled out a chair for each of them with ostentatious courtesy, then himself fetched the coffee pot from the sideboard, pouring for everyone before taking his own seat again. Mr Hammond watched this performance with an expression of surprise, but said nothing. Sophia was surprised too. What did he mean by such attentions? If there were any need for a chair to be held for her, it was the footman's duty to do so, and Froggett would pour coffee. It was bizarre.

But Lord Daniel was smiling at her, a full-hearted smile now, and so all thought of Mr Payne's behaviour flew out of her head.

After breakfast, the rain being too heavy to permit a walk outdoors, the sisters undertook to show Lord Daniel the principal rooms in the house. He accepted this with great good humour, tucking Sophia's arm proprietorially in his and murmuring *'Most impressive'* and *'Very beautiful'* at regular intervals.

They came in time to what was known as the Chinese Room, which housed a collection of objects acquired by a Merrington ancestor on a visit to China. Mr Payne had not expressed any great admiration for this room, merely saying that it was of a style no longer much in vogue, but the cabinets of curiosities and great lacquered urns attracted Lord Daniel's attention, and he wandered about examining everything for some time.

Sophia stood at the far end, gazed through the window at the lake.

"What is so fascinating out there?" Lord Daniel said, coming to stand beside her.

"Mr Payne's orangery," she said at once. "This window will become a door, and beyond it will be the bridge over the river which is also a gallery... and a ballroom." She shivered in delight. "At the far end, just on that rise beyond the lake, will be the orangery."

He laughed. "As if the house is not large enough already. An orangery, I grant you, is an elegant addition to the garden, but a gallery and ballroom? Are there not rooms enough for dancing?"

She stared at him, shocked. "There are rooms, of course, but none large enough for more than a dozen couples or so, and what is the use of that?"

"The entrance hall is large enough," he said.

"Oh yes, but then one would have late arrivals disrupting everything, and there are the marble tiles to be considered. One would need to lay a wooden floor and imagine the inconvenience. Every great house should have a ballroom, Lord Daniel, and in the long spells between balls, it is a quiet gallery where one may take one's exercise in inclement weather and keep all the dreadful old portraits of bewigged ancestors that no one wants in the drawing room."

"The attic is the place for the portraits, and is useful for indoor exercise, too. My brothers and I practise our fencing there."

"But one cannot *dance* in attics," she said with asperity. "Where do you dance at Pentavon Castle?"

"At the assembly rooms in Gloucester, on those occasions when a little jigging about is unavoidable."

"Was the jigging about unavoidable at Marshfields, too?" she said acidly. "What a pity you were so inconvenienced."

He reddened, realising his mistake. "Oh well... that was different, you know."

"Was it indeed," she said flatly. "That is a relief to my mind."

"Of course it was!" With a quick glance around the room, seeing her sisters at the far end of it and proceeding through the door to the library, he took her hand and raised it to his lips. In a lowered voice, he murmured, "It was very different, Miss Merrington, for you were there."

It was Sophia's turn to blush, and although she could not quite forgive him for despising dancing quite so thoroughly, she was slightly mollified.

The ladies all retired early to dress for dinner, gathering in Sophia's room, together with Souter and Kitty, to decide how Sophia should be arrayed. Several gowns were laid out on the bed, and they settled down for a long discussion on the relative merits of each.

After only a few minutes, a tap on the door revealed the duchess's own lady's maid, Allen, bearing a shimmering cream silk gown that brought an appreciative *'Oooh!'* from all present.

"Beg pardon, ma'am," she said in her soft Cheshire accent, "but her grace wondered if Miss Sophia might like to wear this tonight, bein' as how it would suit her so well and her grace still bein' in black."

She held the gown against her, setting the spangles on the spider-gauze over-gown sparkling. Around the bodice, sleeves and hem, more spangles shimmered, and intricate stitchery proclaimed the work of one of London's finest modistes.

"Oh, Mama, may I?" Sophia breathed. "For I have nothing so fine... such beautiful work."

"Aye, his grace insists that her grace only has the best," Allen said with pride. "This was new last year, and her grace has only worn it the once."

"Try it on, dear," Mama said, beaming with delight.

"I can put a few stitches in, if it's not quite right on you," Allen said.

It was a trifle short, for Sophia was taller than the duchess, but Sophia could see from her sisters' eyes and her mother's nodded approval that she looked well in it. Even the rather grainy looking glass on the dressing table showed her a more fashionable and elegant Sophia. Then there was just the matter of ornaments, and the dressing of her hair, and Augusta lent her ivory fan for the occasion, which was a perfect match. Mama donated her own cashmere shawl to add a touch of colour. Sophia descended the stairs with her sisters feeling that if Lord Daniel had any attachment to her at all, he should appreciate her appearance tonight.

He was almost alone in the White Drawing Room tonight, Mr Godley the only other person present. Judging by their expressions, conversation was somewhat laboured.

"Ah, ladies!" the chaplain said, his face lighting up with a broad smile. "Mrs Merrington, how charming you look tonight. Allow me to procure you a glass of sherry."

Lord Daniel stood as if transfixed, that strange expression on his face again. The sisters stood uncertainly. Sophia did not like to put herself forward, yet he made no move towards her. What was she supposed to do?

It was Charlotte in the end who rescued them all by stepping forward towards him, and enquiring if he had received the letter he was hoping for from his mother.

"Robert went into Brinchester especially, despite the weather, for you mentioned that you were concerned about your father."

He nodded, and spoke to her in a low voice, his words rapid, leaning towards her so that Sophia could not hear what he said. She felt oddly excluded. Should she have stepped forward? Yet it would have been presumptuous to assume that he would only wish to speak to her. They were not betrothed, so she must not expect to monopolise his attention. It was for the gentleman to make his intentions plain, after all.

Augusta and Maria sat together on a sofa near Mama, where they quickly became a target for Mr Godley's ponderous gallantry. Sophia was not minded to sit, so she wandered away to the high windows, where plush curtains shut out the incessant rain, and thence to a collection of miniatures on the wall, staring unseeingly at them as she puzzled over Lord Daniel's behaviour.

Gradually the room filled up, the duke's booming voice shutting out even the low murmur of Lord Daniel's conversation with Charlotte. Mr Payne was one of the last to arrive, looking rather flustered. Scanning the room, his eyes lingered on Sophia, and he frowned. He looked at Lord Daniel and the frown deepened. Striding across the room, he interrupted the cosy chat with Charlotte. Sophia could not hear what was said, but a few moments later, all three of them walked towards her.

"Good evening, Miss Sophia," Mr Payne said. "How charmingly you look tonight. Your sister tells me that this is one of her grace's gowns."

"Indeed it is, for I have nothing so fine," Sophia said. "Her grace is very kind."

Froggett announced dinner at that moment, Mr Payne offered his arm to Charlotte, and Lord Daniel turned expectantly to Sophia. For the rest of the evening, he never left her side, but he seemed subdued.

Her own feelings were too muddled to bear close scrutiny. She liked him, naturally, for there was nothing to dislike in him. He was adequately handsome, a fashionable dresser, if one cared for that, and his rank made him eligible, although she had no idea what his income would be. In conversation, he was... well, adequate would be the word again. His manners were gentlemanlike, although with those odd lapses that were hard to account for. He disliked dancing — she remembered his words at Marshfields, where he had said he would prefer a good slice of mutton! Still, not everyone liked to dance and she would not hold that against him.

But ignoring her, when she had put on the finest dress she had ever worn, and looked as if she would not be out of place in Grosvenor Square — that she could not quite forgive. And so, even as he exerted himself to please her, she was unmoved. She would accept him, of course. There could be no doubt on that point. But she felt that it would be some time before she could forget the way he had whispered to Charlotte, and it had been as if Sophia were not even there. It was not the action of a man on the point of a proposal, to slight his intended in that way, and she wondered greatly what he meant by it.

***

Simon made his excuses to the card players and made his way swiftly to Juliet's room. He knocked, but there was no answer. He went in anyway, to find the fire burning low and the single candle guttering badly.

He attended to these matters first, then went to the small figure curled up in the bed.

"Are you feeling any better, sister?"

As she shook her head, he could see tears glistening on her cheeks.

"Did you eat any of your dinner?" He scanned the tray on the bedside table. "Nothing touched. Come now, we will survive this, you know we will."

"Lodgers, Simon?" she hissed, abruptly sitting upright. "Strangers in the house? Aunt Tabitha will turn in her grave."

"I shall find employment. As a secretary, perhaps. Or I could teach... we could set up a small school. At least we have the house, Juliet. If all else fails, we could rent it out, and take rooms somewhere for ourselves."

"Lodgings! Are we sunk so low? I cannot bear it, truly I cannot."

Sighing, he sat on the edge of the bed. "This is not like you, sister. Was it not you who always found some good in every setback? We will survive, you always said. Every time a prospective client faded away, you cheered me up and assured me that one day I would succeed, and then we should have all the money we needed for life's little elegances. I do not like to see you so cast down."

"It is finding out about my mother," she said, sniffing slightly, and mopping at the tears. "Divorced! How can I hold my head up in public with such a blot on the good name of my family? I could suffer the deprivations of our life perfectly well, knowing that I was the daughter of the Earl of Edlesborough, with a long, distinguished lineage. I could be proud of my heritage, even as I despised the current occupant of the family's honours. But the daughter of a woman so scandalous that her husband divorced her — how can I possibly live with the shame of that? It is beyond my capability to raise my spirits in such a situation."

"You are the same person you always were. Her disgrace is not yours, and if your father had protected you as he ought—"

She sat a little more upright. "Yes! Perhaps one cannot blame him for sending me away but—"

"Of course one can!"

"Well, you may be right, but even if he wanted me gone from Edlesborough, he could have paid Aunt Tabitha an allowance to look after me. We should *both* have had an allowance. Nasty, vindictive man! We will survive, brother, if only to spite the old weasel. I could take a position as a housekeeper, for no one could say I am not well qualified. We could both find living-in positions, which would save the cost of lodgings. It would be horrid, but we should not starve, I suppose. The world is full of evil men, Simon. It is so dispiriting. Papa is bad enough, but Mr Thwaite seemed like such a pleasant man. Two years he has had us dangling and it was all a hum. Wicked, wicked man to keep us on a string all this time, and now this!" She rattled the letter at him.

He took it from her, reading again Thwaite's uncompromising words. *'Very much liked your designs but have decided not to proceed... expense... bad time... many apologies...'* He sighed. "Should I bill him for my time? There have been half a dozen full drawings, and innumerable sketches. I spent a month just on ceilings."

"Certainly you should! That fellow with the kennels — he paid for the designs, even though they were never built."

"He paid me fifty pounds, that is all. It barely covered the cost of travelling to his estate, let alone my drawing paper. And since then, nothing," he said frowning. "People enquire, they meet me, I do a few preliminary sketches and then they simply vanish."

"What might we get to rent out the whole house?"

"I have not the least idea. We will enquire when we go back to London."

"That could be any day," she said glumly. "The duke will settle for Richard Merrington's designs for the orangery, I am sure of it. He is just using you to come up with the ideas. Mr Merrington will modify them slightly, that is all, for he has no good ideas of his own. Did you see his original plans? Dreadful! Quite dreadful. Not elegant, like yours. But he will copy yours, and the duke will send us packing and then we shall be reduced to taking paid employment! The humiliation of it!"

"Matters are not yet so desperate," he said gently.

"They would not be if you would only marry one of the Merrington girls. Ten thousand apiece, thanks to the duke! Five hundred a year! Just think how well we should live on such an income. And this son of a marquess comes here with his fancy clothes and his smiles, and makes up to Sophia and you do nothing at all to stop him."

"What would you have me do, Juliet?" he said impatiently. "He is a far more eligible match than I am ever likely to be. Sophia wants nothing more than to marry, and I will not stand in the way of her happiness."

"She could marry you, silly boy! Five hundred a year... we could afford fires in the bedrooms."

"You would make me a fortune hunter, sister. It would be dishonourable."

"Honour! We cannot eat honour, Simon. Oh, go away, do. Slide that tray a bit nearer before you go, will you? I might have a bite to eat before I sleep."

"The snipe is very good. Did they send you any lobster? They did!"

"Snipe! Lobster!" She sighed. "I hope the duke takes a very long time to make his decision."

15: Abandoned

Simon slept badly again, and he was beginning to understand why. When a man's dreams, both waking and sleeping, are filled with a certain face and a certain smile and a certain pair of luminous eyes, the conclusion is inescapable. No matter how many times he sternly told himself he was not in love with Sophia — that he could not afford to be in love with her — still he could not get her out of his head.

Despite this, he held no dislike of Lord Daniel. He was something of a coxcomb, of course, with his fancy clothes and a certain air in his manner of walking and his speech that marked him as a son of the nobility, an air which Simon had either lost or never managed to acquire. But the fellow admired Sophia and was prepared to chase round the country in pursuit of her, and Simon could not fault him for that. If he were to marry her and make her happy, then he might have her with Simon's goodwill.

So although he rose early and unsettled, he was not truly unhappy. A little sad that such a lovely woman would never be his, but there had never been the least possibility of it, so her loss did not weigh him down. In a few more days, perhaps, all would be settled between them, and that would be the end of it. Simon would go back to London with a little ache in his heart where Sophia had crept, almost unnoticed, into his affections, but he would be kept too busy trying to earn money to feel any grief. Or so he told himself.

He passed an hour or two sketching details for the gallery — there was something mesmerising about ceiling designs, so that was mostly where his efforts went — and then Robert appeared with his washing water.

"Heard the news, have you, sir?" he said cheerfully, mopping up a little spillage.

"What news? Not the baby? Or Mrs Richard?"

"No, no, nothin' amiss there. No, it's that markiss's son — Lord Daniel."

It was just as well that Simon was not carrying anything at that moment, for he would surely have dropped it. "What has happened to Lord Daniel?" he croaked, as a myriad possibilities, all of them hideous, passed through his mind.

"Gorn, ain't he."

His eyebrows flew up. That was the last thing he had expected.

"Gone? What do you mean, gone?"

"Just that, sir. Sent for his carriage at first light, and lord, *that* caused a rumpus in the stables, with every last groom havin' to be dragged from his bed, the horses not best pleased either, and his coachman not in his bed at all and havin' to be searched for all over. Found him in the dairymaid's cottage, if you please, and his lordship standin' in the yard waitin' for him. Don't fancy he'll last two minutes once he gets his master home. And away they went, oh, more'n an hour ago now."

"Where has he gone?"

"Don't know. No one knows, or if they do, they're not telling. But he's gone, right enough."

Impossible to make any sense of it. Why would Lord Daniel suddenly turn tail and run away, when all was going on so prosperously with Sophia? It was unfathomable. The obvious answer of an urgent message from home could not apply, because the servants would know of any messenger arriving in the middle of the night.

Puzzled, he dressed in haste and made his way hopefully to the breakfast parlour, where he might hear more.

He was in luck, for James Hammond was alone there. He looked up at Simon and grinned. "Heard about our runaway, have you?"

"Lord Daniel? I have heard. Any idea why?"

"Concerned about his father's health, apparently. The letter he received yesterday was not reassuring, and he decided upon reflection to hasten to his bedside."

"I thought it was gout? Hardly a life-threatening condition."

Hammond laughed. "Exactly so. Myself, I suspect a lover's tiff... or perhaps he just thought better of it, who can say? I am sorry for Miss Sophia, of course, but I think she is better off without him, frankly."

"Do you?" Simon said, startled. "The son of a marquess?"

"The *third* son of a marquess, with no profession or estate of his own, and he looks expensive, to me. He will run through her dowry in no time, and probably end by breaking his neck on the hunting field, leaving her with a string of children and no money. I have tried to make this point to her brother, but he was so excessively pleased at the prospect of marrying her off to somebody — anybody — that I could not get him to see the potential pitfalls."

Godley came in just then, to be told all about it. Simon silently filled his plate and ate thoughtfully. Poor Sophia! She must be quite cast down by this turn of events, for it was clear that Torbuck had taken fright and bolted. Was her proposed dowry not enough for him? Given his high rank, he might have looked for more than ten thousand. Or perhaps the continual hazard of being unable to recognise his beloved in a gaggle of sisters had become too much for him. He would surely have learnt to distinguish her in time, just as Simon had done.

Pyott came and went, and then Hester Merrington, a little sour faced this morning. Richard Merrington and Mrs Hastings came in, ate quickly and then dashed away to attend the new mother again. Simon lingered after everyone else had left, making his final piece of toast last as long as possible in the hope of seeing Sophia.

Finally, the Merrington ladies arrived in their usual crowd, but Sophia was not amongst them. The servants had all disappeared momentarily, so Simon jumped up to hold chairs for them. He wondered what he ought to say to them — should he enquire about Sophia or should he say nothing at all, and act as if everything was normal? They were unusually subdued, which was not surprising, given the circumstances, and he had no wish to distress them further. But he was spared the necessity for a decision by Mrs Merrington.

"You will have heard, no doubt, Mr Payne, that Lord Daniel has gone home?" she said. "A sad day for us, as I am sure you will appreciate."

"Indeed. I was very sorry to hear of his sudden departure. His father is ill, I understand."

"Well, yes, but that would not— However, he is gone, and I do not suppose he will return."

"Perhaps once he is assured that his father is on the mend—?"

She shook her head decisively. "No. He left a note for me, you see, and he made no mention of returning, not the least hint. It sounded very much like a farewell."

"It is very dreadful for poor Sophia," whispered one of the sisters. Charlotte? Yes, he was sure of it.

"To have her expectations raised," said Augusta.

"And so cruelly dashed," said Maria.

"He must be mad!" Simon said forcefully. "Who, having spent so much time with Miss Sophia, could fail to be enchanted by her?"

The sisters murmured in pleasure, and Mrs Merrington smiled and reached across the table to pat his hand. "Ah, how kind you are to say so, Mr Payne. Naturally, we see no fault in Sophia, but perhaps Lord Daniel saw something in her that did not just suit him."

"No, indeed, I cannot allow that," he said, setting the sisters off again. "I had rather suppose that he has hopes of a higher dowry."

"That is true," Mrs Merrington said, brightening a little. "He might have looked for twenty or even thirty thousand, and being a younger son, he will need to marry well since he has no profession. Yes, that may be it — now that he has discovered that Sophia will only have ten thousand, he has decided against her."

"Only ten thousand?" Charlotte said, raising her eyebrows. "Until a few weeks ago, all any of us could expect was two and a half thousand."

"Perhaps that is why we have never had an offer," Augusta said sadly.

"We are just too poor," Maria said.

Simon doubted that was the problem. Four fine looking girls, all well-mannered and educated, and moreover related to a duke should not have any trouble finding husbands. Lack of fortune was not much of an obstacle, for were there not men enough in the world with the wealth not to care for fortune? It was a puzzle.

"Does Miss Sophia keep to her room?" he said.

"She is about somewhere, hiding away," her mother said.

"I expect she wishes to be left alone," he said disconsolately, realising belatedly just how much he had longed to see her.

"Oh no, she is not hungry, that is all," her mother said. "She knows where we will be, so when she wants company again she will come to find us."

There was no reason for Simon to stay any longer, so as soon as Froggett returned to the room, he went out into the hall, and stood irresolute. Where should he go? He was not minded to work on his designs, nor was Juliet likely to be good company. The library wing was liable to bring him into the orbit of Hammond and Pyott, and possibly the duke or Richard, but the prospect of male conversation was not enticing, either.

"Are you in need of assistance, sir?" Froggett said, emerging from the breakfast parlour again.

"No, thank you," he said, turning promptly into the Blue Parlour and thence through a series of chambers to the chapel wing. The chapel... Godley went out for his morning walk at this hour, so the chapel would be deserted. Simon went in, sat on the servants' bench at the back and, by long habit, bent his head in prayer.

Into the silence came a muffled sound. Someone was weeping.

Low sunlight flooding in illuminated every corner of the chapel, and unless the weeper was hiding behind the altar, he was quite alone.

Another sob.

Jumping up, he strode the full length of the chapel, peeked behind the altar, just to be sure, and then back to the centre. No one was there, yet someone was crying nearby.

"Who is there?" he called.

The sounds stopped. Then a tremulous voice from above. "Mr Payne? I am up here."

Above the door, he now saw, was a narrow gallery, partly hidden by an intricately carved latticed wooden screen. He could just make out a pale face peering down at him through the gaps.

"Sophia? Wait..."

He flew out of the chapel, up the nearest stairs and onto the landing where the door to the gallery should be. No door. For a moment, he panicked, then realised that what he had thought was a tapestry was merely a curtain, and behind it was—

"Aha!"

Inside, it was gloomy, and her dark gown made her almost invisible on the bench where she sat, were it not for the white, tear-stained face she turned to him.

"Oh, Sophie! My poor darling! I am so sorry."

Without a single thought in his head except that she was in distress and needed comfort, he sat beside her and scooped her into his arms. She burrowed into his chest, bursting into fresh tears and sobbing as if her heart would break. Or perhaps it was already broken, which made him so angry at Torbuck's fickleness that he would cheerfully have throttled the fellow, were he present. The only outlet he had for his rage was to hug her tightly to him, and rock her gently, murmuring into the top of her head, which was conveniently within reach.

"Hush now, sweetheart, hush. All will be well, have no fear. Sshh, now, my dear. He is not worth so many tears."

At that, she lifted her head and looked up at him. "Oh no! Indeed, he is not. I do not cry for *him*, faithless, deceitful rogue that he is."

Another spasm of crying overtook her and for a while she said nothing more.

When he could bear it no longer, Simon said, "Then what troubles you?"

"I truly thought... when he came all this way to find me... but yet again, a promising man just disappears, and each time, I am a little older, a little more securely on the shelf."

"You will find a husband one day, Sophie."

"No!" she cried, sitting up a little straighter. "That is just it, time is running out. You cannot understand, I suppose, being a man, what it is like to have your hopes constantly raised and then dashed, time after time after time."

"Actually, I believe I can. I have been qualified as an architect for almost ten years now, and any number of potential clients have approached me. They tell me what they want, I make some sketches and then... then they disappear, just like your suitors. My hopes have been raised and dashed, I imagine, at least as often as yours."

"Oh. Then you *do* understand. But I will not allow it to be the same. How old are you, Mr Payne?"

"I am thirty years of age."

"Then you still have many years in front of you to make your name in your profession, whereas I am eight and twenty. I have been out in society for eleven years, I have danced at one hundred and forty-two balls and—"

"Have you?" he said, enchanted with the precision of the number. "One hundred and forty-two? Do you count them as you go along... number seven... number twenty-four... number one hundred and forty-two? That one was the Marshfields ball, I suppose."

"It was. I keep notes about them in a little book. What I wore, who I danced with, that sort of thing."

"That is charming! Is it private? Or would a friend be permitted to see it?"

"You? Are you interested in such things?"

He should perhaps have made some bland answer, but the tears staining her cheeks tugged forcefully at his heart and made him recklessly honest. He ran one finger gently down her face to wipe away the traces. "I am interested in everything about you, Sophie."

"Oh!" She gave a rueful laugh, with a slight shrug of one shoulder. "If only Lord Daniel had been interested in everything about me."

"He is a fool to walk away from you, but you will find a husband, never fear."

She shook her head, the little curls on either side of her face bouncing in emphasis. "No. Not at my age. Who would have me now?"

"I would if I could." It was madness to say such things, but he no longer cared. He wanted her above all to understand that she was a lovely, fascinating woman and by no means without admirers.

"Oh." She gazed at him wide-eyed, her face troubled. "Why can you not?"

"I have no money," he said. "No estate, no allowance from my father, no fortune in the funds. Even my profession brings in nothing."

"But I have money... ten thousand pounds."

"It is for the man to provide for his wife," he said. "Your brother would quite rightly send me packing if I were to approach him for your hand."

"Yet you want to."

"I should love to!" he cried. "You would make any man a wonderful wife, but for me it is impossible. I only want you to understand that... you are admired... valued..." He stopped, suddenly struggling for words. His heart wanted to add *'loved'*, but that was a declaration too far. Even in the throes of this madness of openness, he would not use that word.

"You said something like this once before," she said reflectively, snuggling against his chest once more. "That there might be people who admired me but could not speak because of disparities of rank or wealth. You meant yourself, I assume."

He nodded, quite unable to speak. She sighed, but he could not tell, in the confusion of wild emotions swirling inside him, whether it made her happy or sad. For a while, they sat thus, his arms still tight around her, while her head rested against his waistcoat and one hand crept upwards to his shoulder. The tears had stopped and she seemed content. He was content, too. This was where he belonged, with his Sophie snuggled trustingly against him. If he could never be more to her than a friend to comfort her distress, that would be enough for him.

After a while, with another sigh, she lifted her face to gaze up at him. "This is so pleasant, is it not?"

"It is, yes. Very pleasant. Do you feel better now, Sophie?"

"Much better, thank you. Why do you call me Sophie?"

"I beg your pardon. That was forward of me, Miss Merrington."

"No, no, I do not mind! But why Sophie, rather than Sophia?"

"I have no idea. It just... felt right. I cannot explain it."

"It does feel right! Mama and Papa used to do that — have different names for each other. She used to call him Roly, and he called her Aggy, or Aggy-dear, if he were feeling very affectionate, such as when she had ordered a veal kidney pie for dinner. Papa loved a veal kidney pie. I like that you have a special name for me, too. But what may I call you? There is nothing one can do with Simon, is there?"

"My second name is Harold."

"Oh, that has possibilities! Harry… or Hal! Yes, I think you are a Hal. But only when we are alone."

His conscience began to prickle at this innocent remark. "I am not sure we should be alone, Sophie. Today is somewhat unusual, but it is not at all proper."

She smiled up at him — such a warm and utterly beguiling smile that he melted instantly. "I believe it is quite proper, under the circumstances."

With trepidation, he had to ask the obvious question. "What circumstances are those?"

"That we are as good as engaged… Hal."

"Sophie—"

"You said you wanted to marry me, which is as good as an offer, is it not?"

"Sophie, I do not think—"

"Do you remember sitting with me in the gallery at Marshfields, when you nearly kissed me? I can see that you do. Have you not sometimes wished that we had not been interrupted?"

Simon knew exactly what he should do. He should release her and leave the chapel gallery at once, for to stay would be quite fatal. If he once kissed her, he would be lost, utterly lost and…

He should leave…

He should definitely leave...

He should leave at once...

And yet he could not. Slowly, oh so slowly, she lifted her face towards him and he bent down to reach her.

Then there was only magical warmth and sweetness of such intensity that he almost cried out in joy. Her lips were soft and gentle and yielding, yet they bound him to her with unbreakable iron bonds, and he was lost.

16: A Question Of Marriage

Sophia was in paradise. To be held in Simon's arms was bliss such as she had never experienced before. Her mother hugged her sometimes, or her sisters, in moments of great excitement or distress. But this kind of embrace, enfolded in the strong arms of a man, was something quite different.

And his kisses! She had been kissed before, but never like this, never with such tenderness... such affection. He had said he wanted to marry her and then kissed her, so that was almost an offer, was it not? And since she had allowed herself to be kissed, that was almost a betrothal. She was betrothed! Or as good as...

For a long time, they kissed and cuddled and talked about this and that — she did not press him on the question of betrothal, in case he squashed the idea at once. Best to leave it up in the air, so that at least she could hope.

Eventually, Mr Godley could be heard moving about the chapel below, humming as he went.

"I must go," she whispered to Simon. "Mama will be wondering what has become of me."

Nodding, he released her. Did he seem reluctant? She thought he was. With another quick kiss, she was gone, dancing down the stairs to the ground floor, but not to find Mama. It was not Mama she needed now.

She tried the library and the duke's study, then the nursery. Then Froggett, to see if he knew. At last she ran her quarry to earth in his own study upstairs.

"Richard, there you are! I have been looking everywhere for you."

He was seated at his drawing table, his chin in his hands, gazing pensively out over the gardens. Spread out on the table in front of him were Simon's drawings of the gallery bridge and conservatory, and his own sketchbook, opened to a blank page.

"This is a large house," he said abstractedly. "What do you think of Payne's design? Do you like it?"

"I like it very much."

He smiled at her wanly. "Because it incorporates a ballroom?"

"Not only for that reason. It is very elegant. From the house one will see the bridge arching over the river and the orangery which looks like a Greek temple."

"It is a Roman temple, and indeed it is all very elegant." He sighed. "And expensive, of course, but the duke seems inclined to pay whatever it costs. But let us not talk about this wretched orangery. Did you want me for anything in particular? Oh! Did Rowena send you? Is it the baby? Is anything wrong?"

"Nothing like that. You know that Lord Daniel has left, I take it?"

"Yes, and I am sorry for it. That would have been a good match, if it had come off, but I am sure you will find someone else."

"I have... or at least, I may have. Simon Payne wants to marry me."

For the first time, Richard turned to face her fully. "*Payne* wants to marry you? He has said nothing to me."

"Well... it is not quite agreed yet. He has some scruples about it, but you will not turn him away just because he does not have a great estate or a title or anything of that sort, will you?"

"No, but... he is an odd sort of man. Would you want to marry him?"

Odd? For an instant, Sophia could not breathe. Simon was the best sort of man in the world. How could anyone find him *odd?*

"I should like to marry him very much," she said stiffly.

"Truly? Sister, I will not stand in the way of a love match, but I would urge you not to marry him just because he is willing. That is no foundation for matrimony."

Such presumption! Rage boiled up inside her as she stared at him in disbelief. "No foundation for matrimony? And what foundation did you have when you offered for Rowena? She was better than the supercilious daughters of the nobility, that was all. You proposed to her on the spur of the moment — a mere whim! What do you know of Simon... or of me, for that matter? Nothing at all! So do not presume to judge either of us."

He flushed uncomfortably. "I beg your pardon. I did not mean... I only thought... let me talk to him, that is all, and then I will have an answer for you. Sophia, all I want is your happiness, nothing more than that. If he is the man you would choose above all others, then I will not stand in your way, but I would not have you grasp at any possibility for a husband, that is all. But if you truly like him—"

"I do! I do like him," she said, and the tears, so recently conquered, were not far from the surface again. "You would like him too, if you were to view him dispassionately, as a man, and not as a rival in this absurd competition of yours. He is not *odd*, Richard. He may not be quite like you, but he is none the worse for that."

"You are right, of course," he said gently. "I will try to see him as you do, I promise you, and if he is the man to make you happy, then he will have my blessing."

"And my dowry?"

He smiled. "That too."

***

Simon sat motionless in the little gallery for a long time, his thoughts churning and his pulse tumultuous. Such madness to allow himself to be drawn into temptation. He should never have gone there at all, never have held Sophie and certainly he should never have kissed her, but now that he had, he was held fast in her spell, so sweet and affectionate as she was. If only he could marry her! If only...

Down below, Godley's humming stopped. The chapel door opened and closed a few times, as some of the servants trickled in for the noon prayers. Then a waft of perfume as some of the ladies came in, followed by Godley's voice intoning the prayers, and a low murmur of responses. Simon found himself saying the familiar words under his breath, too. It was a comfort, in all the turmoil of his mind, to be part of the brief service, to know that even though he had behaved badly and surrendered to weakness, God understood his heart and forgave him his trespasses.

The service was soon ended, and the chapel fell into silence once more. Heartened, Simon made his way towards his own room, where at least he could hide away and think about Sophie and remember the joy of holding her tight.

He had not taken three steps when he was hailed by Froggett.

"One moment, sir!" he said, puffing up behind Simon. "If you would be so good, sir... Mr Merrington would be... obliged if you could... spare him a few moments... of your time, if convenient... and attend him... in his study."

Simon could not help smiling at the butler, struggling to maintain his dignity while trying to catch his breath, but he said only, "Of course. Thank you, Froggett."

He found Merrington staring out of the window at the light rain painting the gardens a bleak grey.

"You wished to speak to me?"

Merrington turned and regarded him thoughtfully. "You have offered for Sophia."

"Um... not precisely."

"Then what *precisely* has passed between you? She told me you wished to marry her."

"Indeed I do... if I could. I have explained to her why it is impossible."

"Then explain it to me, Payne, because although Sophia does not need my permission to marry you — or anyone else — she needs my approval to release her dowry."

"I cannot possibly marry Sophia, or anyone, since I have not a farthing to my name. Well, that is not quite true. To be precise, I have eighty-seven pounds ten shillings and fourpence remaining from the last gift from my mother and my winnings at the duke's whist table, but nothing more. I live on my sister's charity, for the most part. I could not conceivably afford a wife."

Merrington gave a huff of surprise. "That is honest, at any event. So what were you doing talking about marriage to her?"

"She was despondent at Torbuck's defection, thinking she would never find a man who wanted to marry her. I intended merely to reassure her that there is at least one man who would love to marry her, if money were not an issue. She seemed to think that her dowry would solve the problem. Although I thought I was very clear that it would not, it seems she believes otherwise."

Merrington gazed at him, nodding slightly. "Why do you want to marry her?"

Simon's breath caught at such directness. "For the usual reasons, I suppose."

Merrington smiled. "Which are what, *precisely?*"

"Precisely... how hard it is to be precise about... about one's emotional state. I know to the penny how much is in my purse, but what is in my heart? That I cannot say, not with precision."

The smile widened. "That is very true. I find it hard to put into words just what I feel about my wife and daughter. I only know that I could not bear to live without them. I was terrified that Rowena would die in childbed, and that fear hung over me like a black cloud. Now, I am so grateful, I feel light-headed with relief. But when I met her, I offered for her... not on a whim, exactly, but on the spur of the moment. I had to marry, and Cousin Hester had whistled up three appalling daughters of an earl. Rowena was the serene antidote to their screeching arrogance. When she said she was going to leave, I offered for her on the spot. I was not in love with her, not then, it was not even a rational decision. I just knew I wanted her to be part of my life. So I do understand how difficult it can be to express feelings in words, Payne, but I need to be sure that you will take good care of Sophia, if she were to marry you."

"It is impossible!" Simon said, shocked. "You cannot want your sister to marry a penniless man."

"As the duke reminds me constantly, there is no shortage of money in this family. Besides, you are not an idle good-for-nothing who has wasted a fortune and wants to marry to replenish the coffers. You have a profession and it is not your fault that no one has yet commissioned you."

"It must be my fault," Simon said, startled. "Who else might one blame? There must be some deficiency in my work."

Merrington shook his head decisively. "No. I may not like the expense of your ideas for the orangery but they are both beautiful and practical, and who could ask for more than that? The plans for your country houses are, in my view, comparable with the very best of our modern architects. It is unfathomable to me why you have not been commissioned to build even one of them."

Simon opened his mouth in astonishment, closed it again when no words came. Merrington actually liked his designs?

"Oh," he said eventually, nonplussed.

With a laugh, Merrington said, "I know, praise from me is unexpected, is it not? And I am no expert. I have never been trained, as you have, but even I can appreciate the quality of your work. Cottages — that is all I am good for. Labourers' cottages, with two parlours and a kitchen below, and two bedrooms above. I can produce those endlessly. But the vision to create a great country house — a Blenheim or a Chatsworth or even a Staineybank? No, that is beyond my capabilities. I know my limitations, I t rust."

"I never finished my training," Simon said pensively. "Five years articled, but then I should have spent two years in Italy, and if I had won awards out there, that would have set my career on the proper path. But I could not afford to go to Italy, and so I have always struggled, and there is no end in sight. I have just heard from a man who has been talking about a country house for two years now. I have prepared any number of designs for him, but now he tells me he will not proceed after all. It is disheartening. So you need not tell me I am ineligible to marry Sophia, for I know it all too well."

"Let me consider the matter," Merrington said. "I shall discuss it with Mama, and consider what we might be able to do for you. The duke should be consulted, too."

"So... you are not saying no?"

"I am not saying no. Neither am I saying yes, not yet, but I want Sophia to be happy, so let us see how it might be managed. I am good with money, so perhaps we will yet find a way to increase your income."

For the first time, Simon felt a gleam of hope.

***

Sophia went to the morning room to sit with her mother and sisters. Naturally, they talked endlessly about Lord Daniel's perfidy in running away, and gave no credence to the excuse about his father's health. At any other time, such gloominess would sink her spirits utterly, but now she had something else to think about. So even as the others chattered on about the loss of her hopes with one man, she was warmed inside by thoughts of another man altogether.

'You would make any man a wonderful wife... I want you to understand that... you are admired... valued...'

Such glorious words! To be admired... to be valued... to be *loved*... He had not said it, but every word, every little gesture implied it. The way he had looked at her, his eyes shining, his voice soft and gentle... everything he said and did proclaimed him as her lover.

As her sisters chattered on, she was blissfully untouched by it. How could Lord Daniel hurt her now? Simon loved her and Richard had as good as said that he would approve their marriage. They would have her dowry, and that would be enough to live on, would it not? She was sure it would. They would manage. She could economise... she would learn to economise.

Then there was Simon's profession. Architects became rich and famous sometimes, so there was still that possibility, and — oh! A sudden thought — there were other ways to make money, besides building the houses. The designs alone could be valuable. Yes, *that* was something he could do.

The duchess and her maid, having been at Mr Godley's midday prayers, came in just then with a new journal that had arrived, and Sophia took the opportunity to slip away, running light-footed up the stairs to Richard's study. He was not there, but the book she wanted was on a shelf there. She skipped away down the landing. Where would Simon be? Her first thought was to check the gallery above the chapel, but as she expected, he had gone from there. Probably he was downstairs with the other gentlemen, in the library or the duke's study, but she did not want to explain her idea to him in company.

She would write him a note! The very idea was thrilling — to write anything at all to an unrelated man was something quite outside the bounds of propriety, as a rule. But she and Simon were as good as engaged, so it was perfectly acceptable. That was what she would do — pen a brief note, tuck it inside the book and leave it in his room.

She went to her own room to write the note, which took her longer than expected, for it was not easy to explain precisely what she had in mind, and then there were a multitude of crossings out and corrections. By the time she was satisfied with it, and had written it out in a fair hand, the afternoon was wearing away. The duke dined early and before long everyone would be coming upstairs to dress for dinner. There was just time, she thought, to run to Simon's room and leave the book where he would find it.

Her light slippers made no sound as she skipped along the landing to Simon's room. As she approached, she heard voices — a male rumble, which she recognised at once as his. She could not mistake that melodious sound. He was there already, and her note would not be needed after all. But that made her hesitate. She could hardly enter a gentleman's bedroom if the gentleman were inside it.

There was another voice, however, and the door was ajar. Perhaps his valet was there, in which case it would be permissible to talk to Simon, at least, which she could do without crossing the threshold. She crept nearer, therefore, not wanting to interrupt, merely to determine whether it was safe to speak to him.

She was quite unprepared for what she heard.

"I thought you would be pleased with me, Juliet," Simon said. "This is just what you wanted, for me to marry one of the Merrington girls."

"But it is so uncertain," Lady Juliet said. "The brother's words are not encouraging. *'Let us see what can be done.'* It is hardly a resounding endorsement, and besides, only two and a half thousand is guaranteed. The mother said so. She *might* get more, but she might not, and if that is all, then we shall be completely taken in. How shall we manage?"

Her voice rose to a low wail, and Simon's reply was inaudible.

Sophia did not wait to hear more. Rage boiled up inside her, eliciting a squeak of outrage. This was the man who had spoken such sweet words to her, and talked of honour and propriety and restraint. He had made her believe he admired her… *loved* her. He had not said so, not precisely, but it was in his face, in his eyes, in his kisses. Oh, his kisses!

And it meant nothing to him. All he wanted was her dowry.

Marching straight up to the door she pushed it open wide, and was greeted with two very startled faces.

"Sophie…" he began.

"How dared you!" she hissed. "How dared you pretend to care about me when all you want is my money, you wicked man! How dared you make up to me, when all the time you were scheming and plotting! You never cared tuppence for me, you only wanted my ten thousand pounds. Well, you can whistle for it! I shall tell everyone what you have done so that none of my sisters will be fooled by you, and if you both end up in a debtors' prison, I shall not care a bit. I hate you, Simon Payne! I shall hate you to my dying day!"

So saying, she turned and fled.

17: Friends

Simon had encountered many disappointments in his life. His father's rejection of him at the age of fifteen was perhaps the largest of them, but even then he had had a place to go and a future to hope for. Even his repeated failures as an architect had never quite depressed his indomitable spirit. There was always another possible client, another house to design, another opportunity. He had Juliet's unflagging support, a house to live in and his own optimism to drive him forward.

Sophie's rejection was of another category altogether.

At first, there was no time to think about it, for Juliet collapsed, wailing, and there was all the worry of that, and women thronging his room with vinaigrettes and burnt feathers, and the apothecary to be sent for, with the result that he missed dinner altogether and had to ask Robert to bring him something on a tray.

Then Robert handed him The Book. That was how he came to think of it, later, with capital letters, and probably underlined three times. At the time, it seemed just a footnote at the end of a difficult day, a day that had started with the abscondment of Lord Daniel Torbuck, had segued into that glorious interlude in the chapel gallery, the surprisingly positive interview with Richard Merrington and then the calamitous encounter with Sophie.

His thoughts had been so despairing that he could not but think his life was over. He did not care about being destitute — while he had his health he could always find employment of some sort, after all. He might even be able to care for Juliet, as she had cared for him all these years.

But he could not face a future without his Sophie. After sternly repressing any thought of marrying her for weeks, having the possibility dangled enticingly before him rendered her loss too bitter even for his usually buoyant spirits. How could he possibly survive without her now? It was too dismal a future to be contemplated.

Then Robert had brought his tray up, and as he left, he had bent down to pick something up near the door.

"Here's a book you dropped, sir. Got a bit crumpled where it fell. Oh, there's a letter too. Put it over here for you, shall I?"

A book? His own books were neatly piled up on the table where he worked. He crossed the room to the small side table near the fire where the book lay, and picked it up. *'A Collection of Designs for Cottages, Both Modern and Healthy, Suitable for the Accommodation of Labourers and their Families, With Complete Estimates of Materials'*, the cover stated. *'By A Gentleman'*.

Several pages had become bent where the book had fallen. Carefully, he straightened them out, then began leafing through them. Cottages, a multitude of cottages. He could not help smiling, thinking of Richard's comment that cottages were all he was good for. *'Labourers' cottages, with two parlours and a kitchen below, and two bedrooms above.'* Page after page was filled with just such designs.

On the side table, where it had been hidden by the book, he now saw the letter that Robert had mentioned. Was it—? Oh! It was to him — from Sophie!

'Simon, This is a book of designs that Richard drew. It was published three years ago, and there have already been two further editions, and now he has been commissioned for a second volume, of stables and such like. He was paid £100 for the first one, £200 each for the second and third, and royalties of £150 so far. They sell very well, and they are not such beautiful designs as yours. If you were to write to the publisher, he might commission you for a book of country house designs or town houses. That would be a good way of getting your name known, and earning some money, too. Your affectionate Sophia.'

He smiled. *Your affectionate Sophia.'* Whatever happened in the future, however lonely and miserable his life might become, he had those words to warm him and remind him that once, just once in his sorry existence, someone had liked him well enough to want to marry him, however briefly.

At once he sat down to pen a letter to the publisher. For a moment, he agonised over whether to use his real name or to hide behind the label *'A Gentleman'*, but the question was speedily settled. Richard Merrington, a gentleman of means and the heir to a dukedom, might choose to conceal his identity, but Simon need have no such qualms. He owed no duty of discretion to his family, and his purpose of making his name as an architect would hardly be served by anonymity. So he signed himself *'Simon Payne of Edlesborough'*, which had the virtue of being entirely true. The publisher would no doubt be astute enough to remember the Earl of Edlesborough, and look him up in the Peerage to assure himself that Simon was legitimate.

But he did not want the fellow writing to Edlesborough, so he put his London address on the letter, and added, *'Currently residing at the Duke of Brinshire's seat, Staineybank, Brinshire.'*

That should get the man's attention!

He then sat down to eat his now cold dinner, washing it down with several glasses of the duke's excellent claret. After this, he felt somewhat heartened, and consoled himself with the thought that at least he had the possibility to make amends with Sophie while he remained at Staineybank. There was no need to despair, not yet.

This comforting thought lasted for precisely one hour, when Robert arrived with the news that the duke would like to see him in the library at once. Unlike the summons from Richard, there was no *'would be obliged'* or *'whenever convenient'*, but such words from a duke, who could not be gainsaid, would be mere flummery.

Simon went, therefore, with no inkling of trouble, and was surprised to find the duke's eyebrows at their lowest and most threatening ebb. He was attended by James Hammond and his father, and by Richard, all looking serious.

Before Simon could do more than bow, the duke rounded on him.

"What is this I hear about you seducing a lovely girl like Sophia Merrington into a betrothal, eh? And you with not a penny to your name."

"I—"

"My cousin, to be deceived by a veritable fortune hunter? It is not good enough, Payne. Not good enough at all."

"Is it true?" Richard burst out. "That your pursuit was only to do with her fortune? For I was deceived myself, Payne. You made a very convincing case."

"Of course it is not true!" Simon cried, stung. "As if I would do such a thing! I never made any secret of my lack of fortune, and I have been studiously avoiding any hint of pursuit of the lady, as it pleases you to describe it, until today, when I came upon her in great distress after Torbuck's defection. Even then, I explained to her very carefully that it was impossible that we should marry, however much I might desire it."

"Easy words to say," the duke said, with a snort of derision. "You must think us fools, Payne. You made no move to attach poor Sophia until she had the promise of a dowry of ten thousand pounds, and then as soon as Torbuck is off the scene, there you are, drawing her in with sweet words."

"And kisses," Richard said. "She has admitted that there were kisses."

"Ha! He does not deny *that!*" the duke said triumphantly. "Well, I will not have it, Payne, and so I tell you. I cannot abide that kind of low deception against a poor, sweet child who deserves all your respect. And to think I admired these foolish designs of yours. Well, there is no chance I will ever build your grandiose schemes now, so you can forget that. Whatever Richard dreams up, that is what will be built, and you may take yourself and your mendacious sister with you. I want you both gone from this house tomorrow, understand?"

There was no point arguing against such a tirade, so Simon merely bowed again. "It shall be as your grace wishes."

"Your grace, if I may..." Mr Hammond Senior had a soft voice, but everyone turned to him. "Lady Juliet is most unwell, and it would be a great risk to her health to force her to leave her bed and undertake the arduous journey back to town, especially in the present inclement weather. Whatever Mr Payne may have done, and however heinous his actions against Miss Sophia may appear, he cannot impose upon her any further, and therefore I see no harm in permitting him and his sister to remain at Staineybank, at least until Lady Juliet is well enough to travel."

The duke grunted. "Very well. I am not heartless, I hope, and would not ask a sick woman to leave her fireside. However, you had best keep out of my way, Payne. I do not wish to see your face again."

"As your grace pleases."

"Now get out of my sight."

Simon was more than happy to comply.

***

Sophia hardly knew what she felt. Her anger burned like the sun for perhaps an hour, and then, abruptly, fizzled into nothingness, like a bonfire in the rain. For a brief time — just a few hours, that was all — she had been engaged to be married. Her whole future life had shifted from the grey lowlands of perpetual spinsterhood, which was all very well but a little dreary, and transformed miraculously to the sunlit uplands of marriage and motherhood and being a person of consequence, to Simon at least, if not to the whole world.

And the worst of it was that she liked him... she *loved* him. She had been held in his strong arms and felt utterly content, as she never had before. Not that she was discontented with her life with Mama and Richard and her sisters, but Simon was special. Or at least, he had made her feel special, which was almost the same thing.

At the back of her mind was the niggling thought that he was the only man who had ever wanted to marry her, and that she was a fool to turn him away just because he had no money. He had never pretended to be rich, had never truly deceived her, and if he wanted to marry her for her ten thousand pounds, what was so wrong with that? She would have a husband who kissed her with an ardour that set her pulse racing and warmed her inside, and they would have enough money to live on without too much scrimping. And one day, he would be a famous architect, and none of it would matter.

He wrote her a kind little letter, thanking her for the book and the idea of publishing his own work, which he hoped to do very soon. He had addressed her as *'Miss Merrington'*, which was sadly formal after he had whispered *'Sophie'* into her ears, but he signed it *'Yours, Simon Payne'*, which was much more promising. Was he still hers? If she reached out to him, would he smile and hold her and kiss her again?

She shivered. The letter was safely hidden in her reticule during the day, and tucked under her pillow at night, and the maid had contrived to get it to her without Mama or her sisters knowing anything about it. It was her little secret, and somewhere, deep in her heart, was another secret — that if ever Simon should offer for her again, she would snap him up at once and never let go of him.

***

For several days, Simon kept out of the duke's way by rarely venturing beyond his own room or Juliet's. He went early to the breakfast room, seeing only one or two of the men, who treated him with cool civility. That was reasonably safe, since the duke breakfasted in his own apartments. Dinner was too dangerous, so he dined with Juliet in her room, trying to tempt her appetite with the delicious treats sent up by the kitchen. They, at least, showed nothing but good-natured respect towards them. He went for a walk in the garden after breakfast, keeping out of sight in the woods and seeing no one but the gamekeeper. The rest of the time, he sat with Juliet, reading to her as she huddled listlessly by the fire, swathed in a shawl, or else compiling some of his drawings into groups suitable for inclusion in a book.

He was fired with enthusiasm to have a book of his own. Richard's cottages were all very well, but there must also be a market for more ambitious schemes, and while he awaited a response from the publisher, he played with ideas for such a book. He had sent a short note to Sophia to thank her for the suggestion and let her know that he would pursue it. He received no reply, but he did not expect it. He knew there could be no further contact. Perhaps, one day soon, he would leave Staineybank and never see her again. It was a grief too deep to be borne, but bear it he must, by keeping busy, occupying his mind and his hands, avoiding anything which reminded him that she was lost to him forever.

One day was so wet that he could not take his usual walk in the gardens. There was nowhere in the house that he could walk without the risk of bumping into someone he had sooner not see, so he bethought himself of the chapel gallery. At least it had happy memories.

As soon as he opened the door, he knew she was there. Even before he saw her, he was aware of the faint hint of her perfume, and the rustle of her gown as she turned towards him. And there was her sweet face, and all the anguish inside him boiled up and tore at him with such pain that he could only stare at her, drinking in the wonder of seeing her again.

"Simon?" she said tentatively. Her voice was calm, with no trace of the anger which had infused their last encounter.

"I—" Somehow the words would not come.

"Come in," she said. "I promise not to snap your head off."

He carefully shut the door, then sat himself at the furthest edge of the bench.

"How is Lady Juliet?" she said. "They would not let me see her. Is there anything I might send, to cheer her up?"

"She is a little better, but still not well. I do not know what she might like... some bonbons, perhaps. She is very fond of bonbons, but we cannot afford them very often."

"I shall buy her some next time we go to Brinchester. And you? Are you well?"

How to answer such a question? Honestly, he supposed. "I am... well enough."

She nodded, her face pale even in the gloom of the screened gallery. "So am I — well enough. Getting through the days one by one. Simon — I am sorry I said those things. I did not mean any of them."

"Oh!" It was more of a long sigh of surprise.

"I do not hate you, not at all, and even if you only wanted to marry me for my fortune, what is wrong with that? It is what everyone does, after all."

"But I did not!" he cried, stung into speech at last. "It was not *only* about money, Sophie. It was never that."

"Oh, I know," she said, with a quick smile. "Richard told me everything you said, how you denied it vehemently when the duke accused you of being a fortune hunter, but you did not deny kissing me. And..." She looked down suddenly, her fingers pleating and unpleating the folds of her skirt. "When you kissed me... that was... not about my fortune. That was how you truly felt."

He nodded, his throat tight. She understood! She knew how much he loved her.

She looked up at him, and oh, that smile! He was so grateful for that smile of reconciliation. Even if they could never marry, at least she did not hate him, and they could be friends.

"In fact," she went on, "nothing happened between us until Lord Daniel left and you consoled me. Well... I suppose if we are being honest, something almost happened at Marshfields, did it not? But there again, you were consoling me, trying to reassure me that there was at least one person who admired me. You were comforting me, not trying to secure my affections to yourself."

"I only ever wanted your happiness," he said slowly, still unsure whether he could trust his voice.

"Was that why you never interfered when Lord Daniel was around?" she said, laughing suddenly.

"I did interfere, in a way. I helped him, when he could not recognise you."

"Not recognise me? What do you mean?"

"Did you not notice? When he saw you with all your sisters, you look so alike that he could not tell which was you. I gave him a little hint when I could. *'That blue dress suits Miss Sophia',* that sort of thing."

She sat up straight, the smile wiped from her face. "I do not look a bit like any of my sisters."

"There are differences, certainly, but they are not enough to tell you apart. Usually with four sisters, there is a plump one, a tall one, a plain one and one with yellow hair, but the four of you all have the same colouring and shape and size. In fact, if it were not for a few wrinkles around her eyes, one might take your mother for one of you, too, and your habit of always going around together makes it worse. I had terrible trouble distinguishing you from your sisters at first. It was not until after Marshfields that I knew you every time, and I still make mistakes with your sisters. So when I saw Torbuck having the same problem, I helped him out."

"Oh! So that was why he sat and talked to Charlotte that last evening, and ignored me, and I had put on quite my finest gown, too. I was mortified. But when you arrived, you brought him over to me, I recall. You saw that he had made a mistake and... oh! How foolish I feel now! But it never occurred to me that he would not know me."

"How should it? To you, your sisters are all very different, but I assure you, when you are assembled as a group, you look very alike."

"But you can recognise me?"

"I can. I would never mistake you for your sisters now."

"That makes me wonder if that is why he ran away," she said, with a low chuckle. "Poor man! Now I feel sorry for him. I recall a set of brothers in Norwich who looked very much alike to outsiders, although two of them truly were identical — twins, you see. But I used to make a joke of it — especially with the youngest, who had bright red hair and was quite different from the rest. *'Now tell me, which Foster are you?'* I would say to him, and he always laughed about it. But how foolish not to mention it, if he truly could not tell us apart."

"It is awkward, if one is supposedly courting a girl, yet cannot pick her out of a crowd."

"Hmm. I suppose you are right. Well, he is gone, and I cannot say I am heartbroken over him. Whereas you..."

Simon's breath froze. The sensible part of him deplored such talk, but he was finding it very difficult to be sensible, when she was so close, looking at him in just that way, her head tilted speculatively to one side, and such words in her mouth!

And then she made all rational thought fly out of his head by sliding down the bench to sit right beside him, placing her tiny white hand in his larger one.

"Simon, I do not want us to be enemies."

"Nor I!"

"But nor do I want us to be friends."

"Oh!"

"At least, not *just* friends. I know we cannot marry, and perhaps we will never be able to. Where money is concerned, Richard is implacable, and now that he has you labelled as a fortune hunter, he may never approve of you sufficiently to release my dowry, and you may never earn enough to offer for me anyway. I understand all that. But I cannot — I *will* not — simply let you go, as if you had never existed... as if we had never shared those wonderful kisses. What I should like is for us to be betrothed — no, do not speak yet, I implore you. Not publicly... a secret betrothal, only known to the two of us, so that I can sleep soundly at night knowing that there is one man in the world who would marry me if he could. And we can meet here occasionally and... and share kisses again, which would be lovely, would it not? And you need not tell me that it is improper, for I know all that, but at my advanced years, I feel a little pushing at the boundaries of propriety is not too heinous a crime. And when you go home, as you will before too long, we will have pleasant memories to keep us warm." She squeezed his hand. "What do you say?"

How could he speak? His heart was overflowing with joy at her words, and even a simple affirmative was too difficult. So he answered her in the only way he could, by leaning across the narrow gap between them and pressing his lips firmly on hers.

18: A Visit From Mr Thwaite

The following day brought Simon a letter from the publisher. He liked the idea very much, and was very honoured to be entrusted with the publication of such an endeavour by a gentleman of noble family. He was sure it would be a great success, but the artistic nature of the contents and the high cost of the best quality of paper, and the finest binding, as such a prestigious enterprise would require... and so on and so forth. In short, he wanted Simon to pay the cost of publication himself.

So that was the end of that little scheme.

Simon could not be too downhearted. There were other publishers who might be more obliging, and besides, how could he think of such mundane matters when he was betrothed to his Sophie. It was not a real betrothal, he knew that, but every morning before breakfast, they met in the little gallery to talk and kiss. Mostly to kiss, if he were honest. And every day stored up more memories against the dreary day when he would have to leave Staineybank.

The day that brought the publisher's letter brought another event, of a most unexpected nature. Simon was reading to Juliet in front of the fire in her room when Froggett came in.

"Beg pardon, sir, but there is… a *person* to see you."

"A person? What sort of person?"

"A male person, sir. A tradesman, by appearance. He says his name is Thwaite."

Juliet uttered a squeak. "Oh, Simon! Perhaps he has changed his mind."

"I know Mr Thwaite," Simon told the butler. "He is a client of mine."

Froggett's face cleared. "In that case, sir, I shall place him in the Blue Parlour."

"This is such good news!" Juliet said, as soon as Froggett had gone. "Thwaite would not come all this way just to pass the time of day and talk about the state of the roads. He must want to commission one of your designs at last."

"We shall see," Simon said neutrally. He no longer had much faith in good news.

Thwaite was standing in the centre of the Blue Parlour, a glass of claret in his hand, gazing at a vast portrait of an ancestral Duchess of Brinshire in a lace-encrusted skirt, with more lace covering her head. Simon could see why Froggett had mistaken Thwaite for a tradesman, for his clothes were ten years out of date at least, and although the quality was good, they were not such as any gentleman might wear.

"Mr Thwaite! What an unexpected pleasure!"

"Ah, there you are, Payne. Well, this is a right fine house and no mistake. Is this what ye'd build for me, happen I wanted it?"

And the accent, of course. Simon smiled at him. "Something like it, yes. Perhaps not quite such a large house, since you are not a duke yet."

Thwaite laughed heartily at this little jest. "Not yet, Payne, not yet. Maybe I'll be a lord, though, before too long. I've had some very gratifying approaches lately, if only—" He stopped, with a sudden frown. Then, remembering the wine in his hand, he downed the contents in one. "Is this a good wine, would you say?"

Simon refilled his glass. "The duke keeps an excellent cellar. But I am sure you did not come all this way to talk about wine. To what do I owe the pleasure of this visit, sir?"

"To my conscience, Payne, to my conscience. That letter I wrote you... well, I'm a simple man, not clever, like you, but I deal honestly with folk. Always have done, and always will. Noted for it, I am. A man knows that when he deals with Timothy Thwaite, he'll get a fair deal and no funny business. And that letter I sent you... it wasn't honest, and that's a fact. I'm not comfortable with it, so I've come to explain, on account of it's best done face to face and not written down."

That was so surprising that Simon poured himself a glass of claret, and topped up Thwaite's glass again. "I am listening, Thwaite. Will you sit?"

"Thank 'ee, but 'tis best said upright, if it's all the same to you. When you first came to my notice, Payne, I had every intention of building a house — something suitable to my current position, and a place where the children, who've had a proper education and learnt to be fine young ladies and gentlemen, can show off to their fancy friends a bit. It wasn't for me, so much. We've got the grand house in town, so now I was all for having a fine place in the country, and you were just the man to build it for me, you being an earl's son, and knowing all about these things. And that was fine for a while."

He took another gulp of wine, as Simon waited patiently for him to get to the point.

"But then... a man came to see me. Lawyer type, I'm sure you know the sort I mean. Very civil, told me I was being considered for elevation to the peerage — that was how he put it, '*elevation*'. Is that the proper term?"

"It is. Nobles are supposedly higher than commoners."

"Ha! Well, perhaps, or perhaps not. But this fellow intimated that giving work to you would hinder my *elevation*. There were those who were prepared to sponsor my *elevation*, but only if I keep you dangling but don't actually give you the work."

"Good heavens!"

"Aye, you might well be surprised. I was myself. But I'll wager you can't guess who was behind it?"

"My father," Simon said at once. "No one else is vindictive enough to play such games against his own son."

"Well, don't that beat all! You already know what sort of man your pa is, but then who'd know him better, I suppose? Quite took me aback, I can tell you, when I eventually found out. I had no idea for a while, but eventually I got wind of who it was. And him an earl, too! An honourable, like you, and not a shred of honour in him, in truth."

"An earl is addressed as The Right Honourable," Simon said with a wry smile, "but no, my father has not much honour about him. Very affable to his friends, and despicable to his own family. So your story does not shock me, Thwaite, and you may be sure I bear you no ill-will. I should have enjoyed building your country house for you, but if it cannot be me, I can at least give you a list of others who would do a fine job for you."

"Well! That's noble behaviour indeed, sir!" Thwaite said. "I thought at the very least you would rant and rave a bit, and with every justification, but you take it as calm as anything. I salute you, sir."

"Ah, but you have given me something I have sought these many years," Simon said, "and that is a reason why I made no progress in my chosen profession. I thought, you see, that it was my own fault — that my designs were inadequate, or my person or temperament gave cause for disgust. But if it was all my father's doing — I can live with that. My opinion of him could not be any lower, but my opinion of myself is raised up a little. So for this boon, I thank you, sir, most sincerely."

***

Simon was not inclined to rant and rave, but Juliet was very much minded to do so.

"Do you mean to tell me," she said, eyes flashing as she abandoned her slumped posture to sit bolt upright, "that all this time our wretched father has been turning off clients and keeping you in poverty? Well! Of all the low-life, despicable, disgusting, abominable, infamous, unbelievably *detestable* things to do! I have not the words to describe how much I loathe that man!"

After which she found enough words, and with very little repetition, to abuse him soundly for a half hour, at least.

"But what can we do?" she said at length, her railing having wound itself down into no more than intense irritation. "What *can* we do, if every client can be bribed or blackmailed or cajoled into dropping you?"

"About the clients? Nothing, except to find some who are not afraid of him, perhaps. But I shall tell you what I *will* do, Juliet. I am going to

Edlesborough to confront him, and ask him what he means by it. Do you know what is the worst of it? When I left Edlesborough, he made me promise not to go into society, and not to go to White's, for I was already a member by then. In essence, I was not to take my place in society, and meekly I did as I was bade. I did not want to shame him by letting it be known that there had been a breach between us. I abandoned my friends from Eton, who might have been some help to me. I could even have lived in some degree as a gentleman, instead of hiding myself away. I kept my side of the bargain, and all he did was cut my feet from under me."

"I suppose we are lucky he did not take away my little inheritance," Juliet said.

"He had no power to do so," Simon said. "The house was Aunt Tabitha's, and her small amount of money, and when she left all of it to you, her executors were duty bound to see it done. Even our father cannot overturn the majesty of the law."

"I would not put it past him," she muttered darkly, making him laugh. "Simon, you are remarkably sanguine about this. You should be outraged. Why are you so calm?"

He laughed again. "Nothing can dent my good humour just now, sister, for I have a pocket full of gold." That was not the only reason, but there was no need to tell anyone about his secret joy. "Thwaite cannot commission me to build his house, not without prejudicing his own future, but I persuaded him to recompense me for my time over the last couple of years. Five hundred sovereigns, in gold, if you please, no linen, so nothing traceable. Nothing that my father will ever know about, anyway, and enough to keep us in coal and claret for quite some time, and to pay for a post chaise to Edlesborough. Will you come with me?"

"Me? Go back to Edlesborough, and see that man? I could not! I have avoided him all these years, and that can continue indefinitely as far as I am concerned."

"You could ask him about your mother."

"I would not ask any favour of him."

"Are you not curious to see him?"

"No! To turn up at Edlesborough and say, *'Good morning, I am your daughter whom you sent into exile at the age of three'*? Indeed, I could not do it. How he would sneer at me, at what I have become, because of him."

"What have you become?" he said gently.

"A pathetic spinster, brother. Unwed and unwanted at the age of forty-one. He would laugh at me and the servants would pity me. I could not bear it."

"No one would know you there. In fact, we could have some fun with this. You could go there with me under a false name... I know, you could be my rich bride, being taken on a wedding tour to visit our various relations. That would annoy him so much, to think me rich after all his efforts, would it not? And he would vent his spleen against me, and not you."

"I have no clothes for a bride," she said. "A rich bride would have a vast new wardrobe to show off."

"Oh. Trust a woman to think of that."

"Trust a man to forget about it. Besides, I am far too old a bride for you. No, Simon, no subterfuge. If we are going to do this, let us at least be honest — which is more than he has ever been."

"Very well, but I hate to appear before him so... so *shabby*. You could borrow some clothes from the duchess, for she is much of a size with you. I have no wish to appear in front of our father like a whiny schoolboy, complaining of ill-treatment. Much better to take a position of strength.

We expect nothing from him, after all, but at all costs let us not show him how low he has brought us."

The duchess, who never refused an opportunity to improve a woman's wardrobe, responded to the idea with enthusiasm. Since she did not hesitate to broadcast the story of Mr Thwaite's visit and the Earl of Edlesborough's perfidy throughout the house, Simon found himself unexpectedly drawn back into the duke's favour.

"I always knew Edlesborough was a snake, but this is beyond anything," he said, having summoned Simon to his study to commiserate with him. "It is bad enough to cut off a son, but such things do happen. Who knows what goes on in families and what differences there might be, and what cause a man might have to cut out the dead wood of the family? Not that I say that description applied to you, Payne, I dare say, for you seem a respectable enough man in most respects."

"Thank you, your grace," Simon murmured, amused.

"Apart from the business of little Miss Sophia, of course," the duke went on, the eyebrows lowering ominously. "Still, you have had your hair combed over that already, so I say nothing more about it. But this! To deny a man the right to follow his chosen profession — that is not the act of a gentleman. I cannot abide such scurvy dealings. I am minded to build your orangery, and that fancy bridge too, just to spite the man, and I should tell everyone about it, too. My support still carries some weight in society, I believe."

Simon laughed out loud at that. "Your grace is very kind to suggest it, but I would not have you commission a design of mine for such a flimsy reason as that. If you choose it, make it be because you like it better than any alternative. I do not wish to make my name because my father treated me badly."

"Ah, you have your pride," the duke said. "I cannot quarrel with that. Very well, whenever Richard has finished his own designs, I shall choose the one I like best... or I might leave Rowena to choose, since it is in her honour. Do you wish to borrow one of my carriages for your journey, Payne? The ducal arms on the door will give Edlesborough pause, eh? He will know that you have at least one influential friend in the world, for I am not quite nobody, I believe."

The secretary and comptroller laughed dutifully at this witticism, and agreed to offer whatever assistance was in their power. Simon's crime of aspiring to Sophie's hand was, if not quite forgotten, at least set aside in the interests of putting Lord Edlesborough's nose out of joint. So while Juliet was rigged out in the duchess's unwanted finery, attempts were made to bring Simon up to the mark, too. Sadly, only Mr Godley was of a size to donate clothes to him, and the chaplain's attire was even shabbier than Simon's. In the end he had to make do with supplies of linen, silk stockings and soft leather gloves from Richard.

Three days later, in the duke's own carriage, piled high with luggage, and accompanied by a valet and maid, two footmen standing behind and two grooms as outriders, Simon and Juliet set off for Warwickshire to confront their father.

***

Sophia was delighted to have Simon restored to favour, so that they could meet openly again. They were both too discreet to make any show of affection in public, but there was a pleasure in being in the same room each evening. She dressed with more than usual care, and although she never dared to sit beside him, there were shared glances sometimes and one evening she sat opposite him at the vingt-et-un table. It was a pity his change in circumstances meant that he would soon be leaving Staineybank, but he would return very soon, as he made sure to tell everyone.

They still met in the chapel gallery, and there was one part of their private discussions which she felt compelled to convey to her sisters.

"Do you think we look alike, sisters?" she said as they sat in the morning room one day.

"Not in the least," Charlotte said robustly.

"We are quite different," Augusta said.

"We never dress alike," Maria added.

"No, but we do wear each other's gowns and jewellery," Sophia said, "and we have the same style and colour of hair. To anyone who does not know us well, it might be confusing."

"I do think there might be something in what you say," said the duchess, looking up from the fichu she was hemming. "Just at first, I did have trouble telling you apart, but I soon got into the way of it. Charlotte is most likely to be with Cousin Hester, wearing an apron. Maria is usually the one with a book in her hand, and Augusta is often to be found wearing a riding habit. As for Sophia, if I cannot find the latest journals, I know where to look. But the gentlemen, who see you less often, do have difficulty, I believe. James Hammond said once that he simply calls each of you *'Miss Merrington'.*"

"Do you think perhaps that Lord Daniel had trouble, too?" Sophia said. "He got to know me at Marshfields, where I was the only Miss Merrington, but then when he came here—"

"Oh! That is entirely possible," the duchess said. "You do like to go round together, the four of you, too, which compounds the problem. I wonder if that was why he left so suddenly."

"But we are not truly alike," Maria said robustly, "and a man who had formed an attachment would not be confused, surely? He would know his love in any company."

This was a daunting point, and the ladies fell silent. It was as well for Sophia that she had Simon's affection to cheer her spirits for otherwise she would have been in a pitiable state at this point. The very thought that Lord Daniel had, perhaps, abandoned his courtship because he could not recognise her was lowering in the extreme. But Simon knew her, he *'knew his love in any company'*, and she needed no other.

Lord Daniel's defection had no power to hurt her, for her heart was whole and in the gentle hands of another.

19: Lord Edlesborough

Simon and Juliet travelled in the utmost comfort. A spell of dry weather and the lengthening days meant that they could, at a pinch, have made the journey to Edlesborough in a single day, but they chose instead to make an overnight stay in Kidderminster, where the duke's livery brought them impeccable service and an excellent dinner.

Juliet was in excellent spirits. Her fine new clothes, even though only borrowed, and the deference accorded to anyone travelling under the auspices of the Duke of Brinshire, gave her a new confidence. Although she worried a little about the expense of their journey, the sight of Simon's bag of gold from Thwaite brought an astonished *'Oooh!'* to her lips, and after that she said no more about it, even when presented with a dish of woodcock and a lobster, with a bottle of the best claret.

They made an early start the next morning, aiming to reach Edlesborough by noon. That way, if they were able to see the earl, there would still be plenty of time to return to Kidderminster before dusk. Simon expected to be thrown out peremptorily, in which case they would be on the road again even more swiftly.

As they travelled, Juliet became more and more subdued, until Simon noticed that every attempt at conversation foundered with a monosyllabic answer.

"Are you quite well, sister?" he said gently.

Mutely she shook her head.

"Do you wish to abandon the enterprise? We can turn round and return to Kidderminster, if you wish it, or we can stop at the next inn we see, if you are unwell."

"No, not unwell," she said, hunching her shoulders miserably. "It is only that... must I come inside with you? I am not sure that I can face... *him.* I should like to see Andrew and Luke again, for I have some vague memories of them, and I should very much like to meet the countess, to thank her personally for all those little presents she sent us, but Father? Must I?"

Simon was very aware of the valet and maid on the opposite seat, studiously looking out of the windows and pretending not to hear.

"You need not come inside if you had rather not," he said. "In fact, I shall not be surprised if I fail to set foot over the threshold myself."

"Might I wait for you in the carriage? You need not even mention me. That would be best, would it not?"

And so it was agreed.

Before long, the villages they passed through began to look familiar to Simon, and then they were in Kingsley Heath, with its church, smithy and inn, bringing back a thousand jumbled memories. The villagers walking about or tending their gardens turned to stare as the carriage passed by. A woman hanging washing bobbed a curtsy, and several men doffed their hats, seeing the mark of a nobleman on the carriage door. Then they were turning down the lane beside the church, passing between bare fields and finally sweeping through open gateposts into Edlesborough.

There was only a short distance between gate and house, not long enough for Simon to tame his thoughts into composure. After fifteen years, he was finally coming home. There was the south lawn, a little ragged at this season. Over there, the stable yard was hidden behind a stand of trees. To the other side, a wide path led round to the formal gardens and the deer park.

Memories tumbled over themselves as he gazed avidly through the windows. There was the tree where Luke had fallen and broken his arm when he was showing off to the Dillon girls. At the bottom of the lawn was the flat stretch where they had practised their archery, and Andrew had once shot a peacock. Where was the pool where Matthew had almost drowned, before Simon had hauled him out by his feet? Somewhere behind the shrubbery, he thought. But the memories from inside the house were less happy — the library where his father ruled like an emperor, or the dining room where meals were punctuated by dyspeptic outbursts. Worse, the attic room where he was banished for some imagined transgression, even his sketch books taken away from him.

He shivered. Perhaps staying in the carriage was a sensible response, or simply turning round and heading straight back to Kidderminster. But they were already passing under the great arch to enter the courtyard and sweeping round to halt before the steps to the front door. One of the footmen leapt down from the back to open the door and lower the steps.

"Good luck," Juliet whispered.

So... was he going to do this? Was he a man or a mouse? He stepped down onto the drive, and strode forward, his boots crunching on the gravel, and took the steps two at a time.

His hand reached for the knocker, and fell back, nonplussed. It was draped in black crêpe. His arrival was inopportune if there had been a death in the house. One of the aunts, he supposed, or perhaps one of the children... Andrew's, maybe. That would occasion a certain amount of grief, even from his unfeeling father, but clearly not a great deal, for it was a very small amount of crêpe, barely enough to silence the knocker. A girl, then. He had never cared about the girls.

While he stood, irresolute, on the step, one side of the great double doors opened and a footman in black appeared.

"This way, sir, if you please."

An invitation to enter could not be refused, however unexpected. Simon followed him into the familiar hall, a good fire blazing in the massive hearth. His father had always kept the place warm, that at least could be said for him. He never stinted on coal or wood, or candles, either, he recalled, his eyes almost dazzled by the giant chandelier.

"You may wait in here, sir," the footman said, holding open the door to the Ante Chamber.

That was puzzling. It was almost as if he was expected.

"I am here to see the earl," Simon said, just in case there had been a misunderstanding.

"Yes, sir. I will notify him of your arrival."

"But..." Simon said, but the man had gone before he could point out that he had not yet given his name.

Had the footman recognised him? No, he thought not, for he was too young to remember the gangly fifteen-year-old who had left Edlesborough so long ago. Besides, if he had known him, he would either have refused him entry altogether, or else shown him into the more commodious Blue Room. The Ante Chamber was where the lower orders, lawyers, bailiffs and messengers, were placed before being admitted to the Presence.

Still, there was a good fire burning, an array of drinks and pastries laid out, as if someone was expected, so he poured himself a glass of something to fortify his spirits while he waited.

After a few minutes, the door opened again, and an older man walked in, the well-remembered shape of the butler.

"Good morning, sir. You are here to see his lordship, I understand."

"I am, yes, but—"

"He will be pleased to receive you shortly."

"Will he?" Simon said, startled. "Then he has changed a great deal."

The butler looked startled for a moment, before he permitted himself a wintry smile. "I believe he is much as he ever was, sir."

Something caused him to look more carefully at Simon, and his expression slowly passed through bewilderment, then surprise and finally, a pleased excitement. "Master Simon? Is it you?"

"It is, Spearman. Why are you still here? Surely it is past time for that little cottage in the village, and days spent at the Plough playing cribbage."

The smile broadened. "Soon, Master Simon, very soon now. I have just been waiting— Well, not long now. Wait a moment, sir, if you please."

He opened the door, and gave some hurried orders to the footman manning the hall, who loped off into the interior of the house.

"Well, my goodness, sir, you got here so quickly. We never expected you so soon. We thought you were the attorney or we should never have put you in here. Heavens, but his lordship will be so pleased to see you! He has spoken of you constantly these last few days, but of course we knew it could be a while. Yet here you are! And so well grown! My goodness, sir, how you have filled out and a good head taller than when you left us, I swear! And looking so well. Such a fine thing to have you back at Edlesborough after all these years. I am so pleased that the Good Lord spared me this long, to see you again."

Simon made no attempt to interrupt these effusions. No doubt when he saw his father, he would find out just why he was so keen to see him.

The door burst open and a great crowd of people poured in, and on their faces, too, he saw nothing but smiles of welcome. How strange! How very unlike the Edlesborough he remembered, as a subdued place, with nary a smile to be seen, except in company.

His father was not one of those beaming at him. Three of his brothers, the wife of his eldest brother, several people he did not recognise and an older woman... Oh, he knew *her*. Yet there was a difference. That dreadful haunted look had gone from her eyes.

"Mama?"

"Simon! Oh, Simon!" She fell into his arms and burst into tears.

Simon laughed, and over his mother's head, buried on his chest, he said to his eldest brother, Andrew, "This is not the reception I expected, but I am very pleased to see you all, naturally. I even recognise some of you. Lady Kendle. John. Matthew."

"Do you not recognise me, brother?" said one of the ladies. "I am Rachel, and this is Elizabeth, and... where are you, Martha? Ah, there you are, and this scamp is Mark, and that is Ruth, who should not even be here. Have you slipped away from Miss Towers again, young lady?"

"Well, how could I recognise you when you were still in the nursery when I left?" Simon protested. "And Ruth, I think, should be there now. How old are you, Ruth?"

But she only sucked her thumb and clutched a doll to her chest.

"She is six," Andrew said. "The very last, unless Mama has a surprise in store for us."

They all laughed, even Mama, but Simon was stunned. When had he last heard laughter in Edlesborough? It had never been a happy place, but now... his father must have changed indeed to cause such a happy transformation.

"We have overwhelmed him," Andrew said, still smiling.

"You have, rather," Simon said. "I confess, this is not what I was expecting, Kendle."

His brother nodded. "You were always very correct, brother, but I suppose you are in the right of it. I do not take the title officially until after the funeral."

After the funeral? Take the title?

Simon's jaw dropped. "Then you mean... he is *dead?*"

So that was why his mother looked so different. Finally, she had escaped from tyranny.

They all burst into excited speech.

"Then... you did not know? You have not come in response to my letter?" Andrew said.

"I saw no letter. I came on a matter of my own. Well, if that does not beat all," he said, suddenly outraged. "I came all this way to finally confront him and give him a piece of my mind, and the old buzzard has gone off before I could tell him precisely what I thought of him. Well! Now I shall never have the chance. That is the most infamous thing."

They all laughed again, and Andrew shook his head. "Simon, you must be the only person in the entire Kingdom who is sorry he is dead. Well, maybe his hunting cronies, perhaps, but no one else. Certainly no one else in this room. We have been quietly celebrating, I assure you. I wrote to you and Juliet within an hour of his death."

"Juliet!" Simon cried. "She is waiting in the carriage outside."

The entire crowd streamed out into the hall and down the steps, the carriage door was wrenched open and Juliet urged excitedly out.

Andrew said to the footman who had followed them out, "See the carriage sent round to the stables, the luggage unloaded and the postilions seen to. Mr Simon and Lady Juliet will be staying here."

***

The ladies bore Juliet away to some feminine fastness, but Andrew sent the rest of his brothers away, and led Simon to a small office cluttered with boxes of papers in a far corner of the house.

"Come in here, brother," he said. "I need to talk to you, and I am settled in this room for the moment. The steward's office."

"You do not wish to use the library?"

Andrew visibly shuddered. "Too many bad memories. What will you have — Madeira? Canary? Port?"

"Claret, if you have any."

"Good idea. I'll get Spearman to fetch some up. The cellar is full of the stuff, but we were never allowed to touch it before. Unless there were guests, of course."

Thus fortified, the brothers settled into a pair of chairs set either side of a small table in the window.

"So tell me what happened," Simon said. "It sounds as if it was sudden. Did Mama poison him? He always said she was trying to."

"No one would have blamed her if she had," Andrew said sombrely. "He treated her abominably. But it was his own fault — he *would* eat lobster and it never agreed with him. His digestion had only got worse over the last few years, and this time he had only taken a mouthful or two when he just dropped like a stone. Served him right, frankly. He always said it was Mama's fault when he overate. Do you know, he put a clause in his will that if he were to die after eating something, Mama should be arrested for murder," he said, in outraged tones. "The man was pond scum. Fortunately, Dr Caffrey has better sense than to do anything of the sort. He said Father had always suffered with his digestion and this was just a particularly virulent bout of it, and the foaming at the mouth was not unusual in such extreme cases. We have all seen him do it before, after all."

"I never remember him doing so," Simon murmured. "But that was a long time ago."

"Far too long," Andrew said, smiling. "But you are looking so well, brother, and Juliet, too. You both look as fine as fivepence."

Simon, laughing, told him of their borrowed finery. "But how are you?" he said gently. "You do not look as robust as I recall."

Andrew pulled a face. "I am worn to the bone, brother, but there we are. We cannot control our health. I trust I will go on better now. But tell me, were you truly planning to confront Father? That would have been a sight to behold."

Simon explained to him the discovery he had made of his father hampering his career.

"I felt it could not be allowed to pass without challenge," he said, "so yes, I was planning to confront him. Since he had already ruined my attempts to become an architect, he could hardly do me further harm. Did you know what he was about?"

"Interfering with your clients? I suspected. Early on, I tried to put my friends in the way of giving you business, but one of them blabbed the whole scheme in front of Father, so of course he put a stop to it. Said you were unreliable... implied you were barely sane, in fact. The physicians allowed you to pretend to be an architect but it was all an illusion, something like that. After that, he leaned on me pretty hard to break all contact with you, and Mama, too. He had us followed, you know. He had always had Mama followed, thinking she was up to some mischief or other, but after that, he had me followed, too, and so I never dared to come and see you."

"I understand that."

"You never blamed me?"

"Never. I know what he is like... *was* like." He paused, grimly forcing himself to remember. "In some ways, I almost wish he had simply hit us. It would have been easier to deal with, but the constant sniping, and never a good word. The best one could ever hope for was to be ignored. And worse for you, of course, being the heir."

"Worst of all for Mama," he said, tossing down the claret remaining in his glass and reaching for the bottle. "At least my mama escaped, in a way, but yours—! God alone knows how she dealt with it, day after day, week after week, year after year. But we got our vengeance, in our different ways."

"Did you?" Simon said, with a sudden smile. "I am glad of it."

Andrew smiled, too. "It was not much of a reprisal. Not as much as he deserved, anyway. Mama... well, I never asked what she did, but it is true that in recent years his digestion became much worse."

"No! Not poison? Not really?"

"As I say, I never asked. No one ever asked, but it started after Ruth was born. I think Mama had just had enough, by then. Father was not kind to her, in their intimate life. But I... I went a different way."

He stopped, then sighed. "I had to marry, of course. You will remember the fuss — it was not long before you left. He gave me a choice — three women, all from the nobility, wealthy, accomplished, extremely eligible. Trouble was, not one of them was acceptable to me. It was bad enough Father managing every detail of my life, but I could not have borne a wife with the same temperament. I cannot tell you, Simon, how that man has ground me into the dirt. You had the courage to escape, and John and Matthew went to Oxford to be ordained, so they avoided his notice somehow. But his eye was always on me, and I had not the courage to stand up to him, not ever. I never once defied him or refused to do what he asked of me. Such a despicable travesty of a man that I am."

"You must not blame yourself for his faults. You were the heir, it was inevitable that you had all his attention."

Andrew shrugged. "Perhaps. But I felt that, whatever his faults were, there must have been some weakness in me that kept me supine, and I had no wish to pass my failings onto another generation. So I put off marrying as long as I could, but... well, you know what he was like."

"All too well, brother," Simon said.

"Lavinia was different from the others. She wanted children, but she was nervous about it. Two of her older sisters had died in childbed, so naturally she was afraid. I did not want children at all... at least, not sons. So we made an agreement — only daughters."

"How on earth did you manage that?"

Andrew laughed. "Lavinia has one surviving sister — her twin, as it happens. She lives in Scotland and they were always very close. So... Lavinia pretended to be *enceinte*, but ill with it, and you know how Father was with any form of physical illness."

"Except his own."

"Precisely. So Lavinia would be banished to Scotland, and in due course she would return with an infant and a wet nurse. We have acquired four daughters in that way, and there are four peasant families in Scotland which are a little better off than they were, and know that one, at least, of their offspring will grow up in wealth."

Simon could not help laughing. "Four daughters... but no sons? How ingenious, brother!"

"We thought so. It suited Lavinia as much as it suited me, and as long as she was continuing to produce offspring on a regular basis, Father had no cause to hound her for the lack of sons. But you see why I sent for you so speedily, Simon."

"Me? What is it to do with me? Even if you have no sons, there is still Luke. Surely he had sons before he died."

Andrew's smile broadened. "Oh, several. Three sons and four daughters."

"Well, then. It is nothing to do with me."

"Let me explain it to you. Well, Luke was pressured to marry just as I was. Do you remember his godfather? An unmarried uncle in Newcastle, and Father always hoped he would leave his fortune to Luke when he died, so he allowed him to visit regularly. Luke met someone there, and settled down to reproduce himself in domestic bliss. Father was delighted, naturally. Luke was the golden boy, unlike me, who failed to produce a son, or you, who escaped altogether."

"Brother, why do you look so smug? If Luke left three sons, then—?"

"He never married," Andrew said, chuckling. "Oh, he told everyone he was, and he produced papers which convinced Father, but everything is fake and I have all the evidence to prove it. Once the lawyers arrive, we shall have all his children officially declared illegitimate. Congratulations, brother. When I breathe my last, you will become the 8th Earl of Edlesborough."

20: Visitors From Newcastle

It took many hours of talking before Simon could be brought to appreciate the change in his fortunes. It was Juliet who brought it home to him, as they talked in Simon's room that evening. He was ready for bed, but she was too agitated, and was still fully dressed.

"Now you can marry well, brother."

The thought hit him like an arrow — he could marry Sophia! But...

"What do you mean, marry well?"

"Someone young and pretty, with a good dowry. You could go to Almack's and take your choice."

"I have already made my choice."

"Sophia Merrington? You could do better than that! The Merringtons looked down their superior noses at you when you were merely an aspiring architect, so why would you want anything more to do with them? At last you can take your place in the world as a gentleman, and choose an appropriate wife for a future earl."

Simon huffed in annoyance. "I am still an aspiring architect, and I cannot imagine a more appropriate wife for anyone than Sophia."

"Well, I suppose she is the sister of a future duke," Juliet conceded graciously. "But why do you persist in this idea of being an architect? You do not need a profession any longer."

"I like designing houses," he said, in surprise. "Besides, whatever Andrew may have done in the past, there is still the possibility that he will father a son, so I do not depend upon the inheritance. He has said he will make me an allowance, which is of far more interest to me, I assure you. Assuming that Father cannot interfere from beyond the grave — although I would not put it past him, the devious old weasel — I shall be able to build my career properly, without worrying about the price of coal. Andrew has said he will tell his friends about me, so I could be inundated with business before long."

"So... we just go on as before?" she said, sounding dubious. "We go back to Finsbury Square and carry on as if nothing happened?"

"No, because I shall be married, I hope, and will be a proper architect at last," he said patiently. "Juliet dear, you do not need to return to Finsbury Square if you dislike the idea. You could live here, or in the Payne town house. You could go to Almack's yourself."

"Me, prance around alongside girls of seventeen? I hardly think so! Oh, Simon, it is all very well for you — you are a man and respectable and you will be very wealthy one day, but I am still the daughter of a woman who behaved so scandalously that her husband divorced her. I still cannot find out anything about her, you know, not even whether she is alive or dead."

The topic had been much discussed around the dinner table that evening, but Andrew had only been eight at the time his mother had been banished, and nothing had ever been said about divorce.

"Father forbade any mention of her," Andrew had said. "We knew something bad had happened, and we learnt the bare bones of it later. Well, it was all in the Peerage, so there was no hiding it, but as to why, no one knew the truth."

Two days later, the lawyers arrived, a veritable army of sombre men in black, who took over the State Dining Room for their business, since Andrew still kept the library locked up. The day after that, the late Earl of Edlesborough was buried with appropriate ceremony and very little grief. The gentlemen and lawyers went off with the coffin, perhaps to assure themselves that his late lordship was securely underground, while the ladies sat in the countess's parlour drinking champagne.

Afterwards, there was a reading of the will, in which neither Simon nor Juliet were mentioned, which was enlivened by the governess, trying to be unobtrusive at the back of the room, while being assailed by a fit of the hiccups. This caused an outbreak of giggles amongst the well refreshed ladies, and put everyone in the right frame of mind for the cold collation which followed.

"Poor Miss Towers!" Juliet said, through a mouthful of pastry. "She would not have been here, except that Andrew wanted Ruth to be there, and she was needed to keep Ruth in order. Whereas she was the one needing to be kept in order."

"I think the champagne may have been flowing a touch too freely," Andrew said, "but it was just what everyone needed to lighten the mood. The will was incredibly tedious. All those long defunct settlements to be raked up and people long since gone who knows where to be left a watch or five pounds. Why on earth Father never updated it I cannot imagine. It has not been touched since he married your mama more than thirty years ago ."

"Two pounds for old Timothy Blaine — that was a particularly amusing point," Simon said. "He was dead before I even left Edlesborough."

"Was he?" Andrew said. "Retired, certainly, after he had that apoplexy amongst the red currants."

"Definitely dead," Simon said. "I used to visit him, you know. He had such interesting tales about the village he grew up in, somewhere in Ireland. He dropped down dead in the Plough, over a particularly energetic game of hood skittles. I went to his funeral. These pastries are delicious. What is in them?"

"Lobster," Andrew said, suddenly convulsed with laughter. "It seemed appropriate, under the circumstances."

Nobody could be found who disagreed with him, and by the time they all dispersed to dress for dinner, not a single lobster patty remained uneaten.

***

Sophia had much on her mind. Not unnaturally, her thoughts were often with Simon on his brave journey to talk to his father, who was not occasionally stern but generally benign, as her own father had been, or even grouchy and unpredictable, like the duke, but was something altogether horrid. A man who could repudiate his son, at the age of fifteen, and leave him to depend on the charity of others was the most despicable of men, and his later behaviour, in turning away prospective clients so that his son could never rise in his profession, was unconscionable. His own son!

And even if he had other sons to console him, did he not have a duty to take care of all of them, even the ones he did not like very much?

The question of Simon raised an awkward dilemma in her mind. Her supposed betrothal to him was a private arrangement between the two of them, a delicious secret that kept her warm at night and tranquil during the day. But she had never in her life had a secret from her sisters before. Mama might not perhaps be apprised of every last detail of her conversations with gentlemen, or the interesting things that occurred on occasion during a walk with one, but her sisters knew of everything that happened in her life, just as she knew of everything in theirs.

Now, for the first time, there was a matter that she could not discuss with anyone, and those long and impassioned kisses in the chapel gallery were by no means the least of it. She was not foolish enough to suppose that anything could ever come of this betrothal. It was all pretence, she was perfectly aware of that. One day, he would leave Staineybank and she would stay, and very likely they would never meet again. When that happened, she must try not to mind it so very much. Whatever the future might hold, she had some wonderful memories to sustain her through the dark years to come, as she slid inexorably into settled spinsterhood.

Her other problem was one which could be addressed, however, and discussed openly with her sister. If it was true that the four of them looked very much alike to outsiders, perhaps that was why, over so many years, potential suitors had melted away. A man who admired the girl he danced with at an assembly might arrive on her doorstep the next morning, enthusiastic and ready to be beguiled, only to find himself faced with the daunting challenge of picking a barely-remembered lady out of a crowd.

But what could be done about it? Simon had said that '*usually with four sisters, one has a plump one, a tall one, a plain one and one with yellow hair'*, and that was all very well, but none of them could change their height or hair colour. She determined to ask the younger men of the household. Mr Godley, however, merely turned beetroot red and backed away when she raised the subject.

Her next quarry was Mr Hammond, the duke's secretary. She found him in the duke's study one day, with only his father for company, the two bending over a notebook filled with a straggly scrawl. They both rose as she entered.

"Miss Merrington," Mr Hammond said. "What a pleasure! How may we help you?"

"I should like you to tell me who I am," she said, with a little laugh, as Mr Hammond Senior ushered her to a chair.

"Um... I beg your pardon?"

"Which Miss Merrington am I?"

They did not dissemble, laughing too. "Oh, a home question," Mr Hammond said, sitting back in his chair and steepling his hands. "What do you think, Father?"

"Maria?" his father said. "It could be Maria."

"No, I think it is Charlotte," Mr Hammond said. "Although... no, definitely Charlotte."

"Thank you," Sophia said, rising to leave. "You have answered my question perfectly."

"Were we right... either of us?" Mr Hammond said.

"It is unimportant," she said. "I wished only to determine that you cannot reliably tell us apart, and you have done so. Now all I have to do is work out how to remedy the situation."

"Something to distinguish each of you?" Mr Hammond Senior said. "An interesting challenge. Perhaps if you each choose a certain colour for your gowns."

"But we swap around our gowns, and jewellery, hair ornaments, gloves, shoes... There is nothing that is unique to only one of us."

"A favourite piece of jewellery, then, that you always wear. That silver cross is very pretty, and if you were to wear it every day—"

"It belongs to Maria," Sophia said. "Besides, it is simple enough for day wear, but no one would wear it for evening."

"Then it will have to be ribbons," Mr Hammond Senior said firmly. "You each choose a colour, and, whatever else you wear, you always bear a ribbon of that colour. A sash at the waist, a trimming at the sleeve, in your hair, holding a pendant at your throat... would that work?"

Sophia raised her eyebrows in surprise. Such a simple idea! "I think it might, Mr Hammond. Thank you."

"You are very welcome... Miss Augusta?" he said as he held the door for her.

She smiled enigmatically, and left without another word.

***

With gold in his pocket from Thwaite, and the first tranche of a sizeable allowance from the new earl, Simon was keen to return to Staineybank and claim Sophia.

"I will not stop you, if you must go, brother," Andrew said, as they sat over a bottle of brandy one evening, everyone else long since retired to bed, "but there is one more person coming whom you should meet — Luke's wife. Well, not wife, of course, but you know what I mean. She calls herself

Mrs Payne, anyway. She will bring with her some additional documents to prove once and for all that Luke left no legitimate heir, so that we can tidy everything up with the lawyers and you will be established as the next heir."

"Will I?" Simon said, eyebrows lifted questioningly.

Andrew smiled at that. "I give you my word, brother. Lavinia and I have an arrangement that suits us both. There will be no surprise arrival of an heir."

"Not even a Scottish one?" Simon said. "Lady Edlesborough is still young enough to make that plausible, even if you do not wish to perpetuate Father's blood."

Andrew laughed. "No! Definitely no more children. The earldom is a great burden to lay on a child, and you have already proved you are capable of meeting the challenge. And now you are to marry, it seems. Tell me about he r."

Simon was more than happy to comply, and for some while he described Sophia's many perfections, and wondered wistfully what she was doing and whether she thought much about him, in her busy life. He wondered if he should write to her, to tell her of his new circumstances, but they were not yet publicly betrothed and a letter would be improper. Besides, he would be back at Staineybank in a few days, and what was the rush? They had their whole lives to be deliriously happy, in public as well as in private.

So he stayed on and the very next day, the party from Newcastle arrived. Sally Payne was a plump, smiling woman of around thirty-five, Simon guessed, who was accompanied by her eldest son, Archie, a well-grown boy of fourteen, as well as a local attorney. She brought with her a great pile of sworn affidavits from Sally and Luke themselves, his uncle, her parents, two magistrates, a baronet and the local parson, to the effect that Sally and Luke had never married, and that therefore all their children were illegitimate.

Much of the day was spent closeted with the lawyers from London, who meticulously went through every document and asked a great many questions, examining also the false papers which had convinced the late earl that a marriage had taken place.

"I still do not understand," the oldest of the lawyers said querulously. "Why would any man do such a thing? Why render all his children illegitimate? Such a stain is impossible to eradicate."

"If you had known my father better, you would understand," Andrew said, for perhaps the third or fourth time.

"Yes, yes, but that does not explain anything," the lawyer said.

Sally Payne laughed, a rich, throaty laugh that gave Simon an inkling as to why Luke had been drawn to her. She was from the lower end of the gentry, with a hint of an accent in her voice, and she dressed for comfort rather than style. Although she wore the correct head-to-toe black of mourning, it was of a style that might have been fashionable five years ago. A sensible woman, then, who reused an old gown rather than go to the trouble of buying fresh.

"The late earl," she said to the lawyer, "wished to control his children. His sons in particular, for women were only breeding machines, to him. The only comment he ever addressed to me was that I had good wide hips, and should have no trouble popping out babies. I suppose he was right about that — I managed seven before Luke took ill and died, but still, it's hardly the thing to say, is it? But the way he treated Andrew and Luke! I completely understood why they wanted to thwart him, and I never wanted to be a countess, so it suited me just fine. Uncle Charles left Cherrywood

Place to Luke, and he's left it to me, for Archie, so I'm very well placed now, and Archie understands how it is, don't you, my dear?"

"Yes, Mama," the boy said. "I don't think I'd like to live here."

"No more would I," said his mother. "Horrid great mausoleum of a place! As for the stain of illegitimacy, if we had any pretensions to cut a dash in society, it would be a hindrance indeed, but nothing is further from our thoughts. Archie will be a gentleman of independent means, wealthy enough to help his brothers to profitable careers and his sisters to good marriages, and my family is well-connected in Newcastle and will ensure no one ostracises them. Most of our acquaintances already know of our situation. So you see, gentlemen, everything has worked out for the best, and Edlesborough will eventually be the seat of the only one of the earl's sons who had the gumption to stand up to him to his face."

She smiled at Simon, and his brothers nodded sagely, leaving him surprised. Had he truly done anything so noteworthy? His father had wanted him to go into the army, a career for which he was spectacularly unsuited, and he had refused. What was so courageous about that? He had already decided on architecture by then, and knew that Juliet would take him in, for in those days there had been no bar on communication. It was only later that all contact had been banned.

He was, he decided, a simple man, who preferred the honest, straightforward route to the convoluted schemes dreamt up by his older brothers. They might take satisfaction in appearing to obey their father while secretly thwarting him, but the constant fear of discovery must have worn them down, over the years. Now, Andrew was not the hale man he had once been and Luke had already been felled by illness. What a strange, sad life they had led! Whereas Simon's only concern had been the cost of coal and candles.

Dinner that evening promised to be a lively affair. There were two additional guests who had arrived with Sally Payne, but had not been involved with the lawyers, so this was the first time Simon had seen them. Mrs Granville was a handsome woman of above sixty, her smooth white hair and fashionable clothes only enhancing her appearance. With her was her eldest son, Mr Charlie Granville, a man of almost forty with a cheerful countenance. They were cousins to Luke's uncle and benefactor in Newcastle. He had been the brother of the late earl's first wife, Juliet's mother, so she naturally had an interest in the Granvilles.

"They are my cousins, too, to some degree," Juliet whispered to Simon, as they sat together in the drawing room watching the Granvilles circulate amongst the guests. "She is a fine looking woman, would you not agree? What a lovely gown, and such a magnificent diamond necklace. Mr Granville must be very wealthy. How beautiful she must have been as a young woman! Do you think she might have known my mother? She must have done, surely — Mama was a Granville and this lady married one. She might know something about..." She lowered her voice even further. "...about the divorce."

"Andrew said that the full proceedings in the House of Lords were in the library."

"Oh yes, but it does not tell me anything new, and the man accused of... of doing those things with Mama, did not, did he? The duke said it was all a lie. But if Mrs Granville knew Mama at the time, perhaps she is privy to the truth about it, for I am sure Mama could not have done anything so very dreadful. No doubt she went along with the divorce to get away from Father. Anybody would."

"A divorce is a terrible stain on everyone involved," Simon said. "I cannot imagine any sane person would *choose* to be divorced purely to escape from a difficult marriage."

"She is coming this way! Do you think I should ask her about it?"

"Personally, I think the less said about it the better."

Andrew brought Mrs Granville over to them. She was even more handsome when observed more closely, the only wrinkles of age being a few laughter lines around her eyes, and she moved with all the gracefulness of a much younger woman.

"Here is someone who very much wishes to meet you," Andrew said, smiling broadly. "Simon is the eldest of my father's second family, and this..." He paused, the smile widening even further. "...this is Juliet."

"Oh, my dear!" Mrs Granville said, sitting down beside Juliet in a soft swirl of silk, and taking her hand. "I have heard so much about you over the years, but you cannot imagine how much I have longed to see you again."

"Again? Then... we have met before?"

Mrs Granville gave a low laugh. "Indeed we have, but not for very many years. Not since you were three years old."

"Three? But... I do not understand," Juliet said, wide-eyed. "That was when I left Edlesborough. How can that be? Were you here? Who *are* you?"

"Have you not guessed? I am your mother, Juliet."

21: The Library

For a long, long moment, Juliet said nothing, staring transfixed at the woman who claimed to be her mother. Simon was just as shocked. So this elegant lady, who seemed so eminently respectable, was in fact the scandalous first wife of the late earl, so badly behaved that he was forced to divorce her.

"But what did you *do?*" Juliet wailed at last. "Whatever happened?"

"Do you mean why did he divorce me? Oh, the usual reason, my dear. I was a very bad wife, and he was quite within his rights. Do you want to hear all about it?"

Juliet nodded eagerly.

"Well, then, I shall tell you everything, but I see the estimable Spearman waiting to announce dinner, and we cannot discuss such sordid matters over the mutton. After dinner, we shall creep away to my room where we can be private, and you shall hear it all, and then you may judge me, if you will."

Dinner was a strange meal. Even with the lawyers taking their meal separately, there were still seventeen of them squeezed into the breakfast parlour. The number included Ruth, sitting on a cushion to allow her to reach the table, who was allowed to be present for the first course, accompanied by Miss Towers.

Eventually, the second course was removed, the sweets, nuts and port laid out and the servants withdrew. Lavinia rose to lead the ladies out, but Mrs Granville raised a hand.

"One moment, if you please. Andrew, why do we eat in here when there is a far more commodious dining room on the first floor?"

Andrew pulled a face. "I cannot bear the dining room... or the library, for that matter. I have no happy memories of either place. The rest of the house I can bear, but those two rooms... Lavinia and the Dowager Countess will put in hand a number of improving works, and then I shall be able to enter them."

"It is a very sad thing," Mrs Granville said, "that your father has squashed all the spirit out of you. This is your moment of triumph, Andrew. You should march into both those rooms and shout at the top of your lungs, *'Mine now!'*. Because they are. Everything is yours. Even his name is yours — you are Edlesborough now. He is dead and you are alive, so celebrate. Make those rooms your own and wash away the bad memories. Take down those dreadful portraits of Elizabethan ancestors and put up your ship paintings. Burn his chair, if it will make you feel better, but take possession of what is yours and be glad you are free now. Unlike me, you never had the choice to leave, but you bore it nobly and you won in the end, so be glad."

"You *chose* to leave?" Andrew whispered, his face ashen. "You chose to abandon your own children?"

She took a long, ragged breath. "It was the hardest thing I have ever done, but my life was unbearable. I could not bear it, anyway. If I had stayed, I should have killed myself — or him, possibly. I thought that divorce was the least destructive option."

"Is it not a mother's place to protect her children?"

"Protect you? From him? I could not protect *myself* from him, so what could I have done for you? A father owns his own children, my dear, and nothing I could have done would have changed that."

Andrew would have argued the point, but Simon's mother reached across the table and rested her hand on his. "You must not blame her. She did what she needed to do to survive. I understand it, as you perhaps cannot. A wife experiences the worst of a man's foibles, Andrew. And she is right about the house, too. You must not let your father cow you even from the grave. You have survived him — we have all survived him. Now let us do our very best to forget he ever existed."

Andrew gave a shaky laugh. "I am sure you are right, both of you. Tomorrow, we will eat in the dining room."

"And tonight?" Mrs Granville said. "Shall we withdraw to the library?"

"Let us all go there now," Lavinia said. "The room is large enough that the men can take their port at one end while we discuss domestic matters at the other without hampering each other in the slightest. No need to look so nervous, Andrew. Let us lay the ghosts once and for all."

So they all trooped in a long line up the imposing staircase to the first floor, Lavinia and the Dowager Countess leading the way, then the rest of the ladies. The gentlemen followed silently, while Spearman and his minions, laden with trays of port, glasses and sweetmeats, brought up the rear.

At the top of the stairs, they crowded into a modest ante-chamber, its carved frieze, gold-encrusted fireplace and rich carpets giving the barest hint of the glories to come. Here they waited while the servants scurried about lighting candles and fires before the great doors to the library were thrown open.

It was massive, three perfect cubes joined end to end, each with its own unique fireplace, a marble frieze running round the entire upper third of the three inner walls, the outer wall being almost entirely taken up by high windows. On the panelled walls, long-dead ancestors adopted regal poses and gazed sternly down at them. A few panels were taken up by floor to ceiling bookcases, to ensure that the room was not entirely misnamed, and on the ceiling, dimly seen by candlelight, nymphs and goddesses jostled amidst unidentifiable greenery below thundery skies.

"Oh, how hideous!" Juliet exclaimed, causing a certain amount of laughter.

"It is rather oppressive, is it not?" Lavinia said. "I suppose it must have been three separate rooms at one time. Perhaps we should restore it to its original state."

"No, no!" Simon said in some alarm. "This is how it was designed. It is the Great Chamber, you see, where visiting dignitaries were taken to be awed by the power of the owner. When the monarch came to stay, this would be the royal receiving room, with the withdrawing chamber and bedchamber beyond. I love this room."

Andrew shook his head in bewilderment. "You must be the only person who does, brother. His desk... I cannot even bear to look at his desk. I see him sitting behind it, berating me for my latest transgression, his voice so reasonable, so gentle, yet he always reduced me to jelly. Simon, I do not know how you can find anything to like about this room."

"But it is beautiful," he said, in surprise. "Look how perfectly proportioned it is, and the artistry that created it. It is magnificent. The walls would have been covered with tapestries originally, which is why the panelling is not so elaborate as elsewhere. It is this room that pushed me to become an architect. I used to bring paper and pencils, and draw this and that — the whole room, sometimes. The outside, too, but the interior fascinated me, the way visitors would be led in procession from the hall down below and up the stairs to this room. I still try to do that in my own work, although the idea has largely gone out of fashion now. The paintwork on the ceiling is darker than I remember it, but the figures are still the wonder they always were. I used to come here early on summer mornings, before the light grew too harsh, and just lie on the floor admiring the ceil ing."

Andrew shivered. "This room will look better tomorrow. Spearman, take the port back to the dining room."

"Ah well," said Lavinia with a sigh. "Ladies, shall we go to the drawing room?"

Mrs Granville looked at Juliet. "The fires are lit, and it would be a shame to waste the heat, would it not? Charlie, find some brandy, will you? Shall we sit, and I shall answer all your questions?"

Juliet and Mrs Granville sat side by side on a pair of chairs so ornately carved and dripping with gilt they might have been thrones. Simon pulled up a faded footstool, while Charlie Granville and a footman moved about supplying brandy for Mrs Granville and claret for Simon.

"So what do you want to know?" Mrs Granville said.

"Everything," Juliet said in a low voice.

Mrs Granville chuckled. "Everything it shall be, then. Let me begin at the beginning. I was barely seventeen when I married your father. I came straight from the schoolroom, knowing nothing of society or life or men, to this place. I did not mind, at first. Edlesborough's parents were alive then, and they kept him on an even keel, I suppose, because he seemed normal enough to me then. He was well mannered, gentlemanlike, good company in society. He never showed me any affection, but that was not expected, on either side. Andrew was born, and he was pleased with that. Then Luke, a couple of years later. By that time, his father had died, his mother had gone off to sulk in some Cornish fastness, and good riddance, too, for a colder woman never breathed. But without his parents... Edlesborough began to show his true colours."

She sipped her brandy thoughtfully, then laid it down on a table carved like a lion.

"You will not remember him, Juliet, I am sure, and so much the better for you. Simon will remember what he was like."

"Not much," he said. "He never took much notice of me, and I took great care not to do anything which would attract his attention. Andrew and Luke told me how best to evade his wrath, although they never seemed to manage it themselves."

"Poor boys!" she said. "I felt dreadful leaving them behind, but it was the only way I could keep my sanity intact. Edlesborough had only three moods, you see. There was the genial face he showed the world when he entertained, making sure that everyone had a wonderful time. Then there was his cold displeasure, where he reduced one's character to shreds, so that one felt like the veriest worm crawling about on the ground, worthy only to be crushed under his boot. And then there were the sudden rages, when he would be ill for days afterwards. And there was no predicting which mood it would be at any given moment. We all walked around on eggshells, as you may imagine. And then—"

She stopped, breathing heavily, before taking a long draught of brandy.

"Perhaps it was something in me, but... he had some deeply unpleasant habits which I found... difficult. I just wanted it to stop, but the more I pleaded with him, the more he tormented me. It was not until after Luke was born that I found a way. I had always had admirers. It was fashionable then... perhaps it still is amongst a certain set, for a married woman to have admirers... cicisbeos. I had several, but there was one in particular... There was nothing improper between us, but he brought me to see how Edlesborough was mistreating me... that there could be affection and even joy between a man and a woman. And he showed me how I could escape my marriage, by taking a lover and forcing my husband to divorce me. So that is what I did and—"

"But wait!" Juliet cried. "What about me? I come between Luke and the divorce."

"Indeed you do," Mrs Granville said, smiling at her, and resting a plump hand on Juliet's. "You were the first of my children by a lover."

"What!" screeched Juliet. "Then I am not even legitimate!"

"Certainly you are, since Edlesborough never repudiated you. He knew, of course, but he was not sure what to do at first. Eventually, he decided that he did not want a male cuckoo in the nest to potentially inherit everything, so if the child was male, he would divorce me and repudiate the child, but a girl he could accept, to prevent a scandal. So when you were born, my dear, he accepted you as his."

"But I am not." Juliet's face was as white as the handkerchief she clutched in one hand, her fingers restlessly pleating and unpleating it.

"Legally, you are, but you are not of his blood, no."

"So who is my real father?" Juliet said, her eyes narrowing.

Mrs Granville laughed. "My dear, that would be telling! Best for you not to know, frankly. After that, I had to begin again. There were several more lovers, and eventually I found myself with child again, and this time Edlesborough did not hesitate. I was out of the house within the hour. He threw you out, as well, which was not at all what I intended, but Tabitha looked after you, did she not? I knew my sister would take very good care of you. She wrote to my brother in Newcastle and he wrote to me, so I knew how you were getting on. Tabitha made sure you were educated and brought up properly, as an earl's daughter should be. I always assumed that Edlesborough would relent, in time, and at least see you brought out into society, but I think on the whole you have done better without all that nonsense."

"In what way have I done better?" Juliet said, jerking into a straighter position. "To have no chance of marrying well — or at all? To have no dowry? To survive on one hundred and fifty pounds a year, at best, and most of that is gone now. How is that *better* than being acknowledged as the daughter of an earl?"

Mrs Granville's eyebrows rose. "Well, I must say that you look very well on your hundred and fifty a year. That gown alone must have cost fifty pounds or more."

"It is *borrowed!* All this finery came from the Duchess of Brinshire, and will go back to her when I leave this miserable place, and I will don my own rags again. Great heavens, what did you think would become of me when you abandoned me? Did you think Aunt Tabitha was a wealthy woman, and I would be dining on partridge and turbot for the rest of my life? Did you think about me at all? You are the one who has done well, if you ask me. You are the one dripping in diamonds, after all. How much did *that* cost Mr Granville?"

The eyebrows rose even further, but she said mildly, "There was never a Mr Granville. I took my maiden name and pretended to be a widow. My Italian lover bought the necklace, and left me very well provided for, it is true. I sold the villa when we all moved back to England, and bought a tidy little property near Newcastle. Apart from Charlie here, there are four more children at home, all with their father's lovely dark hair and eyes." She sighed, a faraway look in her eyes. "The dear man is dead now, poor creature, but he has taken good care of all of us, both in life and in death."

"Then I congratulate you, *Mama*," Juliet said, rising to her feet. "What a charmed life you have led, doing precisely what you wished, abandoning your husband and several children to pursue your own pleasure all these years. How happy you must be, knowing that *you* would never have to worry about the expense of a second servant or the apothecary's fees, or be obliged to reuse tea because it was too costly to buy more."

"Oh, my dear..." Mrs Granville began, but Simon stood and wrapped his arms gently around his sister. Her small frame trembled violently in his arms.

"Sister, you shall have all the diamonds you wish for, and the very best tea from now on."

"I do not *want* diamonds!" she cried, pushing him away. "I never wanted anything for myself, only for you to be famous enough that we could move in society — proper society, not the scuffling little set we belong to at present, but this selfish woman has made it impossible. In all the difficulties I have endured over the years, my one consolation was that I was respectable — an earl's daughter, even if he ignored me. I believed that once you had made your name, we would be able to hold our heads up in any company — perhaps you would attract the notice of the Prince of Wales's set, and go to Carlton House or... or Brighton, and be *somebody*. But that will never be, because I am the daughter of the woman who so scandalised polite society that her husband *divorced* her! I shall never, ever be able to hold my head up again, never!"

With a swirl of the duchess' expensive silk, she swept from the room, leaving Mrs Granville watching her open-mouthed.

"Well! I did not imagine she would be so temperamental about it."

"What did you expect — that she would fall into your arms?" Simon said.

"Something like that, yes. I never supposed she would be so unsympathetic. I could not have stayed with a man who tormented me so, no woman could or should."

"*My* mother did," Simon said, with icy disdain. "She bore the brunt of my father's ill-humours and foibles for over thirty years, without once complaining or doing anything improper, and she never, ever abandoned her children, as you did. I am sorry your life with my father was so miserable, but frankly, I hope I never see you again."

22: The Blue Parlour

Simon took his brandy to Juliet's room, where he found her pacing up and down in a rage.

"Insufferable woman! So smug and self-satisfied! *She* is all right, naturally, with her lovers and her villa and her tidy little property near Newcastle! And all the time I thought she was dead, and grieved for her, and set all my troubles at Papa's door, when really it was not at all surprising that he could not bear to have me in the house, a constant reminder of his faithless wife."

"I told her I never want to see her again," Simon said.

"Did you! How wonderful! You are the best brother in the world, do you know that? What else did you say to her?"

"That, unlike her, my mother put up with Edlesborough for thirty years."

"So she did, and sent us so much money over the years. Twice or thrice a year, there would be the two letters and half a bank note in each."

"Christmas, Easter and the shooting season, when the house was full of tipsy uncles and aunts not noticing how much they were losing at the card tables."

"She must be so happy to be rid of the old buzzard at last," Juliet said.

"Everyone is. Sister, I told Mrs Granville I hoped never to see her again, and I meant it. Shall we go back to Staineybank? There is nothing to keep us here now."

"Do you not want to talk to Andrew? You will inherit all this one day, so you should know how it operates."

Simon shook his head. "It could be many years, for he is only forty-five, and I do not want to get under his feet. He must find his own way for a while, without thinking too far ahead. I have something more important to deal with first."

"The orangery?"

He laughed. "Miss Sophia Merrington."

"You are determined to have her, then?"

"Indeed I am. Shall we leave tomorrow?"

"If we must. I hate this place so much. Staineybank is much more friendly. It will feel almost like going home."

"It is what home ought to be," he said, smiling at her. "I will order the carriage for directly after breakfast."

In the event, Simon spent the morning with Andrew, soothing his anxieties and assuring him that he would return often. In truth, he could not find the heart to worry too much about Andrew. He was not robust, it was true, but he had plenty of years left to him, the physicians assured him, and he would grow accustomed to his high estate. All Simon's thoughts now were focused on a certain young lady, and the glorious prospect of converting their secret betrothal into a real and very public one. Now that he was a future earl, and with money enough to support a wife, even without his profession as an architect, there could be no possible objection from her brother or from the duke.

There was one obstacle, however, that he had not considered. When he and Juliet arrived at Staineybank, weary from two days on the road, there was another carriage drawn up at the front door, one with arms painted on the door which he vaguely recognised. Sudden fear drove him to abandon Juliet and leap from the carriage, and race up the steps two at a time, the skirts of his greatcoat flying.

Inside the Marble Hall, much of the household was gathered, including all the Merrington ladies — except one.

"Oh, Mr Payne!" Mrs Merrington cried, rushing forward to grab his arm, her face aglow. "How lovely to see you again, and at such an auspicious moment. He is back... Lord Daniel is back, and instantly requested a private interview with Sophia. Is it not exciting? She is with him now. The son of a marquess... how delightful... how *suitable*, do you not agree?"

She finished on a slightly questioning note, as perhaps she recalled belatedly that Simon was not likely to be quite so delighted.

He barely heard her, and certainly could not have formulated a coherent response. The pain that tore through him rendered him immobile and mute. She would marry Torbuck, and how could he bear it? How could he possibly bear it? All the good of the last few days meant nothing if she could not share it with him.

He might as well be dead.

***

There had been no inkling of Lord Daniel's return in advance. The first Sophia knew of it was when Froggett sidled into the morning room where the ladies were gathered, and coughed discreetly.

"Yes, Froggett, what is it?" the duchess said.

"Lord Daniel Torbuck is here, your grace, requesting a private interview with Miss Sophia Merrington. I took the liberty of showing him into the Blue Parlour and lighting the fire."

There was a twitter of excitement amongst the ladies. Lord Daniel! A private interview! How very surprising.

"Make sure there is wine in there," the duchess said.

"Robert is attending to his lordship," the butler said, then withdrew with a bow.

"Well!" Mrs Merrington said. "So he has returned, has he? This is excellent news, Sophia."

"A private interview?" she said, puzzled.

"He means to propose, of course," he mother said. "Perfectly unexceptionable."

"Is it not rather precipitate?" Sophia said. "Should he not more correctly make his greetings to you and Richard... and the duke and duchess, of course? Be sociable for a while before jumping into private interviews."

"One does not quibble over details with a man in love," her mother said firmly.

Was he in love? That was an interesting question, one to which she might find an answer very soon. But the question of seeing him alone was of more immediate concern. It was several weeks since his precipitate departure, and his face had gradually faded from her memory, superseded by the more agreeable features of Mr Simon Payne. Just at that moment, in the shock of his unexpected arrival, she could not bring Lord Daniel's countenance to mind at all.

A wave of alarm roiled through her. This man, whom she scarcely knew, was waiting for her, expecting her to bind herself irrevocably to him in the next five minutes, or perhaps ten if he should become particularly articulate, and she could not even remember what he looked like.

"Must I see him alone?" she whispered.

"It is usual," he mother said, smiling. "A man does not like an audience at such a moment. Are you nervous?"

"I should at least like to have my sisters with me when I meet him. It would give me courage."

"Let us all go to welcome him back to Staineybank," the duchess said, rising and shaking out her grey skirts. "He may wonder what sort of reception he will receive, given his abrupt departure last time. We will take you to him, and you will see, no doubt, that he is just as nervous as you are."

"Or more so," Mama said. "Roland was such a bag of nerves when he proposed that he could scarcely string two words together. It was most affecting."

"We shall be by your side when you meet him," Charlotte said.

"You need not fear anything when we are with you," Augusta said.

"Come, let us not keep the poor man waiting," Maria said.

Arm in arm, the four sisters made their way to the Marble Hall, with the duchess and Mrs Merrington behind them. Froggett, smiling benignly upon them all, nodded to the two footmen to open the doors and preceded them into the room in a stately manner.

"Her Grace the Duchess of Brinshire, Mrs Roland Merrington, Miss Merrington, Miss Augusta Merrington, Miss Maria Merrington and Miss Sophia Merrington," he intoned.

And there he was, memory flooding back as Sophia saw the familiar face. How could she have doubted herself? She would have known him anywhere, but his expression was not so familiar. She almost laughed out loud at the shock on Lord Daniel's face. And then, as his gaze ranged over the four of them, the strange expression she had seen before — surely that was panic? It was true, then — he could not tell which of the four sisters was Sophia.

There was an awkward silence until the duchess remembered that she was the highest ranking lady and mistress of the house, so must speak first.

"How charming to see you again, Lord Daniel."

"Duchess," he murmured, executing a slightly awkward bow.

"I trust your father is better?"

"My father? Oh... yes, indeed, much restored. Very much restored."

"That is excellent news," she went on smoothly, more sure of herself now. "We have brought Sophia to you, as you see."

So saying, she turned and led the others out of the room. The door shut with a soft click, and Sophia was alone with him. His face cleared a little, now that he knew he had the right sister. He still looked a shade bemused, but there was no panic there. Yet how odd it was, not to be able to recognise the woman he planned to marry! Simon had no trouble recognising her.

But then Simon loved her. The thought warmed her inside, and she smiled so widely, that Lord Daniel smiled too.

"Miss Merrington... Sophia..." There was just the hint of a question about it.

"Lord Daniel. What a surprise to see you again, after all this time."

His smile slipped a little. "You must have wondered... why I left so precipitously last month."

"Oh no, for you told us why. You were concerned for your father's health, which is most commendable. I quite understood. I am glad to hear that his gout is better, for it must have been very severe to cause you such alarm." And then, a mischievous imp wakening inside her, she went on, "I did think, for a while, that perhaps you left because you could not distinguish me from my sisters. Mr Payne had that problem and so we wondered... but you see, we have decided to wear coloured ribbons, so that there will be no difficulty in future. Charlotte... she is the eldest, so she chose her colour first. She chose blue, which is the best colour, in my opinion, but being the youngest, I had little choice. Then Augusta — she is the next eldest, you see — she chose pink, which is also a pretty colour."

She sighed, but he said nothing, merely gazing bemusedly at her, so she ploughed on.

"And then Maria wanted white or cream, so that she could wear a little bit of lace instead of a regular ribbon, and who could deny her that? So I was left with yellow. Well, I could have had red, but that is such an uncompromising colour, is it not? As for green... oh, no. So it had to be yellow, which does not suit me very well, but there we are. And it cannot be a pale yellow, or it might look too much like Maria's cream. Do you like it? My yellow ribbon?"

The smile had vanished. "I did not come here to talk about ribbons," he said tersely.

"What did you come to talk about?" she said blandly, trying to suppress her amusement. He was so easy to tease, and she really should not. "Shall we sit? I should feel more comfortable if we sit."

She perched on a sofa, and at once realised her mistake, for he sat alongside her, his face afire, and seized her hand in his.

"Miss Merrington... Sophia... you talk about ribbons from nervousness, I am sure, but there is no need. You know what I am about to say. My visit to my father was timely, for it enabled me to tell him about you, and you may be sure I described you in the most glowing terms. Be assured that I have his full approval for all that I am about to say, for I know that must weigh with you."

"Must it?" she said, her mischievous imp still driving her.

"Of course it must!" he said sharply. "My father is a marquess!"

"Oh yes! The Marquess of Pentavon — I looked him up in the Peerage. Such a distinguished history, and Pentavon Castle— I beg your pardon, sir. I interrupted you."

"It is of no consequence," he said stiffly. "My father approves of our match, that is the important point, so you need not hesitate on that account. He feels that a connection to the Duke of Brinshire is an excellent idea. And the duke himself has no objection, he as good as told me so. At least, he will give you a dowry, which is the same thing."

"And my brother?" she said sweetly. "He is the one you will have to convince."

"Merrington? Why should he object?"

"I cannot say, but he might. Gentlemen know more about other gentlemen than ladies do, after all, and he might know something about you to which I am not privy."

"Great heavens, is this what you think — that I have some monstrous secret in my history?" Now he sounded quite cross.

"Did I not just say that I do not know what secrets you might have?"

"Well, I have none."

"I am glad to hear it, although I should have supposed it so. I do not think you have the—" Hmm, courage? Imagination? "—the disregard for your family's honour to do anything dreadful."

"Thank you for that, at least. Good Lord, Sophia, you used not to be such a gabble-mouth! Will you let me say what I have come all the way from Gloucestershire to say to you?"

"I beg your pardon, sir. Pray continue."

She bowed her head meekly, but inside her laughter was bubbling up and trying very hard to burst out. She could not wait to tell her sisters about this — but no, a private interview was undoubtedly meant to remain private. Bother! They would have enjoyed the joke, she was sure.

"Thank you. Sophia..." He huffed in annoyance. "You have distracted me so much that I have forgot what I was about to say."

She was so tempted to say *'You were about to propose marriage'*, but the glower on his face deterred her. His patience was wearing thin. So she bit her tongue and waited for him to put his thoughts in order.

"Well, you know it anyway, I dare say. You must have heard it a thousand times — admiration and so forth. Wanting to share my life with you, that sort of thing. Let us dispense with all the flowery nothings and get to the point. Will you marry me, Sophia?"

Flowery nothings? Could he not even be bothered to make some show of affection? A few compliments — she did not ask for much. She was twenty-eight years old, a person of very little account outside her own family, so her expectations were low, and she had no wish for false declarations of love. But he ought to make some effort.

"I do not want flowery nothings, Daniel," she said gently, "but I should like to know why precisely you want to marry me."

"Well... the usual reasons," he said, looking embarrassed. "I... I *like* you, Sophia. I think we should suit very well."

"Where should we live?"

"Oh, that is all settled," he said smugly. "The north wing of Pentavon. My oldest brother has it at present, but when he marries next month, he will move out to the western gatehouse — that is always kept for the heir, you see. So the north wing goes to whichever of the rest of us marries first, and I thought..." He must have realised how unflattering this line of thought was, for he finished lamely, "And I met you, fortuitously, and so I thought..."

That I would do, she mentally finished for him. But she was tired of teasing a man who provided so little sport, so instead she said, "How many rooms?"

"In the north wing? Four — parlour, dining room, bedroom, dressing room."

"That is very small," she said.

"It is perfectly adequate for the two of us, since any children will share the nursery with my brothers' children. You can have the dressing room, if you like."

"How kind. What is your income?"

He frowned. "That is no concern of yours. It will be enough to support a wife and children, that is all you need to know."

"My pin money is very much my concern."

"That will be agreed when the settlements are drawn up. You do not need to worry about that, my dear. Money is a matter for men to decide. I shall ensure you have enough for your furbelows and bonnets."

"I am glad to hear it. Pray tell me something of life at Pentavon Castle, if it is to be my home. How often do you hold a ball there?"

"A ball? What a frivolous question!"

"Not to me," she said firmly.

"We never hold balls there," he said disdainfully. "We go to town for that sort of thing."

"But that is only three months of the year," she said sorrowfully. "How dreadful to have nine months of every year without the prospect of a ball. I shall be very miserable."

"Oh, town is not for the married women," he said. "My sisters go for their presentations, and to prance around a bit, but dancing is not for the matrons. They have too much to do at home and with the children to care about balls and such like."

"Then that settles the matter," Sophia said, withdrawing her hand from his, which had become uncomfortably clammy, and rising to her feet. "I thank you for your most obliging offer, Lord Daniel, but I cannot marry you. We should not suit at all."

He jumped up, too, his face thunderous. "Because you want to make an exhibition of yourself by dancing?"

"I love to dance," she said simply. "I have few pleasures in my life, sir, beyond my own family, but dancing is one of them. If you plan to deprive me not only of my family but of the joy of dancing, too, then I cannot possibly marry you. I would have to be greatly in love with you to make such sacrifices, and I am not. Nor do I think you have that attachment to me which would enable you to understand my character and bend to my wishes, even in so small a matter. I suspect, in fact, that you are looking for a wife who will be there when you require her company and will meekly disappear at other times to tend to domestic affairs, while you do as you please. That is not the sort of marriage I hope for."

"You hope for the moon, then," he muttered.

"No, only a man who loves me passionately and listens to my concerns and wants to share every part of his life with me, and not one who only sees me as a useful means of obtaining his own accommodation. Goodbye, Lord Daniel."

She held out her hand, but he was too angry even to touch her. Without a word, he swept out of the room, leaving the door wide open.

For a moment, she stood immobile, savouring her triumph. Then, slowly, she began to laugh. She was still laughing when faces peeped round the door frame.

"Did you actually turn him down?" Charlotte said in awed tones.

"What went wrong?" Augusta said.

"Why did he look so angry?" Maria said.

Mama strode through the door, but she said nothing. Nor did she need to speak, for her dark countenance spoke eloquently enough.

"I could not marry a man who will not let me dance," Sophia said briskly. "Even you, Mama, cannot expect me to give up every pleasure for the sake of a ring on my finger."

"Oh, Sophia!" Mama said sadly. "The son of a marquess! You will never have an offer even half so good again, as you must be aware. You are not pining for Mr Payne, I hope," she added sharply. "Your Mr Payne is never likely to be able to afford a wife, so put him out of your head at once."

That was easier said than done! Sophia said carefully, "Mama, I know it was an excellent offer and I had no objection to Lord Daniel himself. I rather liked him, in fact. But liking is not quite enough. I have seen what a happy, loving marriage can be, both in you and Papa, and now in Richard and Rowena. You cannot blame me, surely, for hoping still for the same for myself."

"Which is wonderful when it happens, but one must be practical." She heaved a sigh. "Well, what is done is done. I must say, you are a great disappointment to me, Sophia. After all my efforts to encourage this match, you snap your fingers at it. Such an undutiful daughter! Well, I wash my hands of you, that is all I have to say on the matter."

So saying, she swept regally out of the room, head high.

As soon as she had gone, her sisters crowded around her.

"He is back from Edlesborough..."

"...not an hour since..."

"... and when he heard you were with Lord Daniel..."

"...he looked so..."

"Heartbroken!" they ended in unison.

"Simon? Simon is here?"

She did not wait for a reply, flying on winged feet out into the hall and up the stairs. He was back! She must see him at once... *at once!*

23: Despair

Sophia ran out of the Blue Parlour and crashed straight into the solid form of her brother.

"Sophia, a word, if you please."

"Yes, but—"

"The breakfast parlour will be empty."

"Yes, yes, but I must—"

"Now, Sophia."

"Now?"

"Now," he said in that uncompromising tone that she knew only too well.

Dejectedly, she crossed the Marble Hall, and he held open the door for her. At this hour, the breakfast parlour was deserted, the fire already turned to ashes.

"Will you sit?" he said in kinder tones, holding a chair for her.

She had no choice, but it was almost beyond her ability to sit still, so wild was she to see Simon again and find out all that had happened at Edlesborough. He had been expected back much sooner, on the assumption that his father would have refused to see him, but he had stayed so long that surely he must have achieved the interview, and what had come of it? She could not wait to hear it all. If only she could—

"Sophia, are you listening?"

"Oh... I beg your pardon. I was wool gathering."

"What a strange girl you are, to be inattentive at such a moment. I am attempting to tell you, sister, that I have endured a very sticky interview with Torbuck. Mercifully, the stables were very swift to send round his carriage — in fact, I doubt the horses had even been unhitched." He chuckled. "Well, you sent him to the rightabout, and no mistake! Because he expected you to stay at home and not dance again, is that it?"

She nodded, for that was certainly a part of it.

"Foolish man! Trying to keep you or any of my sisters away from a ball is like trying to stop the moon circling the earth. I did not like him very much, to be frank, so I am not disappointed that you turned him down."

"You are not?" That was a surprise. Then, with a quick laugh, "Mama has washed her hands of me."

He laughed too. "She only wants you to be well settled, and it is upsetting for her to have her hopes raised and dashed, then raised and dashed again. All this coming and going... he turned up here after meeting you at Marshfields, which was perfectly acceptable, but then after two days he disappears, sends no word for several weeks, then pops up like a Jack-in-the-box, wanting to propose to you on the spot. It is all a bit havey-cavey, if you ask me, and that business of rushing off to see his father when all he had was a touch of gout — ridiculous. And as for forbidding you from dancing—! Was that your only reason for turning him down? He seemed to think it a trivial objection, but to my mind, I could not be comfortable giving my sister into the keeping of a man who is so implacably opposed to such a harmless exercise. Surely he would wish you to be happy and would therefore indulge you on a matter so clearly of importance to you ?"

"So I thought, too," Sophia said, pleased that he saw the case as she did. "May I tell you why he wanted to marry me? Would it be wrong of me to reveal what was said in a private interview?"

"As a rule, it would be so, but unless he swore you to secrecy, you may certainly tell Mama. As I stand in place of your father, you may tell me, also. But it should not become general gossip."

"Well, then, his only reason to marry is to get his hands on living quarters before his brothers. Four rooms in a corner of Pentavon Castle, Richard, that was to be my home. I thought a pretty little house in Gloucester, but no, I was to have a bachelor apartment, with no servants or kitchen of my own, and the children taken off to the shared nursery. And not much money, either, I imagine. He may be a son of a marquess, as Mama constantly reminds me, but he is a *third* son, with not even a career of his own. He will be dependent on his father for every penny."

"And your dowry," Richard said tartly. "And when his father dies, it will be his brother he depends upon. He is the only one without a profession, did you know that? I made some enquiries, and the second and fourth brothers are both in the army, and the fifth is in the navy. Lord Daniel ought at least to enter the church, for that is where indolent unwanted younger sons tend to find themselves, but he told me very clearly that he had no plans in that direction. In truth, if he wants to live at his ease without a career, he ought to find himself a proper heiress, with more than your paltry ten thousand."

"Is it paltry?" she said, suddenly amused.

"Invested, it would yield some five hundred a year, that is all. Not a great deal to a gentleman, and not enough to support a gentleman's family in comfort. But I suppose he was in a hurry. He met you, liked you, discovered you have a modest dowry and thought to steal a march on his brothers and snaffle the cosy apartment. That makes me dislike him even more."

"You are not cross with me then? I thought you were desperate for me to marry and save you the hundred pounds a year for my board and clothes."

He laughed, his dour face lighting up abruptly. "You cost me a little more than that, sister, and when my income was so limited, I confess I would have been glad to see any of you well married and my purse a little heavier as a consequence. But the duke has more than enough money to house and feed and clothe you all, and seems delighted to do it, too. So do not feel under any obligation to marry on my account, sister dear."

"Well, I must say, you have changed your tune lately, brother, and I much prefer this one."

"I know — I was a bear, was I not? I was so worried about Rowena's confinement that I was barely rational. But now I can see more clearly, about a great many things that I made an unconscionable fuss about before. This orangery designed by your Mr Payne, for instance. An orangery! No, a bridge and a gallery, which would make a perfect ballroom, would it not?"

She nodded eagerly. "The gallery at Marshfields was used for the ball, and I think that inspired Simon... Mr Payne's design."

Richard smiled at her, and said gently, "I think he is very much in love with you. All his drawings of the ball are of you, did you know that? It was as if no one else existed. His sketches of other people are lightly drawn, barely there, but when he draws you… there is affection in every line. Would you still like to marry him?"

"Oh yes, but I know it is impossible. He has no money at present. One day, perhaps, he will be a renowned architect and be able to afford to marry, but it could be many years."

"Or it could be sooner than you think. Now that I am confident that Rowena is not about to be taken from me and can be rational again, I propose to tell the duke that your Mr Payne's design is so much better than mine that I cannot improve upon it, and will withdraw from the competition. He will make at least a thousand pounds in fees from it, and possibly more, and his reputation will be made. In a year or two, perhaps, I shall have the pleasure of leading you to the altar and placing your hand in his."

Sophia could barely breathe. "Does he know this?"

"Payne? No. I should write to tell him, I suppose, since he looks likely to be gone for some time."

"No! He is back, just arrived, but I suppose in all the fuss over Lord Daniel, no one thought to tell you. May I—?"

"Of course. Off you go and tell him the good news, sister."

Thus released, Sophia jumped up and practically ran from the room.

***

Simon somehow found his way upstairs, following Juliet without thought. She led him to his old room, where a maid was hastily lighting the fire.

"Brandy?" Juliet said.

He shook his head. How could brandy help?

"I am chilled to the bone, and you must be too," she said. "Shall I order baths for us?"

Again he shook his head.

"What can I get you?" she said, her voice so sympathetic that he could have wept.

"Nothing."

Without a word, he turned and strode back out to the landing. He had no specific destination in mind, but his feet must have known what his heart intended, for before long he found himself outside the curtained door to the little gallery above the chapel. Inside, it was flooded with light, unexpectedly blinding him. The midday sun, pouring through the chapel windows and undeterred by the carved screen, lit up the tiny gallery. He sat down in his accustomed place on the bench and closed his eyes, but the light was so bright that it penetrated even through his lids. Groaning, he buried his face in his hands.

At first, his despair was so great that nothing could dent it. Gradually, however, he forced himself to think good thoughts. His father was dead and could hinder his career no more. That was something good, was it not? It was very good, for that dark, evil shadow no longer contaminated the world. His mother was free of his malign control, and Andrew — timid, uncertain Andrew — would grow into his new estate.

And perhaps, one day, far in the future, he devoutly hoped, Simon would step into his brother's shoes and become the Earl of Edlesborough. It was a fate that had seemed so remote that he had never given it a moment's thought before. He did not care about the title, and the obligations of rank would be a heavy burden, but the wealth — oh yes, he would enjoy the fortune that came with everything else. Bless Andrew for the allowance he had given him! A thousand pounds a year was enough — more than enough — to support Juliet in comfort, to buy her new gowns and jewels and as many bonbons as she could eat, and still pay for coal and beef and candles, and a few bottles of good claret.

It was enough to marry on. And then he was plunged into despair again.

So his thoughts revolved, as the sun gradually lowered and the gallery fell into gloom again. It was as if he was aboard a benighted ship in a storm, tossed this way and that by the waves, and with no more power to right the ship than the barnacle still clinging to the hull. Unresisting, he allowed his mood to be thrown this way and that, never settling, never even close to settling.

He barely heard the door open — there was no more than a half-imagined click. It was her perfume he noticed first, and then a soft step at the far end of the gallery.

"Simon?"

A thousand emotions roiled through him like a summer storm. He was not ready to face her, not yet! Perhaps he would never be ready, but she was there anyway.

He jumped up, turned to face her, made some strangled sound deep in his throat. Dear heaven, but a man could die of happiness at the sight of her... or die of grief, more likely. Was it possible to die of a broken heart? He was about to find out. Why could she not leave him alone?

She smiled, that glorious smile that he loved and remembered so well. Inside him, the pain receded. No hurt was so acute when she was so close to him, just a few steps away, and smiling as warmly as the sun.

The smile faded, replaced by anxiety. "Are you all right?"

No, he was not all right. Possibly he would never be all right again. But he needed to know, once and for all, where he stood. "Is he...? Are you...? Will he...?"

"Lord Daniel? He has gone, and good riddance." Before he could assimilate this shocking response, she smiled again. "I turned him down."

For an instant, he stood transfixed, unable to believe it. Then he flew towards her and enfolded her tight in his arms, hugging her to him as if he would never let her go. He was shaking from head to toe, but Sophie was there, he was holding her tight and the ship of despair miraculously righted itself. He had come safe ashore at last.

A muffled voice emerged from somewhere in the region of his chest. "Sorry — hard to breathe."

At once he released her, horrified. "Oh my God! Sophie, forgive me! Are you squashed beyond repair?"

She giggled. "Not quite. Oh, Simon, I am so glad you are home!"

Home? Staineybank would never be his home, yet at that moment it felt exactly as if it were. He had indeed come home — to Sophie. Wherever she was would be home, for she was his lodestar.

"I have good news!" she burst out.

"Have you? Tell me all."

"Richard is to recommend your design for the orangery to the duke. He cannot improve upon it, he says, and you will make at least a thousand pounds from it — I do not know how, but that is what he said."

"Fees," Simon said. "The architect's fees are usually ten per cent of the total cost. Well! So perhaps it will be built in the end and you will have your ballroom."

"And you will have some money, and you know what that means."

"What does it mean?"

She looked up at him shyly. "We can be married, Simon. If you still want to."

For answer he wrapped his arms around her again, although more loosely this time. "Of course I want to, but there is a small wrinkle to this pleasing scheme."

"Is there?" Her face was raised again, and the urge to kiss her was almost overwhelming. "Is there... some obstacle?"

"Not an obstacle, exactly, but an unexpected issue. How should you like to be a countess?"

"A countess! Whatever do you mean? Is this something to do with your father? Did you see him in the end?"

"In a manner of speaking," he said. "I saw him in his coffin, just before the lid was nailed shut."

She gasped. "You mean — he is *dead?* Oh!" There was a long pause, while she gazed at a point somewhere around his middle, then slowly lifted her eyes to meet his. "Should I offer my condolences?"

"For form's sake, perhaps, but there was not much grief on display. The ladies refreshed themselves liberally with champagne while they waited for the funeral party to return."

That made her laugh. "How funny! Then I offer my congratulations, instead. But you will have to explain the part about being a countess, for you have two older brothers, do you not?"

So he told her of Andrew's pact for daughters with his wife and Luke's non-marriage. "So you see, one day, many years from now, one must hope, I shall inherit Edlesborough."

"You will be an earl," she whispered.

"And you, my darling, will be a countess."

"Well! That might to some degree mitigate Mama's disappointment that I refused the son of a marquess. The *third* son, with no likelihood of inheriting. And while you wait for your earldom, you will be a world-renowned architect."

"A gainfully employed one, at the very least," he said, smiling down at her. "Well, Sophie?"

"Well what?"

"Should you like to be a countess?"

"Oh! Are you being so obliging as to offer for me, Mr Payne?"

"I am, Miss Merrington."

"Even though we have been unofficially betrothed for some time now?"

He exhaled slowly. "Well... that was all very improper. Lovely, of course, but most irregular, since I had nothing to offer you. But now I have a good allowance from my brother so—"

"Oh, that is kind of him!"

"It is no more than my father should have done all these years. If he had treated me as he ought and not interfered, I should have been established and independent by this time. But now I have money and prospects, and I need not hold back. So... will you marry me, Sophie?"

"Mr Payne, I am disappointed at the brevity of your proposal. Lord Daniel's was much longer."

He chuckled. "You deserve better, I know, but I am not very good with words, I regret to say."

"Oh, neither was he, for he told me in plain terms that he would dispense with the '*flowery nothings*', as he described them. Not that I wish for flowery nothings, but a little animation does not go amiss."

"Do you want me to tell you that I love you? I can do that all day long, if you like."

"That would be delightful, but you have a much more effective way of demonstrating your love."

"Ah. But first, you must answer my question."

"Which question was that, Mr Payne?"

"Will you marry me?"

"Ooh, I shall have to consider the matter—"

"Minx!"

"—very carefully. Matrimony is a solemn undertaking and one cannot rush into—"

"I am going to account that as an affirmative."

"—anything precipitately."

"Sophie."

"Hmm?"

"Stop talking."

"Make me."

So he did, and there was silence in the chapel gallery for a very long time. Then, from somewhere near his left ear, he heard a whisper.

"Yes."

"Um... what?"

"Yes. I will marry you, Mr Payne."

"Obliged to you, Miss Merrington."

She chuckled, and pulled his head nearer to hers again. After that, not another word was spoken.

Epilogue

STAINEYBANK, BRINSHIRE; JUNE

The baptism of Miss Caroline Georgiana Merrington was a rather grander affair than might have been expected, for a great many people crowded into the Staineybank chapel to watch Mr Godley rouse the infant to loud rage by the splash of water on her face. Beside the proud parents stood the godparents, namely Mr Simon Payne, Mrs Georgie Hastings and Miss Charlotte Merrington. Behind them stood the duke, the stern countenance for once wreathed in smiles.

After the service, the principal participant was whisked away to the nursery by her parents to be pacified and cuddled and thoroughly doted upon, while the rest of the attendees drifted into the morning room, where refreshments were laid out. The event would normally have called for the more formal setting of the White Drawing Room, but preparations for a much greater event were underway elsewhere in the house, so that all the principal rooms were filled with footmen rushing about with chairs, the kitchen boy carrying a great mountain of candle boxes, maids with cloths and china and glasses, and the gardeners with vases of flowers. Outside on the drive, an army of local men laboured to erect a vast pavilion on the drive to shield the Marble Hall from draughts whenever anyone entered or left.

Staineybank was about to experience an event not seen for many years — a grand ball.

It was not to be expected that Sophia could sit quietly while all this was going on, so she soon slipped out of the morning room and made her way on light feet to the Marble Hall, where the tiled floor had been covered in protective matting and a wooden floor placed on top for the dancing.

Oh, the joy of a proper ball! The assemblies had begun in Brinchester, and that had satisfied her need to dance for a little while, but there was nothing to compare with a private ball, and this one was particularly delightful since it was in her honour.

Simon soon followed her into the Marble Hall, giving her that intimate little smile that she had grown to love so much. She could not have believed when she first came to Staineybank that she could be so happy.

"Are your dancing slippers ready for the onslaught?" he said, gently pulling her aside as two footmen with a ladder rushed past them.

"Oh yes! I have been ready for days, with two alternative gowns prepared if Lily's modiste fails me. Is it not time that the London contingent arrived?"

"I think it may be precisely time. Do you hear the sound of an approaching carriage?"

Excitedly, Sophia stepped around the artists busily chalking the floor and went out of the front door, then through the partially erected pavilion to the drive. The carriage decanted the smiling faces of Simon's brother

Andrew, the Earl of Edlesborough, and his wife, bearing a well-wrapped package. Behind them, clutching a new bonnet to her head, was Juliet.

"We come bearing gifts!" Andrew cried, as soon as his feet were safely on the drive. "Lavinia has been carefully nursing yours on her knee all the way from town, Sophia, and it slept at the end of our bed at night, too. It is far too precious to be stowed in the boxes."

"Boxes get rained on and thrown around and occasionally fall off and burst asunder," the countess said, "and that cannot be permitted. Shall we go inside and see what Madame Labette has created for you, my dear?"

"Oh yes," breathed Sophia, "but I must know — did you manage to acquire the other thing? For that is far more important."

"Whatever can you mean?" Simon murmured, eyes twinkling. "What can possibly be more important than a ball gown?"

"Do not tease her, Simon," the countess said. "Yes, Andrew has the special licence, so you two may be married whenever you please. Today, if you wish it."

"The day after tomorrow, and not a moment sooner," Sophia said in her severest tones. "Cousin Hester would be outraged if all her careful arrangements were to be set at nought. A ball tonight, a day of rest tomorrow and the wedding the day after that. One does not marry on impulse, just because one has a licence. It is simply not done."

"Indeed!" the countess said, laughing. "Come, let us open this parcel at once, for I cannot wait a moment longer to see your gown."

"I must find my sisters first," Sophia said. "And Lily, too. They would not miss the occasion for the world. Juliet, will you come, too? Did you have a wonderful time in London?"

"Indeed I did," Juliet said, a beatific smile on her face. "I have never bought so many gowns in my life."

"And bonnets," Sophia said, reaching up to touch a gently waving feather.

"Is it not the most delicious confection?" Juliet said, in awed tones. "And I have *four more!* And gloves and boots and stockings and fans and the most beautiful little headband with *diamonds*, Sophia! Diamonds!" She sighed euphorically. "I have had the most amazing time."

"And so have I," the countess said. "There is nothing more gratifying than having a lady to refurbish from top to toe, and at someone else's expense, too. Simon has been very generous."

Sophia giggled. "You must show us everything, Juliet. But first — my ball gown."

And away she went, skipping into the house positively humming with excitement, Juliet in her wake, as the countess, bearing the precious burden, followed more sedately.

***

Simon watched her go, a smile on his face. She was so light on her feet, his Sophie. It was a joy to watch her make her way up the steps with a slight sway of the hips, her delicately lifted skirts revealing an inch or two of trim ankle.

"She will make a wonderful countess in the fullness of time," Andrew murmured at his shoulder.

"To my mind, she is rather wonderful already."

Andrew laughed. "So she is. Shall we go inside? You will want to check the licence."

They entered the house and, stepping delicately past the ball preparations, made their way to the Chinese Room, which had become Simon's domain while he worked on the plans for the orangery. Simon immersed himself in the florid language of the special licence, while Andrew gazed around the room, which had every surface covered in drawings.

"This is the point of access, is that right?" he said.

"Mm? Yes. That window there will be a door leading to the gallery and thence to the orangery."

"Which has progressed to the point of poles to mark the perimeter, I see," Andrew said, amusement in his voice. "At this rate, it will be years before the thing is finished, and the bride it is meant to honour will be a fat matron looking forward to launching her daughter into society."

"Then she will still have years to enjoy it. No, I estimate two years, at most, although the finishing touches to the interior might take a little longer."

"What do you see as the finishing touches?"

"I should like to have the gallery ceiling painted, like some of the rooms in the main house. But it will depend upon finding the right artist."

"And the duke agreeing, of course."

"That too," Simon said, with a rumble of laughter.

"What are these drawings here? This is not the orangery."

"Those are for the book. Richard Merrington is the creator of a book of cottages of various designs, with full costings. We are collaborating on a similar volume featuring larger houses. I design the houses, and he does the costings. He is something of a genius in that way. Most architects never do more than guess at a final price, and naturally there are always unforeseen problems, but he counts bricks and lengths of wood and marble tiles, and then prices everything up. It is quite amazing."

"That reminds me," Andrew said, helping himself to a glass of wine, and pouring one for Simon, too. "I called on your friend Thwaite and took him to the club — had him round for dinner, once, too. Introduced him to one or two people, so I think he will get his elevation in time. At least I hope I have reassured him that I am not like my father, and would not dream of standing in his way if it should happen."

"I am glad of it," Simon said. "I hope he gets what he wants."

"As to that, what he wants just at the moment is for you to build him a house."

Simon almost choked on his claret. "He plans to do it at last?"

"He does. He said to tell you that he wants the first one you designed, with the extra wings, and he has bought that land you recommended in Hertfordshire and how soon can you start? I had to tell him very gently that you are already fully engaged here for the foreseeable future. He said he will wait."

"Oh, I can manage two projects at once," Simon said airily. "The builder will be here next month and once that is underway, Merrington will be able to supervise while I go to Hertfordshire. Well! The first design, eh? That was the good one, of course. I shall enjoy building that, and his purse can stand it. He is a very warm man."

"A very honest one, too," Andrew said. "He freely confessed to his own cowardice — his word, not mine — in allowing himself to be brow-beaten by Father. He wishes he had had the courage to stand up to him. I can hardly blame him for that, since I never had any courage in that line myself. Unlike you."

Simon shrugged. "In my case, it was more stupidity than courage. I wanted to be an architect, I had Juliet to fall back on for support, so I simply left. I had this curious idea that once I was gone, I would be beyond his reach, but I underestimated his vindictiveness against those who thwarted him. You were right not to defy him openly, I think. By doing that, you protected Lavinia and your children from his wrath, and possibly kept him from worse retaliation against all of us. Besides, your form of defiance was ingenious. You and Luke between you outwitted him comprehensively. Do not denigrate yourself, brother. It took the utmost courage to stay at Edlesborough year after year under his malevolent eye."

"Perhaps so, although it did not feel like courage. Every morning I woke shaking and feeling ill, knowing I had to face him. Even now, three months after he died, I still feel queer at first. It is not until I sit down to breakfast and face his empty chair that I can begin to feel comfortable again. I will recover fully, in time, but he has been a dark shadow over my whole life."

"You are looking better," Simon said. "You looked so thin and wasted, I thought you were ill, but you have begun to put on weight again."

Andrew laughed. "Lavinia has been feeding me up, and of course we can put anything on the table now, even the foods that Father was forbidden. So many treats we can now enjoy! But let us not spoil the day by talking any more about *him.* This is a happy time. We have missed the baptism, I assume, but we are in time for the ball and, of course, your wedding. I shall be delighted to stand up for you on the day, brother."

"I hope you will do so before then. Sophia will be opening the ball tonight, but I cannot dance a single step. Will you lead her out?"

"You cannot dance at all? Heavens, that needs to be corrected. Your lady loves to dance, and a husband with two left feet cannot be tolerated. I am astonished that she does not throw you over for some more light-footed fellow."

"She has promised to teach me, but her efforts so far have not been crowned with success. Will you do it? She will not stand up with her brother, and it ought to be someone of rank, but I do not like to call upon the duke. He is very fit for his age but leading a country dance is probably asking too much of him."

Andrew chuckled. "Even now, his courtly manner of walking suggests that he was a most elegant dancer in his day. He would have executed a wonderful minuet. However, a boisterous country dance would be too much for a gentleman of his age. I can only hope it will not be too much for me. I shall be delighted to attempt it. This is excellent claret, brother. I might ask for some to be sent up to my room, to fortify me in preparation for the ball."

"Do you need fortifying against one dance with Sophia?" Simon said, amused.

"No, against the three, at least, that Lavinia will insist upon. I can usually get away with just one dance, and then retreat hastily to the card room, but I suspect tonight will be different. Perhaps I should sprain my ankle when I dance with Sophia, eh?"

"Do you think Lavinia would believe you?"

"No. Women, Simon! Devious, manipulative little creatures, who know just how to get a man to do precisely what they want. You should run a mile before tying yourself to one. It is not too late."

Simon smiled. "Oh, brother, it is far, far too late for me. I was lost a long time ago, and I would not change a thing."

"Then I drink to your good lady, and a lifetime of happiness," Andrew said, raising his glass.

It was a toast Simon could heartily endorse.

***

Until Simon saw Sophia emerge from her room wearing her new ball gown, he had not realised just how beautiful she was. He had always thought her features pleasing, and would certainly have described her as pretty without hesitation, but the vision that confronted him now was something entirely out of the ordinary.

For a moment he was struck dumb, so that she laughed and said, "Well? Do I pass muster, Mr Payne?"

"Pass muster?" he cried, startled into speech. "You must know that if you walked into Almack's this minute, you would shine down every other lady present."

"Would I?" she said shyly, blushing a little. "It is a beautiful gown, is it not?"

"It is the lady who adorns it who is beautiful," he said. "You are incomparable, my love."

"What a lovely compliment! Those flowers you are in danger of squashing — are they for me?"

"Oh..." He looked vaguely down at the beribboned posy he clutched, having forgotten he was holding it. Now he thrust it towards her. "I... I think they are not too crushed, but you drive every rational thought from my head."

She giggled, took the posy and tucked her arm in his. "Shall we go down, my soon to be husband?"

Wordlessly, for speech was extraordinarily difficult just then, he turned and escorted her to the stairs.

He could not remember ever enjoying an evening so much. Even though the last few months had been a continuous succession of wonderful evenings, and there was the promise of even better to come, yet he felt that there was something magical about the Staineybank ball. Sophia's pleasure in the dance was a large part of it, of course, and he spent his time following her about, sketch book in hand, attempting to capture the gracefulness of her movements and the lightness with which she executed the steps.

Yet Sophia was not the whole of it. Whether her enthusiasm had infected everyone else or whether it was the beauty of the Marble Hall that created the joyous atmosphere, there was no doubt that the evening was unlike any other. Apart from Simon, everyone danced, even the duke, once, with the duchess. She, having finally left off her mourning weeds for her dead son, stood up for every dance. The Merrington sisters, naturally, did the same. Even Juliet and Mr Godley, neither of them keen dancers, took part. It was wonderful to watch.

At supper, the duke and duchess sat beside Simon and Sophia.

"Ready for married life, you two?" the duke said genially.

"Oh, yes," they said in unison.

"You have a wedding trip planned, my dear duchess tells me."

"My brother is lending us his Shropshire house for a se'nnight or so, but we cannot stay away long. I must be back when the builder arrives."

"Ah, Rowena's orangery! That is going to be something very special when it is done," the duke said with satisfaction. "It will be mentioned in all the guide books. *'The gallery bridge and orangery, designed by Payne, is something quite out of the ordinary way, and well worth visiting.'* Something like that. We shall be inundated with travellers wishing to view it."

Simon laughed. "We shall see. But I am afraid we shall be under your feet for some time to come yet, until it is finished."

"No need to rush away. So long as my lovely duchess is pleased to be friends with the Miss Merringtons, they are welcome to stay here to keep her happy and amused, and that goes for Mr and Mrs Simon Payne, too.

Besides, Richard is my heir and you are his family, so you have a home here for as long as you want."

"You are all goodness, your grace," Simon murmured. "And does that apply to Juliet, too? She loves it here, and we have been together for so long that we should hate to be separated now."

"Ah, Juliet reminds me of her mother, and I have fond memories of her, so of course she may stay. Do you think her mother might pay a visit here, if I were to extend the invitation? I should love to see her again, and reminisce about our glory days of years ago, and gloat over all our contemporaries who are fat or insane or dead."

Simon grimaced. "I am not sure that Juliet wishes to meet Mrs Granville again, and I am certain that I do not."

"Well, well, I shall perhaps see her in town one of these days. If Richard and Rowena go up for the season next spring, I shall go with them to introduce them about a bit. Perhaps Mrs So-called Granville will be there. Ah, Cecilia! What a girl she was in her heyday! Ah, more champagne. Thank you, Froggett. So wonderful to have so much to celebrate — Rowena's daughter, and your wedding, and yet, how strange it is that you were brought here by that peculiar letter, Payne, just as Rowena was, and there she is married to Richard, and now here you are, about to marry Sophia. It is almost as if your coming was meant to be."

"It was meant to be," Sophia said. "This mysterious Mr Goodenough, whoever he is, meant it to be. He quite deliberately brought both Rowena and Simon here."

"And Juliet," Simon said. "The letter was addressed to her, and not to me."

"Hammond has a theory about it, did you know that?" the duke said. "He thinks there must be some connection between the two letters, and he thinks he sees it. Rowena is the granddaughter of a woman who scandalised her family by conceiving a child out of wedlock and was driven out of the family as a result. Juliet is the daughter of another woman who scandalised her family and was driven out — divorced. So they are both black sheep, you see. That is the connection, according to Hammond."

"That is very tenuous," Simon said.

"And why would this Mr Goodenough even care?" Sophia said. "It is old history, so what is the point of digging it up today?"

"Ah, old history," the duke said. "It never quite goes away, does it? And all families have their skeletons in cupboards, or their black sheep. So perhaps, if Hammond is right, we will see more of these letters from Mr Goodenough. That would be amusing, would it not?"

***

Two days later, Mr Godley's services were called upon once more. The Staineybank chapel was full to overflowing with the duke's household and the groom's family, while the servants crowded into the gallery above to peer through the carved screen at the proceedings.

Sophia was not nervous. How could she be, as she was passed from her brother's care to the safe arms of her beloved Simon? As they all streamed out of the chapel afterwards, Richard joked to Charlotte, Augusta and Maria, "That is one of you gone. Who will be next?"

"We are doing our best, brother," Charlotte said, eyeing the gaggle of Paynes laughing and joking.

"How fortunate that both Mr John and Mr Matthew are unmarried," Augusta said.

"They are both clergymen," Charlotte said.

"I should not mind that," Maria said.

"Nor I," said Augusta. "A clergyman's wife may still ride, after all."

"A clergyman needs an active, practical wife who can keep house," Charlotte said loftily. "You need a wealthy husband, Augusta, who can afford a string of hunters for you, and your husband must needs have a large library, Maria, and not a shelf of tomes in Latin or Greek."

"I could learn Greek," she said stoutly.

Sophia laughed, and shook her head. "Chasing after a husband has never worked for us, sisters. Take my advice, and stop looking for matrimony, and perhaps matrimony will come looking for you."

The three were silent for a minute, frowning as they worked it out. Then Maria shook her head. "No, I cannot think that it will. You were lucky, sister, but we cannot assume that we will be so fortunate. We must make our own luck."

As they drifted away, heads together, still plotting, Simon said, "Is it strange, being the one married sister? You have done everything as a group and now you will be apart a great deal."

"I do not mind, for now I have you," she said, beaming up at him. "I only wish they could be so fortunate."

"They will do better now that they have established this system of coloured ribbons," he said. "Come, wife, to breakfast."

***

A little after noon, the duke's best travelling carriage drew up at the door to convey the newly married pair away to Shropshire for a week of post-nuptial bliss. The bride wore a fetching deep blue pelisse with a matching bonnet sporting three jauntily waving feathers. The groom, having no pretensions to fashionable elegance, was much as usual, although he carried the new hat his brother had brought him from London. The bride thought he looked absolutely splendid anyway.

The farewells were made, the last tears were shed and the carriage rolled away down the drive.

"Alone at last, Mrs Payne," Simon said, stripping off his own gloves, and beginning to wrestle with hers so that he could hold her hand.

"We shall have a week of being alone," she said, willingly tearing off her own gloves. "Shall we be sick of it by then, do you suppose, and be very thankful to return to Staineybank?"

"We shall be glad to return, certainly, but I hope a week is not sufficient to render us tired of each other. I do not feel that even three lifetimes would be enough for me to tire of you."

He lifted her hand to his lips and planted a delicate kiss on the back of it, and then on the palm.

She blushed a little, then said softly, "It is wonderful, is it not? Being in love, I mean. The poets talk about walking on air, and it truly is like that. There is some kind of alchemy to it. The duke said that your coming was meant to be, and perhaps our love was meant to be, too. I know I felt something inside me the first time I ever saw you, standing in the Marble Hall gazing around you in such awe. Everyone else was concentrating on mundane matters but you were entranced by the house. I found that... so endearing."

"I confess, I did not notice you particularly after that first day when you were so kind to me. You became just one of your sisters, until the invitation arrived from Marshfields and I could see the hope and despair chasing each other across your countenance. I realised then that I would like to get to know you better, this girl who so desperately wanted to dance. And as soon as that happened, I could think of nothing but you."

"It *was* meant to be, was it not?" she whispered.

But his lips were already seeking hers and his answer was given without a word being spoken.

THE END

In the next book of the series, The Duke's Portraitist, society painter Lance Chamberlain receives a summons from the mysterious Mr Goodenough; meanwhile, the duke's secretary, James Hammond, and widowed Georgie Hastings discover that a little sympathy is not always a good thing. You can read a sneak preview after the acknowledgements.

For more information, go to my website at .

Thanks for reading!

If you have enjoyed reading this book, please consider writing a short review on Amazon. You can find out the latest news and sign up for the mailing list at my website at https://marykingswood.co.uk.

A note on historical accuracy: I have endeavoured to stay true to the spirit of Regency times, and have avoided taking too many liberties or imposing modern sensibilities on my characters. The book is not one of historical record, but I've tried to make it reasonably accurate. However, I'm not perfect! If you spot a historical error, I'd very much appreciate knowing about it so that I can correct it and learn from it. Thank you!

About the series*:*

Book 0: The Duke's Heir *(a novella prequel)*

Book 1: The Duke's Architect

Book 2: The Duke's Portraitist

Book 3: The Duke's Gardener

Book 4: The Duke's Steward

Book 5: The Duke's Librarian

Book 6: The Duke's Enemy

Any questions about the series? Email me at mary@marykingswood.co.uk - I'd love to hear from you!

About the author

I write traditional Regency romances under the pen name Mary Kingswood, and epic fantasy as Pauline M Ross. I live in the beautiful Highlands of Scotland with my husband. I like chocolate, whisky, my Kindle, massed pipe bands, long leisurely lunches, chocolate, going places in my campervan, eating pizza in Italy, summer nights that never get dark, wood fires in winter, chocolate, the view from the study window looking out over the Moray Firth and the Black Isle to the mountains beyond. And chocolate. I dislike driving on motorways, cooking, shopping, hospitals.

Acknowledgements

Thanks go to:

Allison Lane, whose course on English Architecture inspired me.

Shayne Rutherford of Darkmoon Graphics for the cover design.

My understanding husband: Jim Ross

Beta readers: Charles Crouter, Sharon Flaherty, Melissa Forsythe, Corinne Lehmann, Leann McKinley, Tina Miles, Rosemary Paton, Kristen Pinto-Coelho, Melanie Savage, Wendy Stubbs, Carol Sturz, Jeanne Thomas, Andrea Usami

Last, but definitely not least, my first reader: Amy Ross.

Sneak preview: Book 2 of Black Sheep: The Duke's Portraitist

MOUNT STREET, LONDON: NOVEMBER

Lance Chamberlain made a minute adjustment to the small emerald pin embedded in his neckcloth, and stood back to admire the effect in the looking glass. The pin was an affectation, for in general he followed Mr Brummell's principles of restraint in gentlemen's dress, but it was a signal to the world that although he was only the younger son of a baronet, he was not an insignificant nobody. Besides, the colour matched his eyes.

"You look very fine, sir," Denny said.

"Oh, I am *'sir'* today, am I?"

"It is an auspicious occasion, worthy of a little respect, even from me," Denny said.

Lance smiled. "Auspicious occasion? Today, my friend, is the pinnacle of my existence. I have achieved professional esteem as a portraitist, I have made my fortune and today I shall be engaged to the daughter of a marquess. I have nothing further to wish for."

"If only it might be so," murmured Denny, making Lance laugh. Well, he could afford to laugh, today.

Downstairs, Mama and Papa were loitering in the hall, eyes shining with excitement.

"All ready, son?" Papa said.

"As ready as I have ever been."

"We are so proud of you," Mama said, as he leaned forward to kiss her cheek.

Breakfast was an odd sort of meal. Lance was used to being alone in the Mount Street house at this time of year, or perhaps one or other of his brothers might make a quick dive for the metropolis, but usually they all stayed safely in Surrey, where nothing much ever happened and they were well out of the unpredictable currents of society life. But today, they were all there — his three stolid brothers and their dough-faced wives, his sisters all running to fat with their rustic spouses. And so many clerics! What was it about the Chamberlains that drew them so powerfully to the church? Yet not a bishop amongst them. Not one of them had an ounce of ambition in h im.

Except for Lance. He had ambition enough for all of them, and today all his carefully nurtured hopes would reach fruition.

He had ordered the carriage for half past eleven, but the day was so fine that at the last minute he sent for his curricle instead. It would strike the right note for Grosvenor Square, he felt.

"Do you want me to come with you, or one of the grooms?" Denny said.

"You, of course. Best livery, my friend."

The whole family gathered in the tiny hall to see him off. Lance squeezed past their solid frames, waved to the servants lined up on the stairs, then across the bridge above the area to the street, where Denny waited, with one of the grooms holding the head of the greys. He paused to savour the moment — they were a fine pair, and had cost him a lot of gingerbread, but worth every last penny.

Several of their neighbours, aware of the significance of the occasion, were out on the street or hanging out of upper windows to watch his departure. With a jaunty wave, he leapt into the seat, picked up the reins and whip, Denny sprang up beside him and with a final cheery lift of the hand to his audience, he was away.

He was early, so he tooled about the streets for a few minutes, to run the friskiness out of his team and to settle what nerves he might have. There were few of those. He did not come from a noble family, nor from great wealth, and his family's estate was only modest, but society did not care about that. His talent for painting, and a certain eye for enhancing the features of a subject without outright falsehood had brought him an initial standing in the art world. His own brazenness had done the rest, in offering to paint the Princess Amelia without charge, a portrait which had cemented his reputation. He was a success, and thus worthy to aspire to the hand of a noble lady.

Grosvenor Square was quiet, the maids scrubbing steps long since vanished indoors, and the great and the good who dwelt within these hallowed portals not yet venturing outside. He was expected, however, so a groom materialised as soon as he halted. The Marquess of Pentavon's house was one of the largest on the square, as might be expected, with an elegant little portico sheltering the front door.

Lance raised his hand to knock but he had been watched for, since the door opened soundlessly before him, and the butler bowed him in.

"Good morning, Mr Chamberlain," he said in the lugubrious tones that seemed to come naturally to butlers, as a minion relieved Lance of his hat, coat and gloves. "His lordship is expecting you. Please follow me."

With a final admiring glance around the hall, slightly larger than the Mount Street dining room, Lance followed him past the stairs and into a rear room overlooking a pleasant garden, with the coach house beyond it. How wonderful it would be to own such a place! Or to be married into the family and invited to stay there.

The marquess rose to greet him, and hobbled over to the door, leaning heavily on his stick, as Lance made his carefully judged bow. Not too obsequiously low, but not the light nod that might be expected from a family member. He was not that yet.

"Come in, Chamberlain, do. How are you?"

"Well, my lord, as always. How is the gout?"

"Hmpf. Same as ever. Bassett, pour Mr Chamberlain something. What will you have — Madeira? I have a very pleasant brandy, if it is not too early in the day for that."

"It is a little, my lord," Lance said. "Madeira would suit me very well."

The butler poured two glasses, offered them on a silver tray, and then withdrew.

"Come and sit down, young man, and you can tell me what you want of me, although I might hazard a guess, eh?"

"You might indeed, sir, since I have made no secret of my intentions. I should very much like your permission to pay my addresses to the Lady Patience."

"And you have it." He chuckled at the surprise which Lance could not conceal. "Ah, you thought I would subject you to an interrogation about your prospects, I dare say. No need. I have already sounded out your situation."

"Have you, sir?" Lance said cautiously.

"Found out you bank at Drake's, and Sir James is my cousin… by marriage, but still, that counts for something. I asked him to vouch for you, and he told me you were pretty well set up. Done well for yourself, considering you are only four and thirty. Now, let us get down to business. Patience will bring twenty thousand to the marriage, and a house in Gloucestershire for her lifetime. Only three miles from the castle, so she will still be near her family, you see."

"I do see, sir, and that is exceptionally generous of you, but my work is in town. My father's house is—"

"No daughter of mine will live in Mount Street," the marquess said, with a curl of the lip.

"Then I can rent somewhere else, but—"

"London is not a healthy place for females, especially in winter. Patience will be moped to death if she is expected to live here all year round. Her home will be in Gloucestershire, and during the season she will stay in this house, naturally. If your work causes you to be away in town now and then, she will have her family nearby for society."

Lance said nothing. He could talk to Patience about it later and see what her wishes were. Surely she would want to be wherever he was? That was a wife's place, was it not?

"Well, are we agreed, Chamberlain? Shall I send Patience in to you?"

"Thank you, sir. I am ready to talk to Lady Patience."

The marquess chuckled. "Got your speech prepared, eh? The ladies like a bit of oratory on these occasions."

"Do they, sir?" Lance said politely, not convinced. He had, naturally, prepared a few suitable words, and had even practised a little on Denny, although he was quite prepared to improvise if the occasion demanded it. However, he was not about to launch into a long recitation of Patience's perfections, or the attractions of his suit, and if Patience expected such nonsense, she would be disappointed.

The marquess rang the bell for the butler, who appeared so quickly that he must have been loitering outside the door.

"Ask the Lady Patience to step in here, will you?"

Within two minutes, for Lance was watching the clock, she appeared, head demurely lowered, walking dutifully two steps behind her mother. They were very alike, the two women, but whereas Patience's blonde curls and wide blue eyes gave her an air of innocent fragility, her mother's hair was faded, and a slight protuberance to her eyes and rather prominent teeth made her look like a fish. He wondered idly if Patience, too, would fade with the years, and grow stout round the middle, her gown struggling to contain the extra flesh.

"Mr Chamberlain, how pleasant to see you," the marchioness said, although her smile seemed rather forced.

"Lady Pentavon," he murmured as he made his bow. "Lady Patience."

"Patience, my dear," the marquess said, "Mr Chamberlain has something most particular to say to you. Be assured that he has my approval and your mama's also, but of course you are free to answer as you will."

She raised her head, and there was an odd flash in her eyes. "Thank you, Papa."

He frowned a little at this. "I trust you will consider your answer very carefully, daughter. Now we shall leave you two to talk."

With a soft click of the door, they were gone. Patience watched them disappear, then turned back to Lance, her face blank. She made no move towards him, so he went to her, lifting her hand to his lips and then retaining it, gently stroking her fingers with his thumb.

"Lady Patience, thank you for seeing me. You look wonderful, as always."

"Thank you, sir." The eyes dropped again, but she did not withdraw her hand.

"You know, I think, what I am about to say to you. I am sure you were aware of my admiration when I was at Pentavon in the summer. I tried very hard but I could not conceal my feelings entirely, and there were moments when, perhaps, you must have guessed that my heart was engaged. Yet I never dared to hope... and your father was not encouraging. But when I heard you had returned to town, I was immediately drawn back to your side, as the bee is drawn to the sweet nectar of the flower."

There! That was well judged, he thought, for he had laboured over that particular phrase for some days now. A little florid, perhaps, but one must pay some sort of compliment. She made no response, however, not even lifting her eyes to his.

"Now I can be silent no longer, Patience. I cannot imagine a future without you, for you are all that a man looks for in the woman to accompany him in life. Your beauty, your character, your ability to laugh at my feeble jests..."

That brought her eyes up to meet his, and he saw puzzlement there. Well, that was better than nothing. She must be nervous, that was why this felt like such hard work. Time to get to the point.

"Patience... my dearest Patience... will you make me the happiest man on earth and consent to be my wife?"

"I will, sir. Thank you."

Well, that was brief. Nothing about being honoured or obliged or any such nonsense. Still, it was the right answer.

He kissed her hand again, then smiled. "How happy we shall be, my love! How soon can we be married, do you suppose?"

"I do not know, sir."

"Lance. Surely you can call me Lance."

"It is a strange name."

"Well... Lancelot, then, if you prefer, but I do not like being *'sir'*, not when we are alone, at least."

"I shall try to remember... Lance. Shall we tell my parents now?"

"A moment yet, if you please. May we seal the bargain with a kiss? If you would permit...?"

Without hesitation, she nodded, and there was that odd flash in her eyes again, which he could not interpret. But there would be time — years and years, in fact — to understand her fully. So he gently enfolded her in his arms and bent his head to hers.

The outcome took him by surprise. He had supposed, where he had thought about it at all, that a girl of eighteen, barely out, would not know much about kissing and would therefore be completely passive. Patience was anything but passive. After only a moment's hesitation, she seemed to get the idea pretty well and hurled herself into the enterprise with an enthusiasm that left them both breathless.

Giggling, she said, "That was most agreeable."

"It was, was it not? Shall we just stay here for the rest of the day?"

She giggled again. "Better not. Mama and Papa will be waiting in the drawing room."

Reluctantly, he followed her out of the room, back to the stairs and up to the drawing room, where the marquess and marchioness waited, smiles at the ready, to congratulate them. On the wall, Lance's own portrait of Patience beamed down at them. He had captured her mischievous smile rather well, he thought. She looked ready for any game, and that was what had so attracted him to her in the first place. He had no wish at all for a docile wife. Her initial demeanour today had worried him slightly, and set him wondering what had cowed her, but the kiss was reassuring. That was the real Patience!

He had to listen to the marquess reiterating for the benefit of the ladies the details he had already shared with Lance of the house in Gloucestershire. Patience seemed pleased with the idea, and clearly knew the house well.

"Aunt and Uncle Matheson will move out, presumably?" she said.

That was a surprise, that the house was already occupied.

"Naturally. We can easily find somewhere else for them to live," her father said, with a wave of one hand.

Lance wondered how long the couple had lived there, and how they would like to be evicted at a moment's notice, purely on the marquess's whim. How strange it must be to be a marquess and order the lives of lesser beings with a stroke of the pen. Would he go and see these relations and explain the situation, or would he merely instruct his bailiff or steward to see to it? He imagined the couple, grim-faced and weeping, packing up their cherished possessions. Perhaps he would be able to paint them before they moved out. That would be an interesting project.

Seizing a gap in the conversation, he said, "I hope Patience will not keep me waiting too long before she meets me at the altar rail."

"As to that, I do not foresee an early wedding," the marchioness said. "May or June, perhaps. Patience will want to have another season of freedom before settling down to married life."

There was no arguing with that tone of voice. "That is a disappointment, but it shall be as Patience wishes. Do you plan to stay in town long? My parents will be very keen to meet their future daughter-in-law, and would like to invite you all to dinner one evening."

Again it was the marchioness who spoke, in the same implacable voice. "Unfortunately, we are to leave almost at once for Wiltshire. Our eldest daughter has just been delivered of a son and heir, and the heir moreover to a dukedom, so we are all summoned to celebrate. After that, we shall go directly to Gloucestershire for Christmas."

Christmas... he could wait until Christmas. But she anticipated his thoughts.

"We shall have the house full to the rafters as usual, I fear, with not a spare corner where we could squeeze you in. We shall see you again in the spring, however."

And she smiled benignly as if this was a great concession, and not a separation of several months between a man and his betrothed.

He forced a smile. "At least I shall be able to write to Lady Patience, and you must write to me, my dear, and tell me all that you are doing. No detail is too small to interest me."

Her parents exchanged glances, but Patience smiled and nodded.

And then, in the politest manner possible, Lance found himself ushered out to the street where his curricle already awaited him, and bidding farewell to his future wife for several months without any further opportunity for private conversation, let alone another startling kiss.

"Well?" Denny said, as soon as they were out of sight of the house. "It went as expected, I take it?"

Briefly, Lance outlined both the success and the disappointments of the morning.

"Not even invited for Christmas?" Denny said, disbelievingly. "What sort of betrothal is it, when a man is forbidden from seeing his lady?"

"Not forbidden," Lance said uneasily. "Just... no room."

"As if they could not squeeze in an extra man," Denny said. "Ladies are a different matter, but a man can sleep anywhere. Ridiculous. And as for not marrying until the spring— Well, it is your own affair, Lance, but I would not put up with it. I wonder if there is an inn near Pentavon Castle where a man who wished to see his lady love could put up for a week or two, eh? What do you think?"

"You are a devious scoundrel, Denny. Let it be for now. She is going to write to me, so if she expresses any wish for my presence, I shall consider it."

At Mount Street, Lance was obliged to go through the same conversation with his family.

"Well, what a disappointment!" his mother said. "We had so looked forward to meeting Lady Patience, and Lord and Lady Pentavon, if they should deign to grace our humble dwelling with their presence. However, we shall meet them in the spring, I dare say. Will they want you to be married by licence, do you think? At Grosvenor Square — that would be something, would it not? Such a pity they have to go out of town so soon."

The lamentations went on, but Lance noticed several letters addressed to him sitting on the hall table. Most he recognised, but there was one he did not know. Ripping it open, he read the neat script within.

'To Mr Lancelot Chamberlain, Mount Street, London. Sir, Your reputation being known throughout England, I have been instructed to write to you to invite you to attend the Duke of Brinshire at Staineybank, Brinshire, in order that you might paint a life sized portrait of the wife of the duke's heir suitable for hanging in the library there. Please reply directly to me to confirm your preferred date of travel, and I shall arrange private transportation and accommodation en route. Respectfully yours, A Goodenough (attorney at law), Castle Street, Brinchester'

A ducal commission! And a life-sized portrait, too. That was something like, and more than compensated for the modest setback he had encountered at Grosvenor Square. He could wait to marry Patience if it meant a project of this magnitude. The Pentavons were not the only people who could mingle with dukes.

"Well! Mama, you keep up with the society gossip. What do you know of the Duke of Brinshire?"

"The Duke of Brinshire? Well! He must be above seventy now, but he was a fine looking man when he was younger. I remember him well. There was some tragedy last year... now what was it? His young son died, that was it, and he was obliged to send for a cousin, who is his heir. I believe the heir's wife had a daughter not long ago."

"I have a commission to paint the heir's wife," Lance said smugly. "Since I am not expected to dance attendance on my betrothed, there is no reason for me not to write to this... this Mr Goodenough, and accept. To Brinshire I shall go, then. Where is Brinshire? Does anyone know?"

But no one did, and there was an unseemly rush to find an atlas and pass round the sherry and toast the future of the youngest and most successful member of the family.

END OF SAMPLE CHAPTER of The Duke's Portraitist; for more information, or to buy, go to my website at https://marykingswood.co.uk

Printed in Dunstable, United Kingdom

77778967R00184